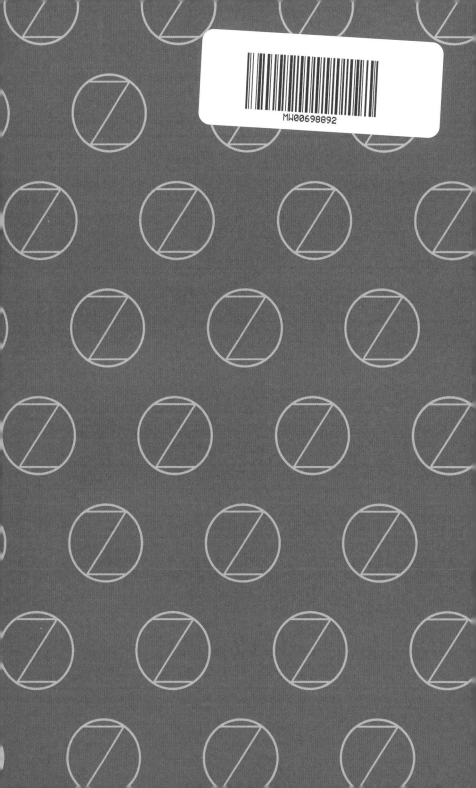

MEET THE AUTHOR

TEASERS,
TRAILERS & MORE...

The Undercurrent

The Undercurrent

Sarah Sawyer

ZIBBY BOOKS
NEW YORK

Library of Congress Control Number: 2024933053
Hardcover ISBN: 978-1-958506-44-8
eBook ISBN: 978-1-958506-60-8

www.zibbymedia.com

Printed in the United States of America

10 9 8 7 6 5 4 3 2 1

I wish I were a girl again, half savage, and hardy, and free . . . Why am I so changed? . . . I'm sure I should be myself were I once among the heather on those hills.

—EMILY BRONTË, *Wuthering Heights*

A girl leans on a metal guardrail at the edge of a brown field. She will not stand here again. She knows this, so she is trying to notice everything: the tall stalks of grass turning into thick stitches of coral and gold, the sun a dark orange marble rolling past the clouds. When she looks down, she sees her toes curling in the gravel, the dents from the hot guardrail burning the soft undersides of her forearms.

If she stays here, facing the field, she can't see the bulldozers, perched like yellow vultures in the cul-de-sac behind her.

She is not allowed to go past the guardrail into the field, even if no one is watching. She has, obviously, because she is thirteen, not a baby, and because cutting across is a shortcut to school, and because she loves this field: its unexpected dips and anthills, the birds that dive open-mouthed across its surface, the snakeskins and velvet butterfly wings she finds on its winding paths. In spring, it is covered with bluebonnets that spread in front of her, undulating and tipped in white, just as she imagines waves might be. When they bloom, she thinks of her fifth-grade Texas History unit, the textbook splayed on her wobbly desk, twenty hand-drawn maps lining the classroom walls. They studied oil first, then gold, then the vaqueros and the missionaries, and then her favorite, Mrs. Lady Bird Johnson, driving from Dallas to Austin to San Antonio, tossing seeds out of the window of her Lincoln Continental with long, glamorous arms. The girl does not know how the flowers got from Mrs. Johnson's car to this field, which touches only some boring, dead-end streets speckled with ugly tan ranch houses, but here they are, all the same.

On spring evenings, the girl likes to balance on the guardrail and watch the breeze brush across the field, painting it cornflower, then navy, and back again, as the clouds billow and roll overhead. Now that it is August, there is no wind, and the sunbaked field has only sharp crabgrass and anthills, but the girl doesn't mind. The summer field is her favorite. She loves the way the mice poke their heads from their burrows if she stands still enough for long enough. She loves the way the field changes but never forgets itself.

Today, she is pretending that it belongs to her.

Nothing belongs to her, though. Not even her own street, which stretches out behind her in a long, snaking line that touches the only places she is allowed to go: her house, her school, the Dewberry Market, the pool. Her father has traced the routes for her many times on the map they keep in the junk drawer in the kitchen, his finger a slow vacuum swallowing the streets on either side as he makes sure she has understood.

She does understand. There are rules. She can't go past the guardrail to play in the field. She can't curl like a pillbug inside the abandoned refrigerator that huddles in a weedy corner of her backyard. Or crawl inside the giant concrete culvert that runs beneath the field and empties into Shoal Creek, then the Colorado, then the turquoise waters of the Gulf. She can't close her eyes and cool her back on its damp walls. She can't read too much or too little. Or play pretend. Play sports. Talk to herself. Shout.

Because of the map in the junk drawer, she knows that directly across the field, over the grassy hump of the culvert and the tufts of brown grass, there is another street, identical to hers. And because of her father's low, urgent voice on the telephone, she knows that tomorrow, the bulldozers that lurk in the cul-de-sac will rip a new path through the tangled brush with their sharp beaks. Dust and the tang of asphalt will fill the air. They will join the two lonely streets together, and the mice will disappear, and the tall grass, and maybe the bluebonnets too.

Probably the girl will be allowed to ride her bike from here to the other side of the neighborhood. The new street will be hers, too, after all. But the field she loves will be gone.

The note she wrote at the dining room table just after dinner is crumpled and damp in her fist. She smooths it carefully on her thigh, refolds it, and shoves it into the waistband of her shorts. With a small grunt, she hops onto the guardrail. Now she can see the whole neighborhood, everything she knows, stretching out on all sides. The field. The dark green cypress trees by the fence. The highway, a glinting white line in the distance. The houses on the other side of the field, turning to blurry slabs of beige as the light fades.

Even though her father has never said so, not exactly, the girl knows that the field is off-limits because of the boys. They are there every day, not all of them, but always at least two or three, loud enough sometimes that she can hear them from inside her house, and so can her father, who frowns in her direction when their voices filter through the windows. "Animals," he mutters. And he's right, in a way. They are a pack, like puppies, like wolves. When they come to the field, they enter from the opposite side in a line and huddle in the darkness between the lopsided wooden fence and the cluster of cypress trees. Their elbows are sharp triangles, their torsos too long. They remind her of the overlapping figures on the urns she has seen on school field trips to the museum at the university, always the same orange and black, always in motion and frozen at the same time, like they are trapped in amber.

There is always a tall one, with black hair. And sometimes, if she is lucky, she sees the one she likes, the one with brown curls bending around the edges of a burnt-orange baseball hat. Once, he stepped out of the line of trees, his hand raised in the air. He wore his hat pulled so low that she couldn't see his face, but she could imagine it anyway: a kind face, a slow smile. Before she could raise her arm to wave back, he was gone, and then she thought she heard two sharp barks of laughter that made her cheeks burn.

He never waved to her again. But once, on her way back from the bathroom at school, she saw him running down an empty hallway just before the fire alarm went off. She does not know his name. All she knows is that her father is wrong. He is not a wolf. He is not an animal at all. He is only a boy.

She wonders if he knows about the bulldozers.

She wonders if he loves the field the way she does.

The girl shapes her body into a star, then a crane, then a star again. She is Nadia Comăneci, her arms fluttering up and down like they are made of white feathers instead of bones. She can feel the heat of the guardrail rise in the marrow of her shinbones as she dares herself to stand in an arabesque for twenty seconds, then twenty more. It rained an hour ago, huge swooping sheets that emptied the neighborhood and made the asphalt steam once it was gone. Now water shines like spilled mercury on the oiled surface of the dead-end street behind her, and shivering lines of fire ants stream from the field to fringe the edges of the new puddles. The smell of crushed honeysuckle is everywhere. Everyone is inside, eating dessert or turning on the evening news.

The girl, though, is waiting.

She is outside because she wants to practice her routine one more time before the bulldozers ruin everything. Because she wants to say goodbye to the field. Because the rain has finally cooled the air, and because she has made a decision: if the boy with the curly hair comes today, she will go to the fence and hand him the note. Maybe she will even talk to him. So she is waiting, pretending to wade through the missing spring blue-bonnets, brushing her hands over their invisible white tips. She keeps her eyes on the fence.

Arabesque, hop, hop, crane, star, cartwheel dismount. She sneaks another glance at the field, but no one is there. The street behind her is quiet. The field is a deep golden color, like a jar of dark syrup held to the light.

Somewhere far away, a dog barks. The streetlights will come on soon, and her father will open the screen door and call her name. She might not see the boy tonight, but she can leave him the note. He will come to say goodbye to the field, just like her, and he will find it. She slides on her flip-flops.

Now, she tells herself.

———————

Up close, the fence is smaller than she thought it would be. It is not solid gray like a child's drawing, but splintered and polka-dotted, with knots as large as eggs. There is no one there, so she crouches low in the space between the cypress trees and the fence, her arms breaststroking her body into a tunnel of shadow and cool, packed dirt. This is where the boys stand together, talking, laughing. She inhales deeply, nostrils flaring. Her heart is pounding. She wants to lie down, to wait for the boy, but the ground is flecked with boogerspit and cigarette butts, and it is getting dark, so she doesn't. She rolls up the note, like an ancient scroll, and slides it between two splintery slats.

The air is thick, still. Everything is the same grayish blue now: the fence, the line of trees, the dirt. She braces herself for the distant sound of her father's voice as she leans her head against the fence, poking her fingers into the holes where the knots have fallen away.

The note is a stupid idea. It's getting dark and the boy hasn't come. He will probably never find it. Or maybe one of his friends will, and they will make fun of him. Or the bulldozers will bury it, deep beneath a pile of dirt and uprooted grass, before he ever reads it.

But the idea of him unrolling it, smiling a little as he sits on the edge of his bed, pressing it flat on the thigh of his jeans, makes her feel happy. Like her body is a balloon, filling with air.

A warm, wet breeze is moving across the field now, the dry grass waving reluctantly in its wake. What if the note blows away before he comes to the fence again? What if it rains again, and the ink runs, and her words disappear? She looks around for something heavy, a rock maybe, but there is nothing, so she takes off her flip-flops and wedges the note between them, like a sandwich. It is hard to stuff the thick bundle back between the fence slats, but now she knows the note won't blow away. She leaves a little flag of paper sticking out so he will see it.

She is picturing his face, trying to imagine the shape of his hands, when she hears a scratching sound, as if a bird is settling in the branches. Then, a voice. A flicker of light.

She scrambles away from the fence and bolts back toward the guardrail, her feet heavy and slow. The edge of the field seems far away now, as if the coming darkness has distorted the distance.

She trips a little at the beginning of the hill that leads down to the opening of the culvert. When she reaches the flat concrete at the bottom, she crouches, panting. She could crawl inside, where he won't be able to see her. The dark mouth of the drain is as wide as her body. It breathes its cool dampness on her shoulders.

If he finds the note, she will know it, somewhere in the palms of her hands, the soles of her feet. She is sure of that. But she wants to see his face, here, the way she has imagined, before the field and the fence and the guardrail are gone forever. She steps away from the culvert and crawls partway up the hill. Her bare feet squish in a thin layer of mud.

He is here.

He is walking out of the line of trees, toward her. It is the same scene she pictured, his long legs moving fast through the dry grasses, *swish, swish,* his eyes fixed on hers. Her mind is whirling, her ears roaring. She is about to say something—what? *Hello?* Would that be enough?—when he opens his mouth. For a moment, he is still too far away for her to hear what he is saying. The light is dim, but she can see that he is frowning, running.

Then, suddenly, she can hear him.

"Go," he shouts.

He is close now. Almost here. He flushes the resting birds from the brush as he runs, and they fly at the girl like bats. He is a black painting on an evening-dark urn. Hercules and the birds, she remembers.

She should be afraid, but she isn't.

It's only that she can't decide which way to go.

Bee

Bee folds the tiny white onesie into a soft brick. It flaps open when she tries to stack it with the others on the bed, its trio of metal snaps gaping like a mouth. There are three stacks now, three wobbly lighthouses in the dark blue wilderness of her bedspread.

"Perverse little fucker," she says under her breath. She wants to stop folding and lie down. She wants to splay across the bed like a sleeping giant, crushing the onesies with her weight.

The onesies do not defend themselves. She is folding, they are unfolding.

Doing, undoing.

"Here, let me have that," Charlie says, appearing in the doorway, his mouth turned down because he is trying not to laugh at her. "You're so . . . bad at it."

"I am. I'm terrible at laundry." Bee gives him a wobbly smile as she stands. A warm dollop lands in her underwear. "Oh Jesus," she mutters.

"What?"

"I'm leaking. Nothing you need to know about."

It has been eight weeks since Attie was born. Bee should not be bleeding. She should only be nursing and cooing. Folding.

She looks down, as if whatever is sluicing out of her will be pooling darkly on the bedroom carpet. There is nothing there but the woolen pink roses and thornless vines, curling around each other as usual. Attie is twitching in her bassinet in the corner, her hands waving in uneven shudders that remind Bee of the jerking frames of a time-lapse video. She is so small, so perfect, and Bee is huge and clumsy.

Charlie looks up at her, frowning, a bouquet of rolled onesies in his hands. "Here, I just roll them. Is that normal?"

"Rolling a onesie?"

He stands and puts his hand on her shoulder. His mouth opens and closes, as if they are meeting for the first time and he is trying to think of the right thing to say. His hand is heavy, warm. "Be serious. The leaking, I mean."

Bee doesn't want to talk about blood, or leaking, or underwear, or anything having to do with the disaster area that is her vagina. "I think so? Yeah? I mean . . . you're the doctor, not me. Plus, you were there, as I recall. It looks like a crime scene down there. Leaking is the least of it."

"Bee, I'm an ER doc, not an OB. Maybe you should call Dr. Calvanese?"

"I'm fine, Charlie. Really."

Actually, though, she isn't sure. Since Attie was born, she has been astonished—that is the only word for it, *astonished*—that women all over the world have babies and go about their lives as if they have just done something ordinary. Bee's breasts are in full-scale revolt. Her hair is falling out in clumps that clog the shower drain. When she stands up too quickly, silverfish twirl at the edges of her vision. She sleeps like a war-zone soldier on patrol, quick snatches that she is sure do not qualify as REM and leave her with shaking hands and clammy, sour-smelling skin. She knows that she is supposed to relish this experience as the miracle that it surely is, but mostly she feels exhausted. Petulant.

Telling herself that she is being childish does not help. Neither do her increasingly desperate efforts to find order in her life: making lists, checking them off, wiping the kitchen counters until every streak is gone, tucking the sheets deep into the corners of the mattress so they don't come loose in the night. She fills notebooks with details of Attie's naps and pumpkin-colored bowel movements, her screeches, her grimaces, searching for a pattern. But there isn't one, or if there is, it is hiding somewhere, mocking Bee's efforts to see the design.

Maybe it is obvious, and she is just too tired to see it.

Bee perches on the edge of the bed, hoping that she will not leak through her sweatpants again. The windows are three glossy black squares against the lavender gray of the bedroom walls. It is already dark, even though it can be only a little past five o'clock. Every November day in Maine is the same: a few hours of feeble light wedged between breakfast and dinner, then darkness that comes quickly, with no twilight. Outside, a thick stand of fir trees edges the yard, like the beginning of a fairy-tale forest, but they are almost the same color as the night now, and Bee can barely see them. She pictures the way she and Charlie must look from the outside, if anyone were hiding in those trees, watching two warm creatures lit up by the overhead light of the bedroom. Laughing together as they make their way through the sweet domestic tedium of the day: baby, laundry, dinner, bed. Asleep with Bee's grandmother's blue-and-white patchwork quilt pulled up to their chins, like Ma and Pa in the Little House books.

And then it repeats, again, again.

In her pocket, her phone buzzes. "I'm going to lie down on the couch for a minute, okay? Do you mind finishing this? You can call me if she starts to fuss." The bed is covered in baby clothes, and there is another pile waiting in the basket. Attie is blinking up at the overhead light, and Bee wonders briefly if it is too bright, if it will damage her unfocused vision.

"Of course. Just try to keep those organs high and tight, okay, Bee? I can't roll all these tiny burrito shirts without you." Charlie smiles, but his eyes are worried.

"Don't worry about me. High and tight. Nothing to see here." Bee laughs because he wants her to.

Downstairs, legs propped, she looks at her phone. There is one new email from work, her boss reminding everyone that the year-end reviews are coming up in December. Bee's out-of-office email must be otherwise effective, as there is nothing else, not even Amina's usual recipe sharing or Luke's seemingly endless supply of *Game of Thrones* memes.

Bee imagines what her year-end review might say:

When she left Grapevine Designs in September, Bee Rowan was pregnant. Some might even say majestic. Now, she is the proud mother of a baby girl who shits her not-insignificant weight in yellowish sludge every single day. The baby is, therefore, quite productive.

Bee Rowan, less so.

Bee hugs the couch cushions so that she can pretend that her sagging belly is just a pillow in disguise. She misses them, kind of. Not the work, but Amina, Luke. Even her boss, Nat, who is nine maddening years younger than she is, a Yale frat boy turned thirty, pale and thin-haired, with a voice that trembles when he stands at the head of the meeting table every morning. She misses the rhythms of the office, the bland humor that arises out of meaningless routine. Monday through Friday. The occasional night out for drinks on Fore Street.

A different kind of doing, undoing.

There is, at least, a product. At Grapevine Designs, there are clients, tasks, data. Boxes to check. You give them something, they give you something. It is satisfying, in its way. Bee works on site design and writes content, which isn't exactly what she imagined she would do with her degree in art history, but what does it matter? She never studied art because she wanted to make money, obviously. She wasn't ambitious enough to become a museum curator or a gallery owner. She just liked the classes, the way she got to sit in the dark for long winter afternoons while some excited professor clicked through the slides and time unbound itself from its usual rules. Venus of Willendorf, luscious and bulging, her breasts two overgrown acorns. *Portrait of Madame X*. The perfect gestural movement of the cave paintings at Lascaux. Frida Kahlo, glaring in the darkness, accusing Bee of something she couldn't remember doing but was equally sure she should feel bad about. "Behold," her professor would say, arms raised, the slides glowing behind him, as if he were a priest, or an ancient philosopher holding court in the middle of a sunbaked agora, not an aging academic at a tiny, snowbound college in Maine. "Behold."

She found him overly dramatic at first. Most professors were, with their grandiose vocabularies, their petty squabbles with colleagues. But then, one late afternoon during her sophomore year, yawning and hung over, she felt her spine lift, bone by bone, from the scratchy orange folding seat in Baxter Hall. On the screen in front of her was a painting she had never seen before, its colors so bold they seemed to pulse. Her arms lifted from her sides like a marionette's, and suddenly there was no room, no screen, nothing between her and the backlit pastels, the brushstrokes. A blue-green angel hovered in the air along with her, and the woman in the painting sat on a strange outdoor bed, floating over a town of angled roofs and windows while Bee's professor talked about World War II and Russian folklore, his voice a muted backdrop to the hammering of her heart.

For a minute Bee thought she had fallen asleep, but then she decided that she had finally done it. She was not dreaming but living.

Beholding, just like the man said.

For the next two years, she took every art class she could. They made her feel calm, composed. She could forget about the calculus test she nearly failed, the roommate who teased her every time she checked the locks before bed, the first-year students who ignored the campus sidewalks to make narrow paths of ugly, mud-crusted snow across the quad. When the slides dropped into place, her breath slowed to match the whir of the projector. Nothing else mattered.

After she graduated, though, she hardly ever thought about how she felt when she sat in those classes. It wasn't that she forgot about them. Not exactly. It was more that she didn't need them anymore. She was busy with her life, its practical, orderly steps: meeting Charlie, getting married, somehow turning herself from a girl into an adult with a steady job and a retirement fund.

Since giving birth to Attie, something has shifted inside her. Broken, maybe, when Attie's head crowned and Bee screamed, the sound echoing down the hospital's tiled halls. Now she sees the same painting every night before she falls asleep, and during the day too, when she steals naps with Attie or lets herself close her eyes in the parking lot of the grocery store. It's the woman, the floating bed. *The Dream* by Chagall. She feels like it is trying to tell her something, so she tries, always, to remember how it felt to be young, sitting in that dark room and lifting from her chair, as if someone had suddenly cut an invisible rope that bound her there.

If she can remember every detail, the shades of lavender and white, the exact tint of the woman's blouse, the way the dust motes floated in the beam of light from the projector, she might be able to do it again.

Living with Charlie in this creaky old house used to make her feel like she was breathing inside a glowing bowl of color. But now, somehow, it isn't enough. She is restless, unnerved. There is the painting and its insistent reappearance. And suddenly she can't stop thinking about parts of her life she thought she left behind a long time ago: her twin brother, Gus, the way he closed himself off to her like an impossible code after their father died the summer they were fifteen. Or her mother, stuck in Austin, sleeping alone in a house built for four. They keep leaking in, a cold, slow-moving wave, no matter what she does to distract herself.

Bee sighs and rolls to her side. Charlie is moving around upstairs, opening drawers and closing them, his footsteps muffled as if Bee is not in the living room but underwater. He pauses in front of the dresser in Attie's room, and Bee knows he is putting the pile of onesies away. When she goes back upstairs, he will have smoothed their blue bedspread so that it is as serene as an evening lake.

She does not deserve him. Or Attie, or any of it: this life she has, something rare, its edges crisp and otherworldly, suffused with color, like the painting in that glowing slide. *Behold*, her professor would say, if he were here, and she would have to confess that she has forgotten how.

Bee opens her mouth. She is about to call up to Charlie and ask him to bring Attie downstairs so that Bee can nurse her. He will settle Attie's humid body against Bee's chest, and she will feel both of their hearts beating, one clumsy and too slow, the other rabbity, feral. But Charlie is humming happily, his feet shuffling in his burping two-step, and she does not want to interrupt him.

She has time for one short nap. Just ten minutes. Charlie won't mind, even if he comes downstairs with Attie squirming and ready to eat and finds Bee sleeping. She can't stop it, anyway—already she can feel her head drooping, her mouth slackening. There is the whir of a projector in the distance, the sound of a slide clicking into place.

"Bee," Charlie calls from upstairs. Bee's eyes fly open and her heart pounds. Attie's wail begins, growing louder until Bee can barely hear what he says next. "Sorry. I think she's hungry."

Bee is half startled, half angry. She is just on the cusp of sleep. Of floating. She is tired. And now Attie needs her again. *Love* is the word people use, but it isn't enough. Bee is attached to Attie with a taut, unbreakable, invisible wire that only the two of them can feel. The wire lifts her from her chair when Attie cries. It pulls on Bee's breasts so they fill the moment she thinks of Attie's hunger.

Her endless, insatiable hunger. Disorderly. Rapacious.

Ridiculous. The hunger of a plague of locusts demolishing a poor family's only field. Hunger that does not care that Bee's nipples are two shredded, undercooked meatballs or that she is in the middle of a dream where she is flying high over extravagantly blossoming treetops, the back of her neck tingling with joy.

At the thought of nursing, Bee's breasts begin to needle and swell, and she shifts again on the couch. It is only, or already, two hours since Attie last ate. Bee and Charlie put the groceries away, swept the kitchen, almost finished folding the pile of tiny onesies before Bee started to leak, and now the time is over, so quickly, a door closing slowly at first and then slamming shut in a breeze, and Bee has failed to notice the moments passing.

If only there were a jolly nineteenth-century neighbor, toothless and aproned, cheeks shining pink with whiskey and lard, to nurse the baby. Bee would pay her anything. She has not yet gone to the bathroom to see what disaster waits in her underwear, and now twin stains of breast milk are blooming on her T-shirt. *No no no no no,* she begs, and yawns a little to clear her ears as she presses her chest, hard. She is a fountain, a sieve. She is worn out, but her breasts are strangely alive. They are purposeful and insistent. Goal-oriented. They would pass a year-end review with flying colors, Bee thinks as she wills them to quiet.

She can tell from the silence upstairs that Charlie has given Attie a pacifier or a finger to suck while he waits for her to answer. Bee can add this to the list of small kindnesses that she has not earned.

She looks again at her phone. No more emails. It's embarrassing how quickly the world has adjusted to her absence.

There are two texts, though, so that's something. One is

from Mary, her mother, the second of the week. They speak on the phone every Sunday, five minutes or less. Mary talks about the price of produce or the real estate boom in Austin or the neighbor who keeps parking his car at the curb in front of her house. The conversation is the same every time, as if there is a script.

Did Mary ever feel the pull of a wire connecting her to Bee? Did she stare at Bee and Gus in the middle of the night, smiling to herself as she brushed her thumb across the velvety down of their cheekbones? It's hard to imagine. Mary never talks about Gus anymore, and Bee never asks. He is unmentionable, a ghost who pops up occasionally in the police blotters Bee finds online but never in conversation. Today is no different. Mary is sending an article about an herbal tonic that will improve milk flow. As usual, the text is just a link to an article, without even a note to say hello or ask Bee how she is doing.

Bee does not need help with milk flow, obviously, so she deletes it without replying.

I'll text her later, she thinks. Her mother is trying, at least. That's more than Bee is doing.

Upstairs, Charlie flushes the toilet, and Bee startles. She can see the first few words of the second unread text—Hey, Bee. It's—but she doesn't recognize the number. Maybe it's someone from work or one of the moms she met at the breastfeeding clinic right after Attie was born and has since ignored.

Bee hesitates, just for a moment, and then opens the message. She is so surprised by what she sees that she fumbles the phone.

It's Leo.

The couch beneath her seems to shift, like it has become an old-fashioned carriage sled sliding on the polished floor.

The text is only a few sentences, but Bee reads it again and again. Hey, Bee. It's Leo, it says. I'm in Portland for a couple of days. I think you still live near here? I'm at the Spoke. Would love to see you.

It doesn't make any sense. Not the message itself, not its casual tone, as if it is from Nat or Amina, even Charlie.

Leo was her neighbor, once. He lived across the street, in a house just like hers, a three-bedroom ranch, except his had peeling paint and an unruly, scorched lawn. Anyone would have said that they were an inseparable trio—Bee, Gus, and Leo—but Leo was Gus's best friend, first and foremost. And even though Bee would never have admitted it, he was her first crush, or maybe love, if love is a thing you can feel when you're twelve, or fifteen, or even twenty, and you haven't ever kissed, or bought a house, or made a baby with someone.

She hasn't heard from Leo in more than fifteen years. The last time she saw him, she was twenty-two years old. The lights of an ambulance washed the pale skin of Gus's face in pinks and blues, and Leo wouldn't look at her.

Bee's thumbs shake as they hover over her phone.

Still there? she types.

She puts the phone on the coffee table. The Spoke is downtown, at least ten minutes away if she doesn't hit a single light. She will have to change her shirt and put on real pants, if she can find a pair that fits. She will have to pump, or nurse Attie, and by then it will be too late, and he will be gone. There is another load of laundry already thumping in the dryer. They haven't eaten dinner, which is only frozen pizza, but still. It is sitting on the counter, wrapped in plastic, the shreds of cheese turning into soggy white maggots.

Charlie won't like it. He will think Bee is dwelling on the past again, and he will tell her, like always, that she needs to let it go. He will remind her that he is on call, and that there isn't time to find a babysitter.

The phone's sudden vibration against the wood of the table is so loud that Bee is startled, confused.

Yup, the message says. Come see me.

Bee stands up, her shirt cold against her body, the stains spreading somehow from below her nipples to the center of her back. She pulls the shirt away from her skin and drips in the center of the living room. She can hear Charlie cooing and singing upstairs, his deep, sweet voice a murmur with no words. She should go upstairs, nurse Attie. Then she can go to the Spoke, just for one drink. Just to see what Leo is up to, what he has to say.

She is just going out to see an old neighbor. A friend. One drink.

Why shouldn't she?

Bee starts up the stairs. Her heart is pounding, and there are tears in her eyes.

"Look, I'm leaking again," she whispers, to no one.

Mary

Austin, Texas
1987

There are shapes in the field, small, rounded creatures that move slowly in the dusk, as if there is nothing out there to be afraid of, no sharp-toothed possum or bobcat or fox. Mary can see them because she has turned off the porch light, and because she has been sitting outside for longer than she should.

She does not want to go inside. Not yet. Leroy is still awake in front of the television, the baseball game blaring. There are dishes in the sink, and she still has to dry Gus's favorite T-shirt. Bee will probably do the dishes, but not the laundry, and Gus will be annoyed if his shirt is damp and stiff in the morning.

She's left the porch light off because it makes her feel invisible. She can sit here, smoothing her hands across her tightening belly, waiting for its answering vibration, and no one will know. If a passing car took a picture of the house, the flashbulb would catch her, perched and watchful on the front steps, but almost no cars drive along this street once everyone is home from work for the day. Even if a car passed, she is sure that no one would notice her.

Mary can match every car on this street to its owner. She watches them coming and going each day, returning at night like game pieces accumulating around a Monopoly board. There is Leroy's truck, of course, in her own garage. Across the street, the Nastasi garage is closed, but Mary knows Diana Nastasi's brown sedan is parked inside. There should be another car there, too, Derek Nastasi's pale blue Ford Escort, but Mary hasn't seen it at all this week, not coming, not going.

Once, she saw that blue Escort leave long after the lights in the Nastasi house had gone dark, but that is none of her business. If she happens to see Derek Nastasi reversing from his driveway tonight while she is sitting here, watching the street, she will scoot back into the shadow under the overhang of the porch so that his headlights will not catch her snooping.

Mary is not snooping. She is just sitting on her own porch. She is just taking a minute for herself. Sometimes, she practices her lines or thinks about whether she should try to find a new school for Gus in the fall or make him practice his guitar out on the back patio, the way he used to. But mostly she watches the field, the way the breezes shift its surface, the way the evening sun gilds the tips of the grass just before it disappears.

Tonight, her watching is tinged with sadness. Soon she will have only the comings and goings of the cars to watch. Starting tomorrow, they are extending this street through the field, plowing through the burrows and nests, connecting it to the neighborhood on the other side to make room for more Monopoly houses, more cars. *For each house, pay twenty-five dollars. For each hotel, one hundred dollars.* By spring, the field will be a line of smooth black pavement, unrolled without her consent.

It doesn't matter, not really. There will be no time to sit alone on the porch in the evening. The baby will be here, and

Mary will be busy with the wiping and soothing and tending that will come. Bee will be fine, of course, and it is time for Gus to learn to take care of himself. The songbirds will find somewhere else to build their nests.

Maybe it's the scuttling of the shapes in the field, or the hint of coolness in the air, but the night is full of a strange, nervous energy. It rained earlier, giant washes of water that poured from the edges of the roof and made deep channels in the beds of pale pink gravel on the sides of the house. There was a tornado warning from neighboring Bell County, but the electricity stayed on. There isn't even any wind. In the Nastasi house across the street, Mary can see lamps lit in two different windows. She has never been inside the Nastasi house, but it is a mirror version of her own, and they're slow to draw the shades at night, so she knows that Leo sleeps in the bedroom diagonal to Gus's. Diana Nastasi has some kind of office where Bee's bedroom would be, and she is sitting there now, as she always is in the evening, working at her desk. The lamp beside her makes a shining crown of her hair. She chews a pencil slowly, thoughtfully, with a mouth that is dark coral and full.

She is a beautiful woman. It is strange, the way Derek carries on.

Mary pats the cigarette she has hidden in her pocket, a single Benson & Hedges Luxury 100 from the gold pack hiding behind the spice rack in the kitchen. She hasn't smoked one in months, not since Bee saw her outside the Pips Playhouse, sharing one with her director after rehearsal. Bee's face was enough to shame the Pope out of being Catholic, as Mary's mother would say. Mary felt like she had been caught with her tongue down the man's throat, and her face still heats at the thought (Bee's face; the imaginary, thrusting tongue). Even if she does not smoke them, she keeps this last pack. Leroy hates the smell of them. The whiff of tobacco in her pocket will be enough to make him tell her that cigarettes are not for a lady, not for a lady of his, and he will roll over in bed, away from her, the tall, hard hump of his belly invisible from the back.

Still, she keeps them. She knows she shouldn't. When she was pregnant with the twins, she smoked just one a day. Everyone did, then. Now, of course, she knows better. There is a warning label on the pack. But if she does not smoke them, where is the harm?

The light from Gus's bedroom presses a square of gold on the lawn as the sky dims. Mary watches the glow turn sharp-edged, the grass around it fading from green to black. How many minutes have passed? Leroy is still watching the baseball game on the television. Soon he will be asleep, head back on his chair, his mouth open as if he is about to shout curses at the ceiling.

There is a rustle in the bushes at her side. Not a snake, which makes a smooth sound, like it is saying the word *delicious* as it slithers. This is some small mammal, a nervous thing with a tiny heart that beats ten times the pace of her own.

There is a tiny heart inside Mary too. A new baby, coming so long after the twins—and at her age—that it feels like an impossible gift, even though Leroy will not think so, and neither will Bee and Gus. But no one has noticed the way her belly has hardened and stretched, and so she hasn't told anyone at all, the way you don't tell anyone your birthday wish, just close your eyes and hope you blow out every last candle.

Mary turns and knocks an elbow against the screen door. The movement in the bushes stops, so Mary freezes, pats her belly, and mouths a silent apology to whatever little rabbit or chipmunk or bird she has frightened. She wills its tiny heart to slow so that the veins and arteries do not explode with the pressure of its fear.

Her mouth is still moving when Gus turns out the light in his room and the whole lawn darkens. The glow of Leroy's television paints the porch a dim blue, and Mary can hear the faint music of the Sunday-night movie. It is somehow later than she realized, darker too, and Mary's pupils expand. She will be able to see anything now: a snake, a tiny rodent, a swooping owl, the cougars that she is always afraid will slink down from the hills to the west and find their way to this quiet, dead-end street.

She knows she has no reason to be afraid. Not really. Leroy has told her for years that her worries are a foolish waste of time. The twins have not drowned, or gotten hit by cars, as she was sure they would when they were small. She has never seen a cougar or even a bobcat. All she would have to do, if some wild, teeth-baring animal decided to pad up to this porch, ready to close its jaws on the nape of her neck, is stand up, turn around, and go inside.

Still, she scoots closer to the door. She has just pulled her feet beneath her when she sees it: something large, bigger than a cougar even, creeping around the corner of the house. It is low, ungainly, scrabbling across the lawn to the tree. Mary's heart hammers, and she hopes that the baby inside her does not feel her fear. She is sure that this misshapen animal will turn at the sound, stare at her with glowing, accusatory eyes. Growl.

The animal reaches the tree, and when it does, it stands. Mary breathes in relief. Of course this is not a cougar, here on Stillwood Lane. Silly imagination. She is not a pioneer wife, out on the wide-open plains with only greased paper windows and a hot poker to protect her.

It is only Gus. He is facing away from her, looking at Leo's house, where the lights glow steadily. She can tell from the tip of his head that he is listening for something, and she opens her mouth so that her own breath will make no sound.

As Mary watches, the light in Leo's room turns off.

The boys are up to something. Mary feels calm, amused even. She is glad Gus has Leo. They are so different. Gus is harsh and angry, Leo gentle and quiet and strange, but when they are together Gus's jagged edges dull, just a little, and Leo's sharpen. Mary has heard from the other mothers on the street that Leo gets in trouble sometimes at school, but it can't be anything terrible. She has known him since he was a little boy. He plants gardens and hatches butterflies. She is glad he and Gus are doing what fifteen-year-old boys should be doing on a summer evening. This is their last night in the field. They should enjoy it. If Bee were sneaking out, that would be different. She is a girl, and the rules are not the same for her, even though Mary would never admit that out loud. It is important to let a girl think she has some freedom, before she learns the truth for herself.

She will give Gus a few minutes to make his escape. Leroy is snoring evenly in the living room. He will jolt awake at eleven or so, patting his shirt pockets frantically, knocking over at least one of the beer bottles at his feet, and then he will shuffle to bed without brushing his teeth. She will feign sleep until he settles in beside her. Early in the morning, before Mary is awake, he will drive himself to the terminal and heave himself into his truck to start the route from Austin to Oklahoma City and back again, stopping to deliver pallets of Cheetos and Fritos and Doritos and whatever else along the way.

Gus is still standing at the tree, watching. She can see his shoulders rising and falling, as if he has been running. There is an inch-wide stripe of bluish gray between the dark form of his body and the thick trunk of the tree. He is not trying to hide, which means that he doesn't know his mother is sitting in the dark shadow of the porch, or he doesn't care enough to turn around. She is not trying to hide either. She is only watching the field and breathing the cool evening air.

Another shape detaches itself from the far corner of the Nastasi house. Leo, of course, running across his lawn, his body a fast-moving shadow. When he reaches the window where his mother is sitting, he ducks. He is only a foot from her, in the bushes beneath her window, but Diana does not look up from her work. When Leo gets to the edge of the driveway, he unfolds himself, turns himself into a boy. If Diana looked over, she might see him, but she is entirely, utterly, absorbed.

Leo has a backpack with him, Mary sees, and it looks like a turtle's hump. She smiles at the image: a boy-turtle, running, like a character in a children's book. The bag is probably full of beer, or whatever he could find at the Nastasi house. Before Derek started doing whatever he is doing, the Nastasis used to have parties, big ones with cars lining the street all the way to the stop sign. It wouldn't be hard for Leo to steal a bottle or two, or something else. Diana would never notice if he took anything.

Mary knows she should call Gus's name, demand that the boys shake out the contents of the backpack at her feet, but she doesn't move. Letting Gus go is easier than trying to stop him now. If she does, they will have yet another fight, and it isn't worth it.

And who is she to judge? She isn't perfect, not by a long shot. She remembers the parking lot, Bee's stricken face, as if she had seen into Mary's most secret thoughts. She purses her lips, lets a long breath of imaginary smoke loose from her lungs.

The boys are heading to the field. They will drink and hang out for a few hours, and then they will come back to their beds, and by that time, Mary and Leroy will have been asleep for hours. Or Leroy will have been asleep; Mary will wait with her eyes on the ceiling, just to make sure Gus comes back safely.

Gus and Leo are the same shadow now. They move together to the end of the street. Leo hands the bag to Gus, who puts it on his own back. The rustle in the bushes starts again, and the more it moves, the more Mary thinks it might be a snake after all. *Delicious, delicious, delicious,* it says, and there is an answering tremor deep in her belly.

A year from now, she will sit on this porch with Gus and Bee, maybe Leroy too. She can almost see Gus smiling at the way the baby will toddle around from one chair to the next, grabbing his knees with chubby hands to balance. Maybe the baby will be another boy. Maybe Gus will play lullabies on his guitar so the baby will sleep. Maybe he will remember the way he was as a child—loving, persistent—before he decided to close himself off to her. Maybe he will return to himself.

In a year, everything will be different. Of course it will.

Mary listens for the noise of the boys' feet crushing the dry grass, but they are far away now, beyond the end of the street, heading for the fence. There is a burst of laughter, then silence.

Across Stillwood Lane, Diana Nastasi is still at her desk, her dark hair escaping the bun at the top of her head. She is looking up now, out the window, and for a moment Mary worries that Diana can see her, hiding on her own front porch in the dark like a fool. But this is silly, as is the idea that Diana is nodding at her, just a slight incline of her head, a tiny lift of one corner of her mouth, before bending back to the pile of papers in front of her.

Mary stands, but she doesn't go inside right away. Leroy has stopped snoring, and she can't see him in the bluish darkness of the living room. He must have gone to bed and forgotten to turn off the television. There are still the dishes to wash, and the counters to wipe, and Gus's T-shirt to hang on the line. She will clear the beer bottles Leroy has left behind and wipe up the spills. She will remind Bee about getting the yarn for her community service project and set the coffeepot for the morning. And after that, she will wait for Gus to return from whatever he is doing, wherever he has gone, and she will not say a word.

Bee

It is Wednesday, so the Spoke isn't full, even though it's only a block from the candlelit restaurants and craft breweries on the waterfront. Bee pauses at the door and tries to peek inside. Behind the door's amber-colored glass panels, blurred shapes join into pairs and then split apart again. Muffled laughter escapes when a smoker sneaks past her into the alley. Bee used to come here all the time, when she first moved to Portland, before she met Charlie. The familiarity of it is jarring.

Bee sucks in her stomach. She is nervous. The skin of her hand looks papery and old on the door's brass handle. These are her mother's hands, not hers, although her mother would have at least bothered to trim her cuticles and file her nails. Bee needs to drink more water, maybe. More something, like collagen or powdered kale. The morning after Attie was born, she found a single white hair, curling like a viper over her right ear. When she showed Charlie, he just laughed. "You'll make a beautiful granny," he said as he hugged her. Bee knew he was teasing, but she plucked the hair out just the same. And the next one, a day later.

And now, what will Leo think? Will he even recognize her? It's been seventeen years. The last time she saw him, she was twenty-two, lean and tan from a summer of farm work. Now she has a banana-boat maxi pad stuffed into her underwear, so thick she is afraid she might waddle. She is still wearing maternity jeans with a spandex waistband that reaches to the bottom of her nursing bra. She is fat. She used to look in the mirror when she brushed her teeth at night and smile, just to see the shine of her cheeks, just for the joy of it.

She is being ridiculous. Vain. She knows she is. Leo is not a date. He is not even a friend, not anymore. She hasn't seen him since Gus collapsed on his bedroom floor at the farm, so high on whatever he was taking that his eyes rolled back in his head. Bee and Leo had been fighting for weeks by then. Leo insisted that Gus was fine, that Leo could take care of him, that they didn't need to get anyone else involved. And then there was Gus, his eyes the unseeing marble of a statue, his skin pale and cold. Bee called an ambulance, and then she accused Leo of being a selfish coward who cared more about his job on a fucking farm than he did about Gus.

She hasn't spoken to either of them since. For years, though, she has traced the faint dotted lines of their lives on the internet, watching the computer screen as they move up and down the East Coast, new addresses popping up every few years like clues. Leo's Facebook page is public but has only two posts: a black-and-white photo of overgrown railroad tracks and one of birds perched like musical notes on telephone wires. Otherwise it is empty, just a gray avatar where his face should be. She has no idea what he looks like now. She's not even sure that the profile belongs to him.

She tells herself that she tracks Leo to keep tabs on Gus, to make sure he is okay. There's a logic to this, even though it's not the kind she can explain. Gus and Leo disappeared from her life at the same time, and they are more like twins than Bee and Gus ever were. Find one, find the other.

She goes as long as she can between searches. She has a rule: if she lasts a whole month without typing their names, she allows herself one hour of diving into Google, like rewarding a month of abstinence with a single drink. The rule is supposed to keep her safe from missing them too much. But since Attie's birth, it hasn't been working. Her searching has become unruly, unhinged, disorganized. Late at night, when Charlie is asleep and Attie has been burped and changed and rocked, she types in the names of the Walnut Creek Pool and the roller rink and Zilker Park, trying to find photographs from her childhood so that she can zoom in and look for her own face, for Gus's, for Leo's. She looks at the 1987 archives of the *Austin American-Statesman*, reading and rereading the account of her father's crash, then his obituary, which is always the same three terse lines. "Born in 1941, Leroy Rowan attended school in Oklahoma before taking a job in . . ."

It's just natural curiosity, she tells herself. And yet her stomach somersaults with guilt every time she types their names into the search bar. She deletes the web history before she crawls back into bed next to Charlie's sleeping body, as if she has been cheating on him somehow.

And now Leo is here, in Portland, inviting her out for a drink, like a sign, as if the years have dissolved. Before she got his text tonight, she'd nearly convinced herself that it didn't matter anymore. Gus and Leo should remain in the past, or wherever your childhood goes when you're not looking, and they should stay there, where they belong. She has her own life, her adult, permanent life, even if she feels like she's bobbing along its river inside a boat with no oars.

She knows Leo, even now. She knows he must have a reason for reaching out after so long.

The reason can only be Gus.

When she opens the door, Bee feels like her ears have popped after a long plane ride. It is loud, and the sounds are garbled and harsh after the quiet of the street. There are more people here than it seemed from outside. There is a group waiting for drinks at the end of the bar, another group stuffed into a booth with stools pulled up alongside. Bee stands stranded at the door for a moment and scans the room, her hands two sweating fists in her pockets.

She doesn't see him.

There is a group of people gathered in front of a dartboard, and Bee steps forward, trying to see their faces.

"Bee." Leo is behind her.

"Hey, Leo." Bee makes herself smile and turn slowly, hoping that he can't hear the frantic edge in her voice, that he can't tell that her heart is pounding unevenly as they hug. And then that he can't tell that she is measuring him, the new width of his shoulders, the familiar smell of crushed lemon balm rising from the crook of his neck when they hug.

Does he hold her just a moment too long before he lets her go?

He doesn't say anything else, just turns and walks over to the bar. She remembers this, the way his shyness disguises itself as gruffness, the way she always wants to jump into his sentences to help them flow more easily.

He has always been the opposite of Gus, who is all sparks and misfires. Or used to be. Bee doesn't know how Gus is now. He could be a monk, or a realtor, or a carpenter, for all she knows.

Leo must be here to tell her something he can only say in person. Maybe Gus has gotten arrested again. Or he is back in rehab. Or homeless. He is lost somewhere on a hike he started in a quest to finally find himself.

She is running through the possibilities in her mind when she realizes that Leo is standing next to a pair of empty stools by the bar, motioning for her coat. She shakes her head. She can feel a cold bloom of milk on her chest, and she does not want him to see it. She sits on the closest stool, and he sits next to her, their shoulders almost touching. Bee has the urge to lean toward him, just a little, but she doesn't.

"It's kind of cold in here, right?" she begins.

"Maybe? I'm a few beers in, to be honest, so I have no idea." He is smiling, but his eyes are worried. His face is tipped slightly to the side, as if he is afraid she might slap him, and his cheeks are flushed. He is drunk, Bee realizes. He is looser, easier to be around, when he is drunk. Before everything went wrong at the farm, they would sit around a fire at night, and Leo would pass her jelly jars of wine and talk, the words tumbling out in a way they never did during the day. Bee always wondered where the stories came from; they spent their whole childhoods together, so how did she miss the time their fourth-grade teacher called the class a bunch of asshats, or the time Gus threw someone's abandoned lunch at the bus driver? Leo wasn't the type to make things up, but she didn't remember any of it.

She remembers so little. She notices this all the time. For everyone around her, time seems to polish the edges of the past, make it shiny and simple and clear. Charlie can describe touch football games he played at recess when he was ten years old, the dramas and fumbles fresh in his mind as if they happened last Tuesday instead of decades ago. It doesn't make sense, not to Bee. For her, it is hard enough to pay attention to the day itself, with its tasks, its tiny hills of feeling to climb up and slide down just to get from dawn to dusk. It's even worse now, with her whole body tuned to Attie, her edges dissolving and reforming to draw a new and unrecognizable contour. Bee can feel her brain softening with each passing day. When she tries to read, the sentences lift at the ends and curl back on themselves uselessly.

Leo takes a sip of his beer and looks at her. Maybe he asked her here for the simplest of reasons: he is in town, he is curious. They are older now, and the edges of the past have blurred for him too. It has been, finally, long enough for him to forget what she said to him as they stood in the gravel driveway of the farm, the doors of the ambulance still open, Gus staring blankly at the sky.

Maybe he has forgotten the shape of her lips, the snarl they made.

Leo's curls are spiky with static. He turns an orange knitted hat in his hands and then sips his beer again. He seems nervous, not angry, but he doesn't say anything.

"It's been a long time," she begins. "You look the same, though." Her voice sounds squawky.

"Do I? I don't feel it. But you do. You look great, I mean." He rubs the stubble of his chin and looks straight ahead, to the mirror that hangs behind the bar. His eyes flicker over her reflection, then away.

It is stupid to protest, so she doesn't. Better to ignore the compliment, and the absurd trembling it creates in her hands.

There is still the trace of a twang in Leo's voice, and Bee wonders if he hears a matching one in hers.

The pause between them lengthens. Bee says, "I was just thinking about you the other day, actually. Did you ever get that farm? I mean, a farm of your own?"

Leo smiles. His drink is almost gone. He raises a hand to get the bartender's attention, but he is too far away, talking to one of the waitresses, who is tying and untying her apron as he loads her small brown tray. The only light is the yellow-and-red faux stained-glass lamp hanging over the pool table. It is probably meant to be ironic, or nostalgic, and it is—it reminds Bee of the old Arnie's restaurants in Texas, where her mother would take them after piano recitals or to celebrate the last day of school. They would put their elbows on the sticky table and order the Hurricane, a sundae made with every flavor and topping on the board. The bar at the Spoke is sticky too, and for a second, the room reels. Bee wishes the stools had backs. It feels hard to hold herself up. Her body is coreless, contracted like a worm's.

"I own a farm now, yeah," Leo says.

"Is it near here? That's amazing," she says. Her cheeks are too warm. "You did it."

"Just bought it a couple of months ago. It's a little to the south of here. Near Portsmouth. I'm planning to grow mostly flowers, some herbs. Some wholesale, some direct-to-customer at the markets. This time of year we have to rely on the winter share. It's kind of brutal, actually. My hands are shot." He looks down at his palms and frowns, as if he is angry at them for letting him talk so much, and turns them over. There is a scar circling his knuckles. The skin is pink and wrinkled. A new one, then. He sees her looking and moves his hand away.

"I didn't realize you were so close to Portland now," she says. He looks up, as if she is accusing him of something, so she adds, "That's great." She smiles and hopes it looks even a little bit like her old one. "You were meant to have your own farm. That was obvious, even to someone who ruined a whole field of cucumber seedlings."

Leo laughs. "I had forgotten that. You were a menace with that tractor. Poor cucumbers." He takes out his wallet, and the bartender turns his head. Leo says, "Do you want a drink? Red wine, right? I think I almost have this guy's attention."

He is so calm. He has always acted this way around her, somehow both formal and warm, like she is an honored guest and a beloved family member at the same time. It used to drive her crazy that she could never figure out what he was thinking. Tonight, though, she is grateful. She can pretend that he has forgotten how unfair she was to him when Gus was sick. Maybe he only remembers the good parts of the farm, the river winding around the fields in an oxbow that protected them in a line of silvery water, swimming after work in their T-shirts. Maybe he never noticed the way Bee blushed and stuttered every time Leo handed her a watering can and his fingers brushed over hers. Maybe he only remembers the beginning, when it felt like they were little kids again, banging around on their bikes, adulthood a distant irrelevance.

"Sure. That's perfect. Thanks," Bee says. She can almost pretend that she's a normal woman, out at a bar with a friend, except that her heart is pounding and the stain on her shirt is widening, shifting. Under a microscope, it would be teeming with everything good and life-giving: proteins, antibodies, minerals. And soon, wine. She has not had anything to drink since Attie was born.

I am not a good mother, Bee thinks.

Leo orders their drinks and watches her sideways. He does not seem to have noticed the stain, or the flap of flesh that is threatening to escape the elastic waistband of her jeans and collapse in on itself like a fold of kneaded dough. Bee pulls her jacket tighter.

The farm was a fantasy, at first. They sat in scuffed white plastic chairs around a firepit after work, the river gurgling behind them in the dark, the smell of overturned earth and sour sweat in the air. Maybe they smoked a little weed. Leo once held Bee's hair while she vomited a bottle of homemade wine into the potato field, and even though he never mentioned it again, Bee couldn't look at him the next day. They drank, they tumbled into narrow beds to sleep. They worked, they ate, they swam, they drank again.

But the way Gus drank was different from the start. He didn't drink like a college kid, maybe because he never was one. He drank like a man just reaching the end of a desert trek, as if his body had some empty vessel somewhere that he had to fill, with liquor, with who knows what else, stuff he got from people he met at the warehouse where he used to work when he was living on a blow-up mattress in Leo's dorm room, or in bars and back alleys, or in places Bee couldn't even imagine.

Bee wasn't sure—she still isn't—when Gus got so sick that he couldn't get better, but by the end of the summer she knew that she couldn't watch anymore. "It doesn't matter, it doesn't matter," Gus would say, his cheek resting on the side of his bed, his hair darkening with sour sweat while Leo smoothed his forehead and tried to get him to drink water, the two of them encircled in their own closed system.

A booth opens, and Bee takes it, watching Leo as he waits for their drinks at the bar. She lets her eyes linger on every part of him: the small curls lying on his neck, the purplish bleach stain on the right shoulder of his navy T-shirt. He is entirely still as he waits, as if he knows she is watching, as if he is inviting her. She sits up a little straighter and lets the breath she was holding escape. Her phone buzzes, but she flicks the switch to silent and does not look at it.

A moment later, Leo slides into the booth and smiles. He pushes her glass across the table, and Bee feels her lungs squeezing shut as he looks at her.

Charlie, Charlie, Charlie, she thinks. *Attie, Attie, Attie.* She picks up the drink and tries to focus.

What she felt for Leo, either when she was a kid or during those strange, bewildering months on the farm, doesn't belong here, in her life. There is no space for it, no way to make it fit.

But Leo's eyes are a dark, shape-shifting green. They look almost brown in the light of the bar.

"So," he says, and then pauses for a beat too long. He clears his throat. "I heard you got married a couple of years ago. Charlie, right?"

Bee nods. "I did. He's a doctor."

God, Bee. Try not to be such a dick.

She starts again. "We actually just had a baby." She pauses.

"Oh yeah? That's amazing. Congratulations." He is twirling a coaster, as fidgety as the boy he used to be. He has never touched her on purpose, not beyond friendship, a hug to say hello, goodbye, but she has imagined it so often that she feels like she knows how gently his hands would move across her cheeks, how slowly they would tuck a strand of hair behind her ear.

He is looking down at his hands again. They open and close

while he stares at them, as if they don't belong to him. "Boy?" he asks. "Girl?"

"A girl. Attie. I named her after my sister. I don't know if you remember, but—" Bee has said this a hundred times, to everyone from her boss to her mother-in-law, but every time, she loses control of the skin on her cheeks, her chin. Attie is named after the baby Bee's mother lost the summer Bee and Gus were fifteen, just before their father died. Back then, Bee thought the word *lost* made it sound like the baby was misplaced, waiting somewhere to be found. But now she has her own baby. She knows that *lost* means divided. Separated. Gone.

Leo takes a long swig, his throat moving as he swallows. "That's—" He stops. "It's a beautiful name," he says, wiping his mouth with the back of his hand. He clears his throat. "You'll be a great mom."

The tiny hitch in his voice makes Bee want to reach across the table to him, grab his hand, smooth her fingers over the scarred skin of his knuckles. She is older now. She is better than the girl who let Leo believe that Gus's problems were his fault, his responsibility. She has practiced her apology a hundred times, in the shower, in the mirror, to Attie as she slurps away in the middle of the night. She can recite it from memory, like a prayer.

She is about to begin when Leo asks, "Have you been home yet? To bring Attie to see your mom?"

The question seems casual enough, but Bee can feel Leo's legs bouncing under the table.

"Not yet. She'll come for Christmas, maybe." Charlie already asked her to buy the tickets so Mary can visit, but Bee can't imagine having Mary in her house, opening her refrigerator, sleeping in her guest bedroom. Leo is right: she should go to

Texas. She should bring the baby to meet her mother because that's what people do. They schlep their babies across the country to meet their mothers, even the ones who don't seem all that interested. "Hopefully Charlie can get the time off."

Leo nods. There is a pause. Bee starts to open her mouth, but before she can speak Leo says, "I think Gus would love to meet her too." He is looking at the table. "And to see you. I know it's been . . ." He runs out of words. "I mean, do you think you might be open to . . ."

Gus. Bee feels something rising inside her. This is the way it's always been: Leo and Gus in their closed system, Bee on the outside.

"Right," she says, eyes burning. "So you still talk to him." In the center of the room, the empty pool table glows. Dust motes float over its surface, and a rack of glistening balls waits.

Leo grabs her hand. It startles her, this sudden intimacy. It's not like Leo, or the Leo she used to know, and it's different from the hug when she first entered the bar. He is cupping her hands in his, holding them tight, and Bee can feel that hers are too squirmy and sweaty. The grassy, lush smell of him is a dark green meadow rising between them. And now that he is here, holding her hand, she remembers the way she lights up like the bulb in a child's homemade circuit in his presence.

Bee pulls her hands away and shoves them into her pockets. "I haven't heard from Gus since the day we sent him to the hospital. What was that, seventeen years ago? You know that, right? He hasn't said one word to me in all that time." She is shaking. "And neither have you."

Leo looks down. Behind them, someone breaks the pool balls with a crack that sounds like a gunshot.

He says, "I know. He wanted to, but…"

The noise of the bar fades until there is only the booth, the pounding of her blood. "What do you mean, he *wanted* to?" Her voice is too loud. The waitress passing their booth slows a little. Bee is fifteen years old again, left out of their plans. She is twenty-two, standing in a doorway, watching Leo kneel to tie Gus's shoes. Time has dissolved, and nothing has changed. Gus and Leo have each other, always, and she misses both of them, all the time.

She has to leave. She starts to move to the edge of the bench seat, but when Leo reaches his hand across the table, she stops.

"Bee, I'm sorry," he says. "I don't see him. It's not like that. He's . . . He doesn't live around here. He splits time between here and Mexico. Or not here, exactly. Maine, Massachusetts. He travels around. He has a van, I think? I'm not really sure. But he called me last week. It's been . . ." Leo doesn't finish his sentence.

Hives march up from Bee's collarbones in long, itchy lines, and her lips are slick with her own snot. She doesn't care that Leo is watching.

"I think he would want to talk now, if you wanted to," Leo says. "I think he would want to see you."

"Oh." She tries to laugh, but it comes out sounding like a hiccup. Suddenly, shame floods her like nausea. This is not Leo's fault. He should be mad at her, not the other way around, and he is here, trying to help and giving her the news she has wanted to hear for years. He is good, like always. Bee is the one thinking about the shape of his lips and crying like a grotesquely amplified version of a hormone-addled new mother. "Leo," she says, "I'm sorry. I don't know why I'm acting like this. I'm just so tired. And Gus, and everything that happened... I don't know. It's been so long."

Bee stands. Her pants are too tight now, and she resists the urge to roll down the waistband. She wipes her face with her sleeve. The bartender is polishing the rims of a rack of steaming glasses with a bleached-white cloth. He looks up and raises an eyebrow at her.

At home, Attie is in her crib. She is curling and uncurling in her fierce, jerking motions. Bee can picture it perfectly, as if she has the video monitor propped on the table in front of her. Charlie is leaning over her, patting her rump, trying to delay the moment when he will have to pick her up, when her tiny hyena lungs will split the room.

"I'm leaving," Bee says. At Leo's stricken face, she softens. "Ding-ding, time's up. I need to feed Attie. I'm kind of a glorified cow these days." She makes her voice hard so that it will not wobble.

"Of course. Yeah. Listen, Bee—"

"It was great to see you." She fishes a twenty out of her wallet and puts it on the table. "Thanks for letting me know about Gus." Leo nods, his lips tight. He is holding his breath. Somehow, she manages not to look back until the door is safely closed behind her.

Outside, the night air is cold and damp on her face. She walks past a row of parked cars, their side mirrors folded in sheepishly. The streets are shining in the lights of the store windows, and in the darkness she can see the lights of the small islands that decorate the flickering water of Casco Bay. She walks quickly at first, in case he is following her, but soon she has to admit that there are no footsteps.

She turns off the main road toward her house, then turns

back again. She has forgotten the car. This is a new low. She will come back for it tomorrow, when this night is in the past, or when it reveals itself to be some kind of exhaustion-induced fever dream. If she wakes up and the car is in her own driveway, she will know that none of this ever happened, that she is not the kind of woman to leave her sweet baby, her sweet husband at home to meet an old crush at a bar, hoping for . . . hoping for what?

Something, anything, to make her aspic brain fire its synapses, she admits to herself as the line of stores comes to an end. A little gallop in the heart.

A chance to feel herself lift, weightless, into the air.

The streets widen as she leaves the center of town. The houses she passes are mostly dark, just a light or two in their deeply slumbering centers, a forgotten oven light or a nightlight plugged into an upstairs hallway. She keeps walking, as if she is only passing time. Sleet clings to her coat in tiny, jewellike beads.

In an hour, she is home. Her hands are numb and her breasts are as hard as boulders. She stands at the end of the driveway and looks at the house. The second-floor bedroom is dark, but all the windows downstairs are brightly lit. Bee can see Charlie in the kitchen, holding Attie. He is dipping and swaying, his mouth moving. Bee knows the song he is singing, a tuneless version of "Let It Be."

Let it all be, she thinks. Leo. Gus. The trip she knows she will take to Texas to see her mother.

The hammering of her heart.

Diana

Austin, Texas
1987

Outside the window of Waggener Hall, the light is too bright. It drains the peach tint from the limestone university buildings, leaving them the same whitish gray as the sky, and the leaves on the live oaks look ashen through the glass. Diana blinks, then turns her back to the window. Her torso casts a shadow across her desk.

She only has an hour to work before Leo gets out of his summer job at the Zilker Park snack bar. He will want dinner the minute he gets home. If she isn't there in time, he will go across the street to the twins' house, the way he has done since he was a little boy, and Diana will be able to steal a few more minutes for her research. Mary Rowan doesn't work and never has; she is home all day, every day, making sure that Gus and Bee don't take one step outside without her knowledge. She is probably pulling a tray of chocolate-chip cookies from the oven at this very moment, fixing her hair in the mirror, staring at the back of the front door and listening like an eager dog for the squeal of their bike brakes. Mary has fed Leo dinner a thousand times. One more night won't make a difference.

One more hour in the library won't make a difference either. An hour isn't nearly enough time to fix the mess Diana has made of her project, a three-year study of Book 4 of the *Aeneid*. Scattered on the floor around her carrel are the discarded scraps of her most recent attempts at originality. During the academic year, she teaches intro classes on classical mythology and intermediate Greek, but it is summer, so she is supposed to be focusing on her book. She has to. She is crawling at a snail's pace along the tenure track and the committee is losing patience with her missteps. Diana is the only woman in her department, so she has dutifully published articles on the Vestal Virgins, the household gods, the role of the female body in Athenian drama, the fragments of Sappho, the endless rapes and decapitations. They are old territory in more ways than one, and the results have been predictably unimaginative. In the morning, she is supposed to give a report on her progress on this new book, and she has nothing to say.

Nothing to say about the *Aeneid*, anyway.

The men on the tenure committee don't know, or, more accurately, they don't care, that her marriage is falling apart at a pace inversely proportionate to the one she is following in her academic career, or that she cannot think clearly because she worries about Leo constantly, as if her fear for him is as essential as breathing. During the last school year, she had to meet with Leo's principal once a month, and the last time he warned, almost gleefully, that Leo's grades and his discipline issues put him in danger of being asked to find "a more suitable placement." As if there were a place in Austin to educate a boy who loves only growing peas and marigolds in the small garden he keeps in the backyard and maybe, allegedly, according to that smug and ill-qualified man, setting fires in the lockers at school.

Diana knows what that school thinks of Leo. She knows what the other mothers say about him and Gus. She sees the way they watch them from their porches, as if the boys will smash through their windows and steal their purses. But Leo has never stolen anything. All his fires have been small so far. More like experiments, or pranks. Nothing big enough to cause any real damage. There was the pile of tall grasses that he wove into a crown and burned in the driveway, and the rope he tied between two fence posts and doused with gasoline so that it burned in a single brushstroke of gold before it crumbled into ash. There was the one in the locker at school, allegedly, the one that almost got him kicked out. Probably there have been others, too, ones Diana doesn't know about, but Leo is only curious. Creative, not destructive, she tells herself when she is called into school. He would never harm anyone.

Diana distractedly pages through a concordance for the *Aeneid*, looking for something, anything, to stick. She is focusing on Dido's lament, the unhappy queen throwing herself on the funeral pyre in despair over losing Aeneas, but she can't find anything that hasn't already been said a thousand times. She just needs one clue, one narrow wedge of light to show her where to find the door to the past so she can push it open.

She will give herself sixty minutes, no more, no less. Then she will head home, maybe pick up some food for Leo on the way in case she gets there in time.

She puts down the concordance and picks up a copy of *The Bacchae* from the pile of discarded books heaped on her carrel. Tucked in the jacket, there is a thin brochure for the Archaeological Museum of Brauron, just twenty minutes east of the airport in Athens, according to the map. Probably a quick stop for some eager, well-funded grad student, the brochure just a long-forgotten bookmark. Diana has never been to Greece.

Before Leo was born, she applied for travel grants every year, but she never got one, and now leaving Austin feels impossible, so she has stopped trying. It's better to focus on Leo, on her work.

Diana pauses, peering at the only photograph on the brochure, a black-and-white shot of the interior of the museum. There is a row of small marble statues, children maybe, inside a bulletproof glass case. Sunlight hits the glossy page, and for a moment, she can't read the description.

A cloud moves over the sun, and then, Diana spots a word she has never seen before. *The arktoi*, she reads, *4th Century BCE*. The paragraph beneath explains that they are the she-bears of the cult of Artemis. The cult of Diana. Her heart leaps at the sight of her own name—is this the sign she has been looking for?

In reality, Diana's mother named her after the apple-cheeked, beautiful, and, it must be said, quite stupid best friend in *Anne of Green Gables*, but Diana has always told people she was named after the goddess: Diana in ancient Rome, Artemis in Greece. In either place, the fiercest of them all. Goddess of wild animals and the moon, the crossroads and the countryside. Protectress of women.

When Diana was eight, still stuck in Lubbock, she wore a white bathrobe and a crown made of tinfoil for Halloween. She carried a sheaf of arrows made from wooden dowels she found in the garage and painted in stripes of gold. The neighbors thought she was trying to be an ordinary princess or a fairy. They were uninteresting girls, dressed as cheerleaders and butterflies, but Diana can still taste her disappointment.

Obviously, she was the goddess of the hunt.

The arktoi were the daughters of the Athenian elite, the brochure explains. Tiny girls, some as young as seven, who left their homes for a year to wear honey-colored robes and "act the bear" for the goddess, dancing at altars, roaming free in the woods, crawling on all fours and growling. They were meant as a symbolic offering to the goddess, in hopes that she would spare Athens from plague. They have been hiding in plain sight, and now there is a row of them, staring out at Diana from the photograph. The first girl in the row has plump cheeks and an oddly knowing smile. She is holding a rabbit in her gently curved arms.

A faint memory tickles the back of Diana's mind.

Aristophanes?

Diana scrambles to pull the green Loeb edition from the shelf. *Birds. Lysistrata. Women at the Thesmophoria.* She hasn't opened it in years, and she barely remembers the plays, but suddenly the flimsy, transparent pages are a sacred text, their lines a secret code. The Greek on the left side of the page, the stilted English on the right, both hiding the arktoi behind a screen of curves and lines. It takes her a few minutes, but she finds the lines she is looking for.

I bore the holy vessels
At seven, then
I pounded barley
At the age of ten,
And clad in yellow robes,
Soon after this,
I was Little Bear to
Brauronian Artemis.

Then, the pea-green walls surrounding her study carrel split open, and in through the metal air-conditioning vents comes a thick, animal musk. The marble statue of the girl in the brochure nods, slowly, and puts a single stone finger to her lips.

This is it. All these years, she has been waiting, circling, trying to find a project to match the scope of her ambition and to make up for the fact that she has only traveled from Lubbock to Austin, not even four hundred miles, not the continents she imagined. She wants to do something extraordinary, something that will show Derek and Mark and everyone else that they have underestimated her.

A quick glance at the clock on the wall tells her that she has just fifteen more minutes. She reads frantically, her fingers clumsy and damp on the thin pages. An idea is forming with such force that she is reminded of Leo's birth, the huge, impossible crest of pain, the sensation that she might be splitting in half.

"I was Little Bear," Aristophanes wrote.

This is the wedge of light that Diana has been looking for in the scraps of paper on the floor. As she reads, she feels the door to the past swing open, hingeless and free. She can see the girls so clearly: they flicker through the trees, their robes shades of yellow orange and crocus, like tiny Hare Krishnas transplanted into the Attic forest. Some of them wear scraps of fur tied around their narrow wrists. They scamper down the forest paths, the way that girls do before they realize their bodies are full of weights of all kinds, before their breasts and bottoms jut out, betraying them and making them the handmaidens of gravity rather than a goddess.

Diana knows immediately what she must do. She will abandon her book about Dido. She will find everything she can about the arktoi. It is not just that they are new territory, or that she is certain she will be the first to pursue them. It is that she can feel, deep in the center of her chest, that they must have discovered something, deep in the woods, some secret about being a girl, a woman, that Diana has forgotten, or never knew. She wants to reach into the brochure, tap them on their marble shoulders, tell them that she is listening. The arktoi had a whole year to hold a door closed with their bear hands while the world of marriage and babies and boredom frothed like a giant wave behind it. One whole year to be an animal before all their human girlness came crashing back.

She needs to know how they did it. How did they keep their wildness when they shed those yellow robes and went back to the world? They would have peeked out from the forest and seen their fathers standing in clusters at the temple, waiting to take them home. They would have smoothed down the wisps springing from their oiled hair and rubbed sprigs of rosemary on their skin. They would have felt their muscles tighten and coil, trying to turn them back.

They would have grabbed each other's small, sweating hands. But they knew it could be done: they could be women, and they could also be bears, uninhibited and free.

She needs more time. She needs hours, weeks. A year, maybe. If she is late tonight, Leo will not miss her, and Derek hasn't been home at night for two weeks. It won't matter if she stays until the library closes. Her hands are trembling, but she cuts out the picture from the brochure and tapes it up in her carrel, along with the page from Aristophanes. She is not sorry. They belong to her, and she does not want anyone else to find them.

She closes her eyes and sees a girl, crouching deep in the woods. She has been dancing all day, but she is on all fours now, her thigh muscles quivering and taut with the unfamiliar effort of it, and above her small spine a row of downy fur bristles.

She moves slowly because she is filled with thick honey and blood. She runs her tongue over her teeth, worrying the small chip in the front incisor. There is scrub brush and cypress, a sky so blue that when the girl closes her eyes she can still see the glowing outlines of the marble temples on the horizon.

Another girl is there, too, butting her stomach. She is dressed in the same saffron-yellow robe, cinched tightly at the waist with a hempen cord. Her dark braids, thick and oiled, smell like chopped green chives and the musk that drips between her shaking legs. For a moment, the two girls kneel together, their heads touching. They do not speak.

They growl.

Diana's eyes fly open. The sound is as real to her as if the arktoi are hiding in the darkness of the stacks.

She has to go home to check on Leo. She sighs.

It would be so much better to be a bear, even if you knew it wasn't going to last.

Outside, the sun is still glaring, even though it is past five. Diana walks through campus toward Sixth Street, blinking and rubbing her eyes. She feels like she has just awakened from a long night of perfect sleep. The world is crisp and glossy, and her mind is swimming with thoughts of the arktoi. Tonight, she will sketch out a new plan, one that will impress the tenure committee in the morning. Even though she hasn't written anything yet, even though there is hardly any evidence of the arktoi, they will be sure to renew her funding, and it will not matter that Derek is leaving her with one sadly inadequate academic salary and a ramshackle ranch house in a declining neighborhood. Everything will be fine.

Mark, her old dissertation adviser, asked her to grab a beer with him as she was rushing out the door, the way he does almost every Monday after work, but the thought of being stuck in a dark bar with him makes her feel claustrophobic. If she ever said yes, their meetings would be even more awkward and bumbling than they already are, his sweating hands making foggy swirls on the linoleum top of his desk and smearing his crossword while his laugh booms too loudly down the empty afternoon hallways. She can picture him attempting to kiss her, leaning in, his lips two wet pink worms.

He is repulsive. She can't talk to him about her new idea; he'll talk her out of it before she even starts. *You can't force a round peg into a square hole, Diana,* he will tell her, leaning back in his chair to stop his paunch from splitting the lowest button of his tan, short-sleeved shirt. *There won't be enough research on these arktoi. If there were, someone would have done it long before you. Be rational.* She will nod and make promises, but she won't listen. She will watch him blink behind his glasses, his eyes distorted and huge, and think, *Well, Mark, just because you don't have the evidence doesn't mean that there isn't any.*

When Diana took her graduate school entrance exam, she scoffed so loudly at the questions on the logic section that the proctor threatened to ask her to leave and cancel her score. "Select and indicate the best answer from among the five choices," the test read, when whoever wrote it forgot about the fact that the girl holding two apples will drop one in the gutter because she believes the hole she sees in it might be from a worm, or that perhaps the person giving out the awards to candidates A, B, C, D, and E was sick that day and couldn't come to the ceremony. Diana chose "The answer cannot be determined with the information given" every time, but they let her into grad school anyway because of her essay: "Bad Wife: Portrayals of Clytemnestra."

And, obviously, because Mark is the chair of her department, and he thinks she is beautiful.

It doesn't matter. None of it does—not the test, or Mark and his stubby, grasping fingers, or the fact that she has endured him for years, all the way through graduate school, and now, as a colleague who enjoys reminding her that he is a full professor and she is not. Not her marriage to Derek, which is gasping for air.

Only Leo matters. Leo, and now the arktoi. When she is finished with her research, the argument will compose itself, she is sure, as long as she can find the right format. Maybe it's not an academic book at all but something bigger, bolder, more creative, like a play or a film. Whatever it is, it will be spectacular.

She will stop for a drink, just a quick one, to celebrate her new idea, but not with Mark.

The shadow of the university clock tower makes a brief spot of cool air on the sidewalk. Years ago, a sniper stood on its top, picking off coeds below, and Diana looks up, just in case. It's a stupid reflex, but everyone around her does the same: a quick shift of the eyes upward. Diana wasn't here when it happened—she was only fifteen then, shelving and reshelving books at the Lubbock Public Library after school and waiting, waiting, for something to happen—but she remembers the news story, the marine sniper with the thick, corn-fed face, the students cowering behind columns and rows of shrubbery while he fired at them without reason, without mercy.

Until today, nothing happened at all. Except that her husband apparently started an affair with the university swim coach, who admittedly is much prettier than Diana. And much dumber, and therefore probably easier to live with, like the *Anne of Green Gables* Diana would be. The swim coach's breasts are round and full, the proverbial grapefruits, and she has no children, and especially not a Leo, who sings to the rows of orange marigolds he has planted in the backyard and is difficult in ways that Diana is secretly afraid she will never understand, and sometimes, maybe, sets fires.

The swim coach spends long afternoons telling people to go back and forth, faster and faster, which is pointless, but at least there is an end to it. The race finishes, and the swimmers heft themselves out of the pool, water cascading from their glossy bodies. They put on their clothes and go home. They have won, or they have lost, and the swim coach's purpose shifts accordingly. The swim coach does not wonder what she should do tomorrow, and she does not worry that she is wasting her time, her life.

To the swim coach, Derek is enough.

Diana shakes her head, rolling it in a circle like one of the little arktoi limbering up before a hunt. She will not stop for a drink. She will head home, to Leo, and even if he is already at the Rowan house, he will come home eventually. He likes to hear about her ideas, and he will make a much better audience than Mark or Derek ever could.

The open doors of the bars on Sixth Street yawn like the dark, slobbering mouths of Cerberus. Diana looks away from them, to the center of the street, and concentrates on watching the cars pass. Inside them, she knows, the black plastic seats are so hot they will scald the backs of your legs. She will have to drive with her fingertips so that the steering wheel does not scald her skin.

She does not care. She will hold the wheel tight. Let her palms burn.

At home, Diana stands at the open door, holding up a white paper bag in her fist like a brace of ducks at the end of a hunt. She can do this, at least. Teenage boys love burgers.

"Leo?" she calls. Her voice ricochets off the faux marble floor of their entrance. It is the only spot of luxury in the house, but Diana hates the way it fools you into thinking the house will be something better than it is, just before your feet meet the flattened orange shag of the living room.

There is no answer. Leo is next door already. Diana sighs and moves toward the kitchen, dropping the greasy bag on the counter with a thud.

The house is empty. In her bedroom, right off the kitchen, the sheets are rumpled on one side. Derek's toothbrush is gone. A new development. She sits on the edge of the bed and stares first at her feet, then out at the front yard.

Someday, she will live in a house with an upstairs bedroom so she does not have to worry about robbers or flash floods or wayward cars with no brakes when she sleeps. She will be alone, and there will be two floors, maybe three. She will live somewhere with seasons. Fall, winter. Diana's mind drifts as she falls back on the bed. A foreign country, maybe Greece, in a house with a bedroom skylight that frames a scene of tiny blackbirds swooping in patterns known only to them. The hills around her house will be dotted with broken chunks of marble, the remnants of ancient statues that are waiting for her to discover their meaning. She will live there for so long that she blends in like a native. She will have an office with its walls covered in pictures of Leo and ancient temples and the marble statues of the arktoi. No Derek.

She will work there, undisturbed. She will not feel, anymore, like she has spent her life taking care of other people, while her own creativity dissipates and falters. She will not feel like she is supposed to want to apologize for requiring her own life, with its own passions. Its own ambition.

The tree outside the bedroom window is dying from the top down. The crown is bristling with twigs, and some kind of tar is circling the lower branches and choking them with its viscous black snot. When Leo was small, he used to call her outside to show her how he could climb it with one hand shoved into his jeans pocket, his mouth contorting in a series of taut frowns as he tried to pretend that it took no effort. He and the twins spent hours up there, the leaves shivering when they moved from branch to branch, the occasional face popping out.

But that was years ago. Now the neighborhood kids are more interested in cars and bikes, and they are never in the yard anymore. Diana doesn't know where they go. And why should she? They should carve their own space in the world. That is the private work of children, hers and everyone else's. She doesn't need to know everything. Leo is her boy, her little lion, but he is too watchful, too quiet. He already has the face of the man he will become, and it makes him look too old for his body. The neighborhood boys edge around him like currents around a stuck branch.

It is only the twins who seem to understand him. They know that Leo is quiet because he is thinking of the right words to say. But to everyone else, he is the boy who sets fires at school, the one who drinks and smokes with Gus Rowan in the field. They don't bother to learn more.

She hopes he does not notice this. She knows she should do more to help him, but she is so busy, and he is so quiet, and it seems impossible.

At first, the police lights look like daubs of paint through the windowpane, reds and blues that glow and shift as Diana watches them. She thinks they will pass, as they do often in the evenings, circling the field and the row of convenience stores closer to the highway, but then the pulsing lights grow bright and hover on the glass. The police car is at the curb. Diana moves to the window and watches as two officers dressed in tan shirts and tan pants emerge from the car and make their way up the driveway. They look more like zookeepers than policemen. They are not in a hurry. The one on the left stops, plucks his pants from the fold of his crotch, and pats the gun that sits on his hip like a bulbous tumor.

Leo has set another fire. Diana's body tenses at the thought. A big one this time, now that he is fifteen. Maybe he has ruined the field, or the twins' house, and the police are here to take him away. Her body fills with the familiar fear, the one she feels every time she catches Leo with a lighter, or matches, or the strange contraption he has made from flint and a piece of steel he found in the shop classroom at school.

Maybe it's something to do with Derek, not Leo. The roiling boil begins again in Diana's gut, and at first she can't tell its nature. Is it fear? The bobble-breasted swim coach will have figured out that Derek is a cheating fool. She has found a restaurant receipt, with too much food for a single man, like Diana once did. Or she has followed him somewhere. Maybe the swim coach grabbed her ladies'-style pink pistol from her underwear drawer—

An explosion of sharp knocks sends Diana rushing to the

door. Whatever is coming, she hopes it will not hurt her boy.

"Evening, ma'am."

Diana tries to produce a normal smile, one that you might give to a police officer at your door before you invite him in for lemonade and small, homemade cookies to accompany your civilized conversation. Her heart pounds in her chest.

"Can I help you?"

"Yes, ma'am. We're wondering if you noticed any strange activity in the field right there last night."

Not Leo, she thinks. *Not Derek*. "Last night?"

"Yes, ma'am. In the field. Were you home yesterday evening? Did you see anything unusual? Any lights or anything?"

Diana thinks about Mary Rowan, sitting in the darkness on her porch.

"Lights in the field? Are we talking about aliens?" She laughs, to show them that she is joking and release the strange mixture of relief and disappointment inside her. This is not about Derek. They would have asked her name, or they would have invited themselves in to sit down. *We are sorry to be the ones to bring you this news, Mrs. Nastasi, but your husband . . .*

"No, ma'am," the officer says. "Nothing along those lines. We have a missing person, and we need to locate that person as soon as possible. Nothing you need to worry about."

"Worry about?"

Diana has become a parrot because she has just noticed something: Leo is here. He is standing behind the red oak in the side yard. She can see the left side of his body and the toe of his sneaker, clinging like a root to the bottom of the trunk. The police will not see him, not unless they turn around, which they will not do if Diana manages not to give him away so that he has time to run to the backyard.

She is careful. Leo's face is unreadable, but he puts his finger to his lips and shakes his head once, twice.

Diana feels the cold seeping up from the hallway floor, as if it is real marble after all.

As if she is too.

Bee

When Bee opens the front door, Charlie is standing in the foyer with his coat on and his phone in his hand. It is past nine. "I tried to call," he says. He won't make eye contact with her. He is either angry or distracted, but Bee can't tell which. The wine she drank at the Spoke is making her squint in the overhead light.

She pulls out her phone and looks at the screen. Seven missed calls from Charlie. Two texts. I'm on call, Bee. You need to come back.

Nothing from Leo, she notes.

"Oh God. I'm so sorry. I think I got absorbed in seeing Leo." This is true, at least. She has never lied to Charlie. "It was so weird to see him. Super awkward. It's been such a long time."

Awkward doesn't count as a lie; it's just an incomplete description. Charlie doesn't know Leo, and the stories Bee has told Charlie about her childhood have a wholesome, Three Musketeers vibe, all feel-good pranks and goofy escapades. Stealing a Whatchamacallit bar from the grocery store and then getting caught when the three of them had rings of melted chocolate around their mouths. Pushing each other off the high dive into the bright turquoise rectangle of the Walnut Creek Pool.

It is all true, and at the same time, it's incomplete, like Bee is looking through a keyhole and trying to describe a whole landscape. She can't explain the way it felt when the three of them started to drift apart. Or when she realized she was drifting, alone on her own raft, Gus and Leo together on theirs. They still rode the bus together, and they still had the same teachers, and they went to the same swim lessons at the university pool every July until Leo's mother refused to pay for them anymore. But when she tries to pinpoint the moment it started, she can't; she only knows that by the summer she was fifteen, when her father died and her mother lost the baby, Gus already felt like a stranger to her, and Bee had already spent years longing to be a part of something that was rightfully hers. She hated it. The way she turned into an unwelcome visitor in her own house whenever Gus and Leo were together. Or worse, her awkward attempts to make them invite her when they didn't have to. She would have gone on a bike ride, a trip to the truck stop, the field, anywhere at all, if only they would pay attention to her.

Leo would, sometimes, for just a moment. "Hey, Bee," he would say. "Come outside with us." But Gus found any way he could to get away from her.

It got worse after the accidents. Two accidents right in a row, and then losing touch with Gus years later, after the farm, felt like the third blow, the trio of crises that Bee secretly hopes will keep her safe from harm, as if there is a quota of lifetime sorrows that she has already met. First, there was her mother's miscarriage, which sent her to bed for days on end, her skin pale in the darkness of the master bedroom, her hair unwashed and uncombed for the first time in Bee's memory. Then, less than two weeks later, their father was on his way to work and bent his truck around a tree eight miles from home, his blood alcohol so high that the coroner said he was surprised he got that far.

The miscarriage was their mother's disaster, not Bee and Gus's, not really. It was private. Mary hadn't even told them about the baby yet. Their father's death belonged to all of them, but still, somehow, Gus felt it more, needed his mother more, needed Leo more, and Bee watched her own sorrow like it didn't belong to her. She wasn't even sure at the time if she was sad that her father was dead or that she would never know him better than she did at that moment, when he still seemed blurry to her, or garbled, like a voice speaking from a distant room.

That's what it felt like, anyway, and even though she is older now, and hopefully more reasonable, she still secretly wonders why Gus mourned with such ferocity. Their father was hardly ever home. He never came to the pool to lift them on his shoulders, the way other fathers sometimes did, and he never came to their school plays or field day or anything else. Still, Gus wouldn't leave his room, wouldn't talk to her. Bee could measure the inadequacy of her grief by the intensity of his.

During their senior year, two full years after the accident, Gus would disappear for the whole day, while Bee lied and told their mother that he was on a field trip or staying late for band, and then Leo's gray pickup would pull into the driveway across the street, Gus in the passenger seat, the two of them as still as twin cardboard cutouts in the narrow window of the cab. Gus never got in trouble, not even when their mom caught him. "He's still upset about your father," she would say. "Give him time."

So much time has passed now. The minutes have spread like widening ripples from those three dropped rocks. But Bee still flips the light switch in her bedroom three times when she turns it off at night. The front door of every house she has ever lived in: lock, unlock, lock. She clicks the cover to her gas tank three times, then three more, with a pause in between. These tiny counterspells keep her safe. They keep the door to that trio of disasters closed tight. They keep her family safe.

Bee, Charlie, Attie, she says to herself, every time.

And sometimes, even now, *Bee, Gus, Leo.*

Charlie pulls his car keys from the hook by the door and says, "I bet it was awkward. Leo's the weird one, isn't he? The neighbor who was always setting fires and hanging around your brother?"

"Yeah, I guess so." Bee doesn't remember describing Leo to Charlie at all, but she must have. "He's pretty quiet, I guess. It was good to see him. He just bought some kind of farm near here. I can tell you more when you get back." She glances at the string of messages on her phone again; she is checking for Leo. "God, Charlie. I'm so sorry. My phone must have been on silent or something."

Charlie checks his watch. "The hospital paged again. I have to go. Attie is fine, maybe just needs to get topped off."

This is their joke, that Attie is a gas tank on a fussy old car, but Charlie isn't smiling, and Bee's laugh sounds screechy as it bounces around the walls of the foyer.

"Charlie. Wait. Just—Leo said that he talked to Gus. I—"

Charlie pauses, then raises his eyebrows. "Really? Ah, Bee. That's crazy." He squeezes her and then kisses her forehead.

She is late, and she has made him late. Charlie hates talking about Gus, and Bee is not telling him the whole truth about how it felt to see Leo or what he said. But she is forgiven, without even asking, without even telling him that she needs to be. Charlie says into her hair, "I want to hear all about it, I really do, but I have to get to the hospital. I'll call you from the car?"

"No, that's okay. We can talk about it when you get back." Bee pulls away and presses her hands into her eyes. She will be asleep when Charlie gets home, and the conversation will be delayed a day, a week, even. "Go fix a broken leg or something. I love you."

Charlie grabs his coat from the closet. "Broken arm. Love you too. We'll talk later." He doesn't pull the door all the way closed behind him. Bee pushes it until the latch catches with a soft click.

Upstairs, Attie screeches, a wild cry that lodges in the center of Bee's chest.

"That's my cue," Bee says. Charlie's headlights sweep across the front windows as he drives away.

Attie has been asleep for an hour, and Bee is being a good wife. She has unloaded and loaded the dishwasher, swept the kitchen floor, rinsed the coffeepot and reset it for the morning. The itch to search for them is here, deep in some unreachable place. But she will not allow herself to turn on the computer until everything she can think of to do has been done. She scrubs the downstairs toilet for good measure. Her hands stink of bleach, so she washes them three times, then rubs them with the thick unscented cream that someone gave her for her nipples when Attie was born. She finds an emery board wedged in the side of the junk drawer in the kitchen and shapes her nails into smooth half-moons. After she refolds the kitchen towels into matching stacks the size of sandwiches, she stands at the bottom of the stairs and strains her ears, listening for the baby.

Nothing.

The computer is in Charlie's office. Bee tiptoes up the stairs and gingerly lowers herself into his desk chair. The browser is still open to CNN, and for a minute or two she pretends to read the news: an article about Charlize Theron and the mean girls who tormented her in high school, another about flood warnings in the South. Then she sees that there are two more tabs open. Her shaking hands hover for a moment over the keyboard before she clicks on them.

Charlie has searched *wife + PPD + symptoms*. *Bonding + baby + mother*. The articles scroll down endlessly.

"The Importance of Mother-Baby Bonding."

"The New Science of Infant Bonding."

"Linkage Found between Sleep Deprivation and Depression."

"Maternal Bonding in Infancy Predicts Social Competency in Adults."

Bee is indignant. How can Charlie not understand that Attie is as dear to her as her own leg, her own internal organs? He thinks that having Attie should make Bee happier, but their bond has nothing to do with happiness, or logic. How can he not see it?

It is biology. The magical, binding, irrefutable force of the blood.

Your own baby.

Your own twin brother.

Bee takes a deep breath. Gus is in the world, somewhere nearby. *"I think he would want to talk now, if you wanted to,"*

Leo said. There is something happening, something important enough to make Leo break a silence so long she was sure it was permanent. Bee can feel a steady tug from Gus's end of the line.

She opens a new tab, one she will close before Charlie gets home to see it. She has searched for Gus a thousand times before, and she knows what will happen. She will sit on the riverbank of her desk chair until the rabbit hole appears. She will fall in.

Drink me.

Augustus Rowan, she types. Seeing Leo tonight makes her feel like she will find something new, something that will tell her if she should take Leo's invitation to see Gus again or keep her life the way it is, safe and protected with Charlie. Right away, Gus's first arrest appears, second on the Google page. The article is old, and Bee has already seen it, but she clicks anyway: "September 3, 1998. West Virginia. A twenty-six-year-old man, Augustus Rowan, was arrested yesterday on suspicion of shoplifting. He was apprehended attempting to leave the Foodland in Blair with over $300 worth of formula." Even if this weren't her brother, Bee would have wondered about the man and his Robin Hood–style crime, like he was an example from a high school lesson on ethics. Now, she wonders: How many cans of formula would $300 get you? How many hours without nursing?

There can be only one Augustus Rowan who can't get it together, and there is a string of arrests on the Google rap sheet: the highway stop that revealed packets of heroin scattered across the back seat, the endless thefts of jewelry, money, unattended Amazon packages. And then, for two years, nothing. Usually, Bee has only the public records to go on, but now she has something new. *Gus Rowan + Mexico*, she tries. Nothing. At the Spoke, Leo said that Gus went back and forth. Doing what? Stealing formula for who knows what poor, foolish woman? Trafficking drugs? Living in a van, maybe? (*Gus Rowan + van*, she types, stupidly.) Bee registers the disdain she feels for this life that she knows nothing about, a thickness in her throat that feels a little bit like triumph. Her life went one way, his another, and here she is, with a house and a husband and a baby. Clean marble counters and parquet floors. They are the proof that she has made a good, competent life.

Aren't they?

She swallows. There is still time for Bee's life to go horribly wrong. There are all those studies about twins: separated at birth, they both become marathon runners. Or dentists. Or they end up living two blocks away from each other in New York City, missing each other by a single subway train every morning until one day they stand together on the platform, looking in a freakshow mirror.

You dye your hair red? I dye my hair red too. It reminds me of…

That's your passcode? That's my passcode too!

Maybe the stories are all about identical twins. Maybe you had to at least share an amniotic sac, a ladder of genes, or swim in the same cesspool of piss. Bee and Gus weren't even born on the same day. Bee was first, just before midnight, and Gus came twenty-seven minutes later, the amniotic sac intact around him. Somehow this felt like he was taking the easy way out, as if Bee had to go first, carve a path through brambles and briars while Gus just sailed through, padded and cushioned, taking all the attention for himself.

Bee clicks the mouse again and again, but there is nothing new. She is starting to feel frantic. It's almost eleven. Charlie will be home before midnight because it's just a broken leg. *Arm,* she corrects herself. Attie will be awake soon, her tiny fists pawing at her own creased face in her rage.

Bee pushes the chair away from the desk, then rolls it back again. There has to be a clue here, something that tells her what she should do next, like the Choose Your Own Adventure books that littered Gus's room when they were kids. *By Balloon to the Sahara*, maybe. Or: *The Worst Mistake of Your Life.*

Turn to page 52 if you want to see Leo again.

Turn to page 58 if you want him to give you your missing brother's phone number.

Turn to the end if you know all of this is a bad idea.

She'll start with the old neighborhood. Her fingers are buzzing as they pass over the mouse pad. The Google Earth camera lurches in from outer space so rapidly that Bee feels nauseous. In the darkness of the room, she can see the blue light of the screen glowing on the contours of her own cheeks. Her eyes are tired. The left one is twitching, as if there is the ghost of a butterfly beating its wings on her eyelid. She should try to sleep, just for a little while before Attie wakes up.

Instead, she tries *Stillwood Lane, Austin, Texas*. Her old street is unrecognizable in the aftershock of the Austin real estate boom. The field that used to stretch out beyond the dead end like a miniature prairie is gone, and the rows of identical beige three-bedroom ranch houses have been replaced with a mishmash of faux adobe casitas and what look like two-story boathouses slapped together by toddlers. In one yard, a man is mowing a brown lawn, but it's not Gus. She moves up and down the streets, half-pretending she might find him there, peering out at her from his hiding place on the screen.

There is nothing, of course. She closes Google Earth and

tries searching again, typing the address of their mother's house into the search bar. This is the only way she visits home: as a bird swooping overhead, unnoticed. The keyboard is warm beneath her flying fingers and the sound of her typing is getting louder, faster.

She is fine. She is only filling the minutes until Charlie gets home. He will tell her what to do.

He will remind her that she should not reach out to him, no matter what clue she finds, what path through the undergrowth.

But Charlie is not here, so Bee keeps going. She presses Return, Return, Return. On the screen, the Google page fills with news websites, ones she has never seen before. They are new, just days old. Bee's breath comes quickly, and her forehead dampens with cold sweat.

"Construction Project Reveals New Clues in Cold Case of Missing Girl."

"New Evidence Found in Decades-Old Case."

And then: "Buried Backpack Provides New Evidence."

This last one is from some kind of junk news website, but Bee clicks it first. Her hands are shaking.

She remembers this story. This is Deecie Jeffries.

Construction workers tearing up the sidewalks in the Thrushwood neighborhood of Austin, Texas, uncovered a startling find: a young girl's backpack, buried since before the neighborhood was expanded in September 1987. The backpack is labeled with the name of Darlenia Cora Jeffries, a thirteen-year-old believed to have been kidnapped in August of that year. The police have made no public comment.

Bee realizes with a start that she is inches from the screen. She loads the next page, and the next, her heart skittering strangely in her chest. August 1987. Deecie Jeffries vanished right before the miscarriage, her father's accident, the first two in the trio of Rowan catastrophes. It has never occurred to Bee to count Deecie's disappearance as the third tragedy that summer, the final stick to be pulled out of the dam that was holding the Rowan family together. But maybe, somehow, it was. She remembers it, of course, because it was all over the news, and because Deecie went to her school, and because Bee wasn't allowed to hang out with Gus and Leo outside for the first few days after she vanished. It faded into the background, though, in the face of everything that came after. Until now, Bee never thought about how close together it all was: one family's dam breaking parallel to another's. The end of that summer, that fall, all of it is a wave of sorrow.

For the first few years after Deecie went missing, she appeared sometimes in Bee's dreams, and once Bee was almost sure that she caught a glimpse of her, staring out the window of a passing car. Another time, she thought Deecie was standing in front of her in the checkout line of the Dewberry Market, and she poked Gus, trying to make him see, but he squeezed her arm so hard that she couldn't say anything. The girl turned around at the noise Bee made, Gus's hand like a vise around her upper arm, and of course it wasn't Deecie at all, just some red-haired girl buying milk.

Deecie lived a mirrored version of her own life, not even a mile away. It could have been Bee who disappeared on some hot August evening, as she played outside and waited for something to happen.

Bee has never thought to look for the story online, partially because it happened so long ago, before there was an internet, which makes it feel like it never even happened, like it is a myth rather than a real thing that happened to a real girl. Still, every once in a while, something about Deecie's disappearance floats into Bee's consciousness, and she will remember a girl who did gymnastics during recess, her hair pulled back in a tight ponytail, her wisps tamped down with spit. She remembers the news reporters, scavenging for information on the sidewalks at school because they weren't allowed on the property. A thousand maroon and yellow balloons bobbing in the air on the first day of school, as if any thirteen-year-old girl wanted her school colors at a balloon release.

For two weeks, Bee's mother kept asking Bee and Gus if they were okay, if they needed anything, if they understood what was happening. "We're fine, Mom," Gus always said. "Stop asking."

And then the dominos tipped, and Mary lost the baby. All the way through September, their mother was in bed, and then there was their father's accident, and the funeral, and Deecie stayed missing. No one talked about it anymore. There wasn't any point. Eventually, the neighborhood moms let their children leak onto the streets after dinner, and they nervously clustered around each other for a while, like ants around a spot of spilled sugar, and then the months passed and they went their usual ways, as if nothing had happened.

Bee clicks on every article about the backpack. Then she searches for the *Austin American-Statesman* and pulls up the archives. The articles about Deecie go on for months, from late August 1987 to April 1988, until the headlines drop to the fifth page, then the eighth, and finally disappear. The details are simple: she was practicing her gymnastics routine after dinner, and then she went inside for the night, and then she was gone. Her father didn't notice she was missing until late the next morning, when he went to her bedroom to wake her up and found her window wide open. When the police arrived, they found her footprints in a thin layer of dried silt at the edge of the neighborhood field.

There was nothing else to say. There was a girl, and then there wasn't.

Downstairs, the front door latch clicks. Attie lets out a small squeak. Bee can hear Charlie hang his keys on the hook. The coat closet opens and there is a soft shuffle as he shakes his parka and hangs it inside. Bee knows these sounds by heart. Next he will come up the stairs. He will skip the third step because it creaks and might wake her.

She is supposed to be asleep because Attie is. Isn't that what all the moms in the baby group tell her? *"Sleep when she sleeps. You never know when you'll be able to sneak in a nap."*

"You're still up," Charlie says, his lips at her ear.

She has closed the computer, but she is sitting alone in the dark at his desk. He will know that she was looking for something, and even though she is obviously allowed to use the computer in her own house, she feels like he has caught her doing something bad.

"I know. I should go to sleep."

"Yeah, you'll be tired. What are you looking at?"

Bee hesitates. They have had this conversation before.

"I was just looking at this news story my mom sent me." A small lie, a fib, so minuscule that she will be forgiven. "A girl who went missing from my neighborhood when I was a kid. Did I ever tell you about that? Deecie Jeffries? She was a couple of grades below me in school, and she just . . . disappeared. Right before my dad died. She was on milk cartons and everything."

She doesn't mention Gus, or Leo, who has left the imprint of his warm hand on hers. She was unfair to him at the bar, but she is so tired. It makes her rigid, unreasonable. Leo would never hurt her on purpose. He has always been good to her.

"Hey, Bee. Come outside."

Charlie's mouth tightens a little, but he doesn't say anything. For the thousandth time, the millionth, she is amazed by his ability to sail past these moments, to treat a ground swell like a ripple. He is always patient. He knows about the ache that lives nestled in the curve below her collarbone, but he thinks she can tolerate it. He doesn't worry it will overtake her, or them.

"I'm just checking," she says. "For Gus," she admits, in a quieter voice. She does not say anything more about Deecie Jeffries, whose school portrait is shimmering in the air in front of her.

"Oh, Bee." He looks down at her. He is tired too, she can see. There was the broken arm, and probably stitches and drunk college kids and a hundred other things. She can smell the disinfectant on his hands, and in the deep background of her mind, behind his familiar sweat, the blood. "Is Gus okay? You said Leo talked to him?"

"Gus is fine. I think he is. I—" Attie's cry was just a microburst. It is quiet upstairs, but they both know she will start again soon. Whatever they have to say will have to happen now. "I don't know if I want to talk to him. If I should." Saying this out loud makes Bee shudder, as if she is uttering a curse. What kind of sister wouldn't want to see her missing brother? What kind of sister wouldn't be overjoyed to know that he is alive, somewhere nearby?

Charlie puts his chin on the top of Bee's head and rests it there. His beard is prickly, his head heavy. After a moment, he pulls away and says, "We've talked about this. It's not good for you. You know? The way you always look for him, when he doesn't even try to see you, it's . . . it's like you want to be unhappy." He pauses. "And the way you went to see Leo, after he hasn't called you in years. It's—"

Suddenly, the full force of Bee's exhaustion rolls through her. She wants Charlie to hook his arms under hers and hold her up while she slumps against him. He would do it if she asked.

He is so good.

But why does he always think he knows what's best for her?

"Thanks, Doctor," she says. The words come out before she can think about them. The tone is wrong. She does not want to be cruel or cold, but it is too late.

"Bee, come on."

"No, it's fine. Let's just try to go to bed."

"I don't know why you're mad at me, Bee. I'm only saying something you know. We've been through this a hundred times." Charlie's voice is calm, but he is breathing fast. He hates arguing with her, so they never do.

Tonight, though, is different. Bee wants to fight with Charlie, and then she wants to make up with him, so that she can feel the bond between them stretch taut, fray a little, and then relax again.

"There's something I didn't tell you," she says. Charlie is staring at her, his eyes glassy. She wants to tell him the truth about seeing Leo, the bar, the heat of his hand, the way it made her blood leap along her arm. About the way she wanted to lean across the table and pull him to her, as if she could drag him all the way back to another time, before he left her, before Gus left her too.

Charlie nods, as if he can see her thoughts. He will listen to whatever she has to say. He will be reasonable. Scientific. Kind.

She does not deserve this. So she says, "I'm such an idiot. I left my car at the bar. And by the time I realized, I was halfway home, and the walk felt good, so I just kept going. I'll get it tomorrow. Let's just go to sleep, okay? I'm exhausted. I know you are too."

"Bee, I want—"

In the next room, there is another squeak, then a wail. Attie is awake. There is no time to talk about Gus, or Leo, or anything else. Charlie looks at the door, toward the baby room, and asks, "Is there any breast milk in the freezer?"

"I think so." She is right here. She should feed Attie herself, wine and all. "Don't overheat it," she says. It is an unnecessary instruction, and Charlie frowns, but he doesn't answer.

As soon as he is gone, Bee opens the computer again. The page about Deecie Jeffries is still open. A pop-up ad starts playing some kind of video about an electric kitchen mop. The music plinks like a carnival, loud and tacky, so Bee mutes it. She peers at the photo of Deecie on the page. It must be a school photo: her cheeks shine in the studio lights, and the background is the same turquoise as the deep end at the Walnut Creek Pool. They used to trade these photos, paste them in albums behind thin cellophane. Deecie looks calm, slightly bucktoothed, like every other kid Bee grew up with. Her red hair is dry and snarled at the ends. There is nothing special about her at all.

Still. She was there, and then she wasn't. Something must have happened to her. In the hall, the door to Attie's bedroom opens, but Bee can't tell if Charlie is coming or going. She traces her finger around her chin, her damp forehead, drawing an outline of her own face to match the dim reflection in the computer screen.

In every life, she thinks, there is probably a before and an after. Before Deecie went out to play that day, and then after.

What would it be for Bee? There were too many to choose from: before she had Attie, and after.

Before she married Charlie, and after.

Before Leo grabbed her hand at the Spoke tonight, and after.

Before the farm, before losing Gus, and after.

She is now, it seems, in the after. But what was she before? A girl?

Mary

Mary Rowan is standing in front of her bedroom mirror. "Peter Piper picked a peck of pickled peppers," she says, letting herself spit a little as she speaks. "Rubber baby buggy bumpers." Her thin lips struggle their way around her front teeth. They jut out too far, two white Chiclets, but she has never had them fixed. She lifts one breast in a palm, then lets it drop. Her nipples are uneven, like the googly-eyed beads her children used to paste onto Thanksgiving turkey cards made from tracings of their chubby hands.

She has been rehearsing her lines without her clothes, not because her role at the Pips Playhouse demands it, but because she has been thinking about the Puritans in the play they are performing, *The Crucible*. She studied the Puritans in school, but she has them confused somehow with Christopher Columbus, because grade school was a long time ago and because both lessons involved making ships from damp milk cartons and featured dour men standing at the helms of ships. Arthur Miller's photo makes him seem dour, too, although he somehow managed to marry Marilyn Monroe, whose breasts obviously did not look like a child's holiday craft.

Now Mary is wondering if the Puritans had mirrors, and if they did, whether or not they ever looked at themselves in them, and how pale they must have been, underneath all those clothes and buckles and all that dark, thick, itching shame.

Mary's robe is plum purple and soft. It is nothing that her character, Elizabeth Proctor, would have worn. But Mary, who is a woman who would stand naked in front of her mirror and preen, just a little, is nothing like the righteous Elizabeth. Except.

Except.

"You see, sir, I were a long time sick after my last baby . . ." Mary whispers the line, lets the faux antique grammar become natural in her mouth, adds a wide twang to the closed New England vowels. She knows she sounds more like Scarlett O'Hara than a seventeenth-century Salem housewife, but it fits. At first, she was disappointed at the casting—she would have preferred to be Abigail, or even Rebecca, meaty, dramatic roles that should not have gone to Irene and Marla—but two months ago, when she found herself pregnant, so long after the twins, like a tiny miracle, she felt a new kinship with Elizabeth. Mary is, herself, not brave, onstage or otherwise. Her director tells her regularly to bend, to *move like a regular person for God's sake*. But now she can imagine standing there in court with that growing baby inside her. She pictures it, pumping its tiny fists as she testifies bravely for her husband.

"My husband . . . is a goodly man, sir."

Mary is fifteen weeks along now. Her baby is as big as an apple, her doctor says, so Mary imagines the child inside her as a plump Golden Delicious, its hair a sprouting stem. She turns sideways and traces the curve of her stomach with her hands. This one is swelling her belly so much faster than the twins did, or at least as far as she remembers. It is filling out the bag of skin they left behind with alarming speed. She is worried about her costume, which has a stiff black bodice with laces in the front. But maybe that is the point of the laces, to give you an illusion of shape, even after a lifetime of eating greasy game meat and hard cheeses.

Leroy would laugh if he found her this way, staring at her own body like an insecure teenager. He won't see her, of course, because he is still driving and will be until at least eight o'clock, long after the dinner dishes have been put away and the twins have retreated to their rooms. When she was pregnant with the twins, he told her that pregnant women made him think of aliens, or farm animals, so she has not told him yet. He rarely touches her these days, so he has not noticed.

She sighs.

"Mom," she hears. The voice is a grating soprano, but that doesn't mean anything. It could be Bee or Gus, because even though Gus's voice changed more than two years ago, it is still high when he wants something or when he is upset.

Mary smiles. The woman in the mirror smiles back, but her smile seems insincere, even to herself. *When he wants something or when he is upset.* Gus is always both, or he has been, since around eight years old, when he shifted suddenly, the sunny, sweet boy in him gone. He is a boat tossed in perpetually roiling seas, while his twin sister points her determined ship perpendicular to the waves and sails on.

That, at least, is a blessing. It is important, as a woman, to know what to see, what to ignore.

"Mom. I'm calling you." It's definitely Gus. Bee is never

demanding, not in this way. If Bee asks for something, she does it politely, carefully, and she picks her moments: when Mary is sorting the piles of laundry into darks and lights and singing to herself, or when Gus and Leo have disappeared on their bikes. Bee is discerning. She knows how to get what she wants.

Mary scrambles to pull on her robe.

Mary pulls the sash of her robe tightly over her belly and puts on a pair of underwear. Bleach scents the air. "Coming," she calls. Her hair is caught in her collar, and when she pulls it loose a shiver fills her.

There is a thud and then a crash from the kitchen.

The twins will start to fight if she does not appear soon. Gus has turned into a moody, violent creature. She has no idea where the boy she once knew went.

She gives herself one last glance in the mirror before she goes to them.

In the kitchen, one of her blue milk glass plates has shattered on the linoleum. Tears spring to her eyes; these are her grandmother's dessert plates, and there are only three left. Two now. Gus dropped the first one in the driveway when he was six years old, carrying crackers to the picnic that Bee was arranging for Leo. Bee brought the blue shards inside so carefully, holding them like jewels in her plump little hands, but one of them cut her anyway. Gus was holding her hand, and he was crying, too, so at first Mary thought that he had cut himself on the same shard, and then that he was trying to wiggle his way out of trouble, but it turned out that he was trying to fix Bee's cut without Mary knowing. "I can fix her myself," he said, Bee's blood dripping in his hands. The two of them were like that, back then: when one of them was in trouble, they fused into a single being, a school of fish under attack, shifting and glinting like metal in the sunlight.

Not now. Now they will blame each other, even if it is no one's fault.

The blue plates are a marker of Mary's faults. Her failures. They were a wedding gift from her grandmother, wrapped in newspapers from decades ago, the ink smeared and the thin newsprint creased with age. In a different life, the one she once thought she might have, she would have used them to entertain artists, or doctors, or politicians, or anyone at all. There were six to start, and now there are two, and Mary has a notion that if she sat down with a piece of yellow notebook paper to write a list, she would be able to match each of her faults and failings to a missing plate.

"What happened?"

"Nothing." Gus is looking at the ground. He hasn't looked her in the eyes for months, she realizes as she stares at him, waiting. Maybe years. She is not even sure she still knows the pattern of his irises, the way the brown is flecked with uneven lines of gold that catch the light when he is excited or scared.

Bee's eyes are wide and blinking, like a small child's. But at fifteen, she is taller than Mary and striking, with walnut curls that dip beneath her shoulders and the brown, glossy eyes of a forest creature, full of movement and awareness. Bee misses nothing. She is not beautiful in the way that Mary is, but as it didn't do Mary any good to have breasts that once filled a hand perfectly or legs that still do not meet at the top of her thighs, she is grateful for her daughter's relative plainness.

Her life will be easier that way.

"Obviously something happened. I have eyes, you know."

Silence. She pulls the belt of her robe tighter. Bee and Gus look nothing alike—Gus's hair is thin, like black corn silk, and he moves constantly, the way a tree is never completely still but registers every shift of the animals and the air—and now they are so opposite, so contradictory, that they seem to come from different families.

Except that they are both staring at her, mouths tight, refusing to answer her.

Blue Plate 1: Children refuse to take responsibility for their actions.

"Okay. Can you at least clean it up?"

Bee bends to pick up the glass, and Mary remembers the bright line of red on her tiny hand, the way the blood dripped down her forearm and stained her sleeve. Mary does not stop her, though. Bee is a teenager now, not a child, and old enough to clean up a simple mess, even if her brother is probably the one who made it.

Gus is watching Bee bend in front of him, her eyes at floor level as she pats the ground, searching for shards that might hurt them later. He does not crouch to the floor with her or offer to help.

Blue Plate 2: Child has become unkind, ungenerous. Mary thinks about the pack of cigarettes behind the spice rack. It is waiting there, like a little golden jewel box. What would be the harm of smoking just one?

Gus says, "Why are you wearing a robe? It's the middle of the day."

"What?" She is not sure how to answer this, but she realizes suddenly that she must look ridiculous, standing in her fuzzy purple robe in the kitchen with daylight streaming through the windows. She knows that Gus will use it against her, if not right at this moment, then sometime soon. *At least the other mothers do something with themselves,* she can imagine him saying. *Leo's mom is practically a professor.* He sounds like Leroy when he talks to her like this. He could add *you stupid cow* if he wanted to make the transformation complete.

"Whatever. Can I go now? Leo is outside." For a moment Mary can't trace the thread of the conversation, but when her eyes settle she sees Gus staring at her. It has been a long time since he asked her permission for anything, and she is about to answer, but his eyes have already slid away from hers, and he is moving toward the door, his brief slip into manners forgotten, and when he opens it there is Leo, already sitting on his bike, as if he plans to ride it inside and get dirt and mud on Mary's well-kept beige carpets.

"I don't know. Is it safe?" Mary does not want to be the first mother to let her children outside. The Jeffries girl hasn't even been gone for a week. There could be anything out there: murderers, child traffickers. Wild animals. She shudders when she thinks of how close Gus and Leo must have come to whatever happened.

They were out there, too, the night the girl disappeared. Gus still has circles under his eyes, as if he hasn't slept since. Mary was sitting in her hiding spot on the porch when she saw Gus run from the field, back around the corner of the house. He tumbled into his window so recklessly that she was sure the noise would wake up Leroy. She waited for the thunderclap of Leroy's anger—his open hand slapping the bedside table and making the brass lamp wobble on its pedestal—but there was no sound from behind the closed door of her bedroom, and there wasn't any noise from Gus's room either, not even the shuffle of blankets or a sigh. She thought she heard the slider from the backyard open and close, the hitch on its track like a stifled cough, but there was nothing else. It was the wind, she decided, rattling the back bushes.

She didn't say a word to Gus. And she didn't tell the police about it when they asked the next day. She knows she shouldn't let Gus sneak out like that. Drinking the liquor and who knows what else in that backpack.

It is Mary's theory that the Jeffries girl was taken by a wild animal. A cougar, a bobcat, an ocelot, a bear even, wandering into this quiet neighborhood by mistake, ruthless in its confusion and its hunger, and long gone by now. She knows her fear is irrational, but this neighborhood is safe. It's where she lives with her own children. An animal is the only idea that makes sense to her. Part of her wants to stop the kids from going outside at all, just in case she is right, but she tamps down her fear. She knows Gus would mock her if she said it out loud.

"It's fine. We're going the other way." Not to the field, he means, which is still intact, the construction project delayed while the police investigate. They will head to the elementary school, where he will lie on the slide, the whole sinewy length of him stretched from the platform at the top to the dirt at the bottom. She saw him this way once, on her way to the grocery store a few days before the girl disappeared. Leo was sitting on the swings, facing the other way. They did not look like they were talking, but they must have been. They are always talking, with words, without them. They have grown to be more like siblings—like twins—than Bee and Gus. No matter how hard Mary wishes there were still a bond between her children, they both love Leo more. She doesn't understand it, and she can't fix it.

Bee is moving faster now, her hands brooms that sweep

across the linoleum. Splinters of glass will stick to her palms. When she looks up at the door and sees Leo, she smooths a strand of hair over her shoulder, a quick movement that reminds Mary of a preening cat.

Blue Plate 3: Child is vain, delusional.

Blue Plate 4: Her mother is worse.

"Hi, Mrs. Rowan," Leo says. He is such an odd boy. He smells like lawn clippings. And he barely moves when he speaks, as if there is a core of cold metal inside him where her children have something fizzy and unpredictable, like a geyser field. When he is older, it might be compelling, or even sensual. But now it makes him too noticeable in a crowd.

Leo takes one hand off his handlebars and scratches the back of his neck in a gesture that is both shy and unconscious. It makes Mary want to invite him in so that she can serve him something sweet and cool. He says, "Hey, Bee. Come outside?"

"Just a sec," Bee says, touching her hair again. She must see the older version of Leo too, curling inside him like a seedling in a seed. "I have to—"

"She's not coming," Gus says. "Let's go."

Bee is already standing, but the door closes, and they are gone. Their laughter trails behind them like a smell.

Bee

Snow covers the ground overnight, and when Bee wakes up under the blue quilt in the morning, the bedroom is gray and chilled. She feels drained, but she can tell from the hardness in her breasts that she has slept all night, which must mean that Attie has too.

Charlie is gone. He is on call, so this makes sense, but she does not remember him leaving. There will be a note downstairs, by the coffeepot, which will be full. It will say something like *Good morning, sleepyhead. I'll give you a call later. Love you.*

Outside, the snow begins again. The flakes drift and then turn to rain. When Bee gets out of bed, the sidewalks outside will shine like they have been covered with glossy black paint.

Bee touches the palm of her hand, her lips. She thinks of Leo and lets her hand wander between her legs. She has not touched herself like this since Attie was born, but on this snowy morning she feels different. More awake. As if seeing Leo reminded her that she is actually a woman and not just a walking milk fountain. Maybe he thought she was beautiful, once upon a time, with the soft glow of a firepit tickling her cheekbones, a river glittering with moonlight behind her. He wanted to see her, yesterday, even though he was probably drunk, even though he just wanted to tell her about Gus.

But still. Her hand moves faster and her head turns on the pillow. If Charlie were here, she would join him in the shower: she can picture his delighted surprise. She lifts her shirt so the milk that is now flowing out of her will not stain it, and then she comes. *Leo, Leo, Leo,* she thinks, and the wrongness of it is just her own. Private. Delicious.

Not a fib, but a lie.

Attie is not in her crib, and downstairs, there is no note. *Well, there you have it,* she thinks, like a reflex, even though she knows that Charlie will never leave her. He has told her as much, so many times that it feels as close as anything does to certainty.

She is filling the coffeepot when she hears the front door opening. Charlie shakes the snow from his hair as he enters the kitchen, then grabs a dishcloth to wipe the floor.

"Hey," he says. Attie is a football wedged in the crook of his elbow. She gazes at Bee with steady eyes, a wise old woman who has seen too much of the world to be bothered by a little marital spat. Not even a spat: a tiny drool of emotion. "We went to get the car. Here." He hands Attie over, and she blinks, slowly. Her cheeks are two damp pink rose petals.

As soon as she is in Bee's arms, she begins to sputter. "Is it me?" Bee asks, hoping their usual joke will land.

"No doubt."

Nothing more. She has tilted the balance between them, and

it will take him a little while to right the scale, as he always does. But it isn't her fault. She is exhausted, all the time.

She is exhausted, and she misses Gus. Still, after all these years. That's all it is, and Charlie is getting tired of it, her constant searching and occasional fits of weeping—worse now that Attie is here—in the bathroom while she is brushing her teeth, in front of the case of milk at the supermarket, late at night while she is nursing.

They move around each other in the kitchen, their backs brushing when they both reach for the refrigerator. Charlie cracks an egg into a bowl, stares at it, then cracks another.

Bee is determined not to speak. This is stupid, because she is the problem, not Charlie. She is the one with the family that isn't even a family anymore, while he wants to go to Sunday dinner in Camden almost every week, to sit at his mother's dining room table with placemats and polished wood and dahlias blooming along the fence line in the fall. She is the one who will mess this up, not him.

She will try harder. She says, "Thanks for getting the car. Do you have to go in today?"

Charlie is stirring the eggs in the skillet. They are sticking to the sides anyway. He will leave the pan soaking in the sink until she gives in and washes it, his single, unconscious marital failure. Such a small flaw when she has so many.

"Yeah. I'll just eat this and then I have a few meetings. But it should be an easy day. I'll be back by five or six."

Five o'clock. Ten hours, at least. On a normal day, the prospect of so much time alone would send Bee into a panic. She has notepads filled with schedules that she never keeps. She breaks the day into thirty-minute slots that are absurdly optimistic. She remembers a history teacher once showing her class the schedule of Benjamin Franklin—"Rise, wash, and address Powerful Goodness," it said—and she tries to be industrious, rational. Time for sketching, time for exercise, time for long walks with Attie, perfectly scheduled for her nap and content in the stroller. Arise, clean, wipe, feed. Address Powerful Inertia.

Repeat.

Attie never sleeps when she is supposed to, though, so Bee never accomplishes anything important. Benjamin Franklin was a man, obviously, with a day that belonged to him.

She can't figure out how the other women do it: run businesses with their babies strapped on their backs, bouncing around and looking slightly stunned at all the activity, but quiet. Pull on spandex and jog laps around the Back Cove, pushing strollers with their sleeping babies bundled in mittens and hats. Bee can't even read a magazine.

Today, though, is different. She is full of a skittish, untethered energy. Charlie is scraping his eggs onto a plate, and Bee is thinking of Leo's eyes, the roughness of his hand on hers. A key, a kite. She knows she is both pathetic and clichéd, possibly adulterous, but she can't help it. Leo is here, and Bee is fifteen again, longing for him to reach out for her hand. It is as if a locked, forgotten door inside her has opened. A window. And now she wonders: where has that fifteen-year-old girl been all this time?

Leo used to set fires. Growing, burning. It was an odd combination, Bee realizes now. He had, always, a garden patch of his own in the backyard of the Nastasi house, pushed up against the fence and bursting with dill and parsley and orange nasturtiums that clashed with the rest of the yard, which was only dirt with some scabs of sprawling crabgrass. The fires were colorful patches too: first, a hole in his carpet that grew to the size of his fist before he poured water on it, cauterizing the melting polyester into the black, smoking ring of a tiny volcano. Next, a campfire blaze of old history notes at the bottom of Tyler's locker at school after he pushed Patrick Moynihan to the floor of the bus.

They were mostly small, the ones Bee knew about, anyway. And who could be sure that Leo was really to blame? The fire in Tyler's locker was obvious. No one liked it when he teased Patrick, and Leo was the only one who had the hall pass when the fire was set, even though he insisted to the principal and even to Gus and Bee that he was in the bathroom where he belonged.

Bee has always wondered if Leo set the fire that broke out in the field a few weeks after Deecie disappeared. She was at the pool when it started, and she can remember turning onto her street and seeing the sky darken overhead, then watching the grasses blaze in strange, looping swirls the firemen had to follow with their hoses. By the time they put it out, the field was already a sodden carpet of ash. The dark yellow construction equipment turned black from the soot, and before the company came to clean them, Bee thought they looked like giant black beetles.

Everyone thought it was Leo. It was obvious. Still, no one ever caught him. The police must have asked him questions, because they asked everyone who was home that day, but nothing came of it. Leo would never confess, though, even if he did it. He never talked about the fires he set, and he never asked Bee or Gus to help him. The fires were private, like the garden. An inner landscape, blooming with orange and red, appearing and disappearing with the seasons.

This is the problem, maybe. Leo makes her curious in a way that Charlie doesn't. All of Charlie's landscape stretches out before her like she is standing on top of a mountain on a clear day. If she rotates a bit to the left, a bit to the right, she can see for miles.

But it isn't just seeing Leo again that is making Bee tally the hours she will have alone like beads on an abacus. And it isn't just what he said about Gus either. There is something new scraping at the corners of Bee's mind, making her restless and impatient. Bee wants to go upstairs, open the computer, and search again for Deecie Jeffries. She wants to know what was in that backpack, what the police think it means, what else they know that they aren't saying. Deecie has appeared again, the way she did in Bee's dreams, in that supermarket line, but this time she is real, and she has left something real behind, something Bee could see, hold in her hands.

People don't just disappear. Of course they don't. They take up so much space in the world. They are pounds of flesh, gallons of blood. Teeth, bones, fingernails. It all has to go somewhere.

Bee rotates her coffee cup. The tablecloth twists, and she smooths it out. Attie's lips are pink and slick, and a tiny bubble appears in one corner. Bee sips her coffee, angling away from Attie in case she spills, and a memory resurfaces. A long-ago night at the farm, glasses of wine in jelly jars catching the firelight and turning to rubies. They were telling stories, the way they often did, Gus teasing Leo about his little garden, all of them laughing, the whole scene warm with a rare, joyful ease. Then Bee saying, "Hey, do you guys remember Deecie?"

A sidelong glance from Leo to Gus, their cheekbones lit with orange. Leo clearing his throat, changing the subject. Bee knowing, somehow, that she was on the outside again. That she shouldn't say anything else.

A block of sunlight turns a patch of pale blue on the kitchen wall into dazzling neon, almost white in its brilliance. Bee's half-eaten bagel looks holy, like it belongs in a still life. There is wetness between her legs, familiar and forbidden.

Charlie is chewing slowly, his eyes on the block of glowing sunlight. Attie is in her bouncy seat, its low buzzing a balm settling over the room.

Suddenly, Bee cannot bear it. The room, the quiet, the low buzz. Charlie himself, his forehead furrowed, his inability to hear her thoughts when they are so loud that it seems to Bee that the neighbors will ring the doorbell, ask her to pipe down.

Attie reaches one hand in the air, swiping at one of the plush stars that dangle from the plastic arch above her seat. She misses, once, and tries again. She is too small for this trick, so Bee leans down and unwraps Attie's fist so she can hold it. She clutches it while she stares at Bee. *Do it,* she seems to say.

"Charlie." The idea is now so clear, so sudden, that Bee stumbles on his name. She has to bring Attie to her mother's house, in Texas, where everything started. Or where it stopped, all of it: her feeling that she belonged somewhere, that she had a brother who loved her, a neighbor boy she loved. She is starting to see it, like a blurry slide coming steadily into focus: Deecie Jeffries disappeared, and Bee did too.

She has to go back.

"Hmm?" Charlie looks at her, startled. She can see his pupils dilate as he turns away from the sunlight.

Bee looks down at Attie. She has dropped the star, and it is bouncing gently above her. She is calm, expectant.

"I want to visit my mom," Bee says.

"What? In Texas? Why?" Charlie is focused now. He pushes his plate away and turns to her. "You just—you're still recovering, Bee. You're not ready. She'll come at Christmas. We already have the ticket."

Bee looks down. Attie is watching her, gray-blue eyes open and glossy, and though it's impossible, Bee feels like she is raising her eyebrows and telling Bee to confess. *Fine,* Bee thinks.

"I actually never bought the ticket," she says.

Charlie doesn't look surprised, but he isn't happy. Bee can tell by the time it takes him to push his chair away from the table and carry his plate to the sink. His movements are too slow. He is planning each step before he takes it.

"What do you mean?" he finally asks, facing the sink.

"I mean, I didn't buy it. Yet. I just felt like I needed more time. You know how she is—you remember how awkward it was at our wedding, right? She couldn't even do the toast. She hasn't been to Maine since you finished your residency, or even seen the new house. I'm not even sure she knows our address. It's impossible to imagine her here, eating Sunday dinner with your parents, or—"

"So you lied."

"Charlie, I'm sorry. It didn't feel like lying. I think I was just trying to delay. But Leo said—"

"Leo said you should go see her, so you're going."

Bee is startled. This is not exactly what happened, but it might as well be.

She can't think of anything to say.

Charlie turns to her. "Bee," he says. "Are you okay? You're acting kind of... I don't know." He walks over to her, and Bee can feel his warmth.

"I'm okay," she says, but her voice trembles. She is thinking of Charlie's web searches, the worry for her that he has never said out loud.

"Sure?"

"No, I am. I'm fine." As soon as she says it, it feels true. She takes a deep breath. "I think it will be good. You're so busy. You can catch up at work and everything. And by Christmas Attie would practically be a teenager, anyway. It'll only be a few days." She takes his plate and scrapes it into the trash. "A week, at most."

Charlie is not looking at her. He is kneeling in front of Attie, humming along to the song that is playing from the bouncy seat. Bee knows she should feel sorry for being so impulsive, but she doesn't. She can't even make herself pretend.

He stops humming and stands. "Why now, Bee?"

"What do you mean?" Charlie doesn't answer, so she says, "I want my mother to meet Attie. That's what I'm supposed to do, right? It's just a few days. It'll be fine. I promise."

"Fine. As long as—"

"What?" She makes her voice gentle. She has to, or he will not tell her what he means.

"As long as you promise that you're not looking for Gus. I don't know what Leo said to you last night, but I don't want—I don't want Attie exposed to any of that. We don't know what Gus is doing now, or if he's even sober. It's not just the two of us anymore."

Bee crosses the kitchen and grabs his hand. Relief flits across Charlie's face. Bee thinks of the way he spends his whole life caring for other people—his patients, his family—and she softens. "I know," she says. "I do. I promise. I just feel like seeing my mom. And maybe eating some tacos." She smiles. She doesn't add, *I want to get away from Leo, and maybe search for a missing girl.* "Just for a little while. And hey, you can get a few days of uninterrupted sleep. It'll be a little vacation. From me," she jokes.

Charlie doesn't laugh, but he squeezes her hand, tips her face up, and kisses her.

Then he is gone. As soon as the front door closes, Bee picks up her phone.

She types, Random question: Do you remember Deecie Jeffries?

She clicks the tiny paper airplane and sends her message. Probably, Leo will not answer her. He will have realized that seeing her last night was a mistake.

The phone buzzes. There has hardly been enough time for him to read her message, but it's him.

The girl who disappeared when we were kids?

Bee hesitates. There is a roaring in her ears, distant, but growing louder as she thinks.

Yes, she types. The one who lived on the other side of the field. Remember?

Three gray dots appear as he types, then vanish. He doesn't write anything else.

Attie is squirming in her seat. The square of sunlight is crawling slowly up the wall. The clothes are thumping in the dryer, and Bee's heart matches the sound, jumping wildly in her chest as if the sac that holds it has stretched out and can no longer keep it in place. There are two Bees, like the Frida Kahlo painting, their hearts exposed like two disused placentas. They are connected by a tangle of flimsy arteries.

One Bee is cold, impassive. She can live this life forever.

The other Bee, the one who is in danger of bleeding to death, is leaving.

Diana

Austin, Texas
1987

After Deecie Jeffries disappears, the police scour the field for days. They ask questions in the skating rink and at the Vaquero Drive-In, where truckers stop to refuel and buy foot-long sandwiches they hold in their laps for miles. The police knock on every door in the neighborhood, even the Moynihans'. Everyone knows not to knock there because Jim Moynihan is a vicious drunk, and Diana wants to tell the police to stand in the bed of the rusted El Camino in the side yard and throw a handful of pebbles at the Moynihan boy's window, the way the kids in the neighborhood do when they want him to come outside, but eventually Annie Moynihan opens the door, her face gray behind the screen. After a few minutes the police officers emerge, nod at each other, and move on.

But the girl has been gone since Sunday night, and it is Friday now, almost a week later, and they must know as well as anyone that they will not find her alive. They are focusing on I-35, the parade of trucks that marches back and forth between Austin and Dallas, and have given up on searching the field.

The construction vehicles arrived a few days before Deecie disappeared, but the police have paused the project, so the waiting backhoes and bulldozers crowd the side streets. As soon as the police give the go-ahead, there will be a road from one side of the field to the next, and then houses will rise like anthills along its sides.

Time will pass, as it does.

Since the first visit from the police, Diana has been watching Leo carefully. Half of her thinks it was a trick of the mind, seeing him behind the tree with his finger to his lips, quieting her: an illusion, an aftereffect of her excitement about discovering the arktoi. She can tell that he doesn't want to talk to her. If he doesn't have to go to his summer job at the park, he mostly stays in his room, the curtains closed, their edges glowing orange in the late-August sun. Maybe he is just sad for the obvious reason: his father is gone, with only a few perfunctory phone calls to explain himself. Twice, Diana has caught him staring at Derek's empty seat at the dining room table, chewing slowly, his eyes blank and fathomless. Maybe, hopefully, his is ordinary heartbreak.

On Tuesday, he went to the pool with Gus and Bee.

On Wednesday evening, just after dinner, he stood in the backyard for a long time, his back to the kitchen window, watering the patch of lemon balm and dill, drawing swirling shapes on the back fence with the hose while Diana pressed her face against the window, willing him to move just a little to the left so that she could read what he might be writing. After a few minutes he lowered his hands. The hose dangled to the ground like he had forgotten it, and the water pooled in the hard dirt at his feet, making a dusty river that trickled toward the driveway in two halting lines. Diana thought he might be crying, but when he turned around, his face was calm. The fence behind him was already fading, the shapes blurred into unreadable splotches in the heat.

He is in his room now, sleeping. Diana is sitting at her desk two rooms away, but she can picture the way his face looks, eyelids fluttering as the air conditioner vent next to his bed blows cool air across his cheeks, a book open on the floor next to him. She does not go into his room anymore; there is no reason to, and she is not invited. She sleeps on the couch, even though Derek is not here, because her own bedroom feels like a hotel room in a foreign country. She is sure that every object has been touched by the swim coach's chlorine-covered hands. There is an invisible film clinging to the jewelry on her dresser, the lamp by her pillow.

There are only a few rooms in the world where she feels at home these days: the empty classroom in Waggener Hall where she spreads out her books and journals across the desks so that she can order them, reorder them, as she thinks. The Cowgirl on Sixth Street, where she can drink a dirty martini and eat a whole basket of peanuts by herself.

The carrel in the library where she works, which is not even a room, but more like a bowl of light, and holds a row of dancing girls, dressed in dark yellow, chanting something Diana is straining to hear.

Diana has not been to the university in a week. She longs to go back, to search every inch of the library for evidence of the arktoi so that she can continue her project, but something tells her she should not leave Leo alone. She will not let the police ask him any questions. Not that she is worried; Leo is gentle. Obviously. But she knows that he will be misunderstood. There are those fires. In their last meeting, the school principal called him "troubled," and Diana felt a nauseating mix of resistance and recognition. If Leo already has a label like that, out in the world, he could be blamed for something he didn't do. He might say something strange, or nothing at all, or he will not remember where he was at some important moment. She knows that things could go very wrong, irretrievably wrong. And Derek will not help her because he is not here.

So she stays home, day after day, making herself a buffer between her son and the world.

When the police knock on Diana's door for the second time, she is in the backyard, fixing the broken fountain, so at first she doesn't hear them.

Like the faux marble foyer and the peeling breezeway, which Diana pretends is an ancient stoa when she walks from the garage to the house, the fountain is an incongruous addition to what is otherwise a flat, faded, piece-of-shit three-bedroom ranch that squats like a troll on its concrete slab. "Unassuming," the realtor said when they pulled up to the curb for the first time. She tapped her clipboard as she said it, as if the click-clack of her manicured nails would distract them from the mustard-colored paint peeling from the window frames and the dark, greasy paths in the carpet.

Derek was interested only in the price. That and the yard, which circled the house like a moat and made it feel twice its size. "For my princess," Derek said, which grated on Diana, even at the time, and now makes her think of Rapunzel and Sleeping Beauty, trapped in their castles. When they bought the house, Diana didn't even know the fountain was there. It is nestled in the back corner of the yard, covered in thick ivy and brambles. She thought it was a pile of broken concrete, discarded from some failed home-improvement project, but when she pulled the errant vines away, she could see the algae-covered bowl, the size of a large kiddie pool, and the rusted pipes sprouting like branches from its back.

Derek said he would fix it, but he never did, and he obviously isn't going to now. The missing toothbrush has made that abundantly clear.

She has decided that she will do it herself. She's home anyway, so she might as well do something useful. On Monday, she started with the vines, which unraveled in long swathes that popped and turned her hands green as she pulled them away. Then she poured a bucket of bleach into the basin, rinsing and wiping carefully, turning the emerald to pale lime as the chloroplast dissolved in the wake of her sponge. When the fountain is working again, and she has rinsed the basin a hundred times, she will buy Leo a fish. Something native to Texas, indestructible, accustomed to heat and all forms of deprivation. A school of brown minnows that he can feed with a handful of crushed saltines. A turtle with long yellow stripes on its neck and a cheerful, wise face.

But Leo is not a child anymore, she reminds herself as she pulls on her rubber gloves. He is almost a man, taller than she is, with a row of pimples on his hairline and at the corners of his mouth. Too old to feed fish and turtles and not old enough to find them interesting. He is vacant-eyed, wandering in an interior landscape that admits no adult visitors.

Unlike Diana, though, he is supposed to be walking in this middle world. He is not stuck there. He is not trying to go back in time, to an era he never lived in and would not recognize at all. She brought everything home from the library to her desk, but despite all her work, the arktoi are out of her reach, little ghosts that vanish when she tries to get close to them. Giggling, they dart behind the plum trees as she drags the garbage cans to the curb. They turn into the vapor of the ice machine at the market. She is starting to worry that there is not enough material, not enough substance, to make it work.

The fountain is something real, something tangible. It is a question with an answer. Gravity, air pressure, water. Today, she is scrubbing the pipes with steel wool, trying to clean them enough that she can see how they fit together. One of them is clogged with something, leaves probably, and Diana can't figure out how to clear it. She puts her face on the opening, but all she can see is black muck. It smells like rotten leaves, the cool underside of a rock.

She is kneeling, trying to see into the dark pipe, when she hears someone clear his throat. For a moment she thinks it is Derek; she scrambles to her feet.

But it isn't Derek. It is the same officer who came the other day. He is smiling, one hand hooked to his belt loop. Bee pulls off her gloves and wipes away a splash of muck she feels clinging to her cheek.

"Ma'am, we're sorry to bother you again."

"No bother," she says. She wipes her hands against her jeans to hide their shakiness. "Everything okay?"

He has already pulled out a tiny green notebook. It looks ridiculously out of proportion in his hands. "Sometimes people remember little details as time goes on. We're just here to see if there's anything else you noticed, anything at all, from last Sunday evening. Or even the days leading up to that."

This is not really a question, Diana notices. It sounds like Mark when he "asks" her if she has considered the myth of

Iphigenia in her research. *"The sacrifice of Iphigenia might be an interesting springboard, Diana."*

She shakes her head to bring herself back to the officer's question and says, "No, I'm sorry. I don't."

Leo has never met that girl, she wants to say, but she is not sure it is true.

"Do the kids in the neighborhood play all together? For example, do your kids play with the kids over there, on the side of the field where the Jeffries family lives?" He points, and Diana half expects to see the twins and Leo traipsing through the field's rabbit tracks to the other side, where another line of children stands waiting, like they are in a scene of *West Side Story.* She wants to call out, to stop them from whatever is about to happen next. But from the backyard, she can't see anything at all—only her own back patio and Leo's garden.

Diana wipes her cheek again. "To be honest, I have no idea. I work at the university, so I'm not here all the time. And my son is mostly with our neighbors, the Rowans. They live right across the street. Over there." She walks to the side yard and points to the Rowan house. Their lawn is somehow still dark green, the only one in a sea of brown that stretches up and down the street, and the windows sparkle like dilating pupils. Mrs. Rowan is a wonder. Or a robot. Or both.

"I see. And these kids, they're older than the Jeffries girl?"

"I don't know the girl. But I think the paper said she was a couple of years younger. I don't think Leo knows her at all." Diana wills her voice to settle. She should know her son's friends, his comings and goings. She should know if he was in the field that night, or if he knew Deecie Jeffries. But she doesn't.

"Well, I'm assuming you've talked about this whole thing with your family. At the dinner table and all." The officer smiles, as if he is trying to soothe her. His lips are thin and grayish under his tan.

"No. I mean, yes." Diana flushes, and immediately she is angry. Who is this man, standing in her yard and implying that he knows more about Leo than she does? "He's not. Familiar with her, that is."

She says the word *familiar* too slowly. It sounds lewd somehow. The officer raises his eyebrows and stuffs his notepad into his back pocket. His eyes slide to the pile of vines next to the fountain, down to the streaks of green on her shirt, then back to her face.

Diana knows she has to convince him that she is calm. "I'll ask him about it again and get back to you. If you have any magic tricks to get a teenage boy to talk to you, let me know," she says, and puts a smile on her face. She rubs one hand slowly down her neck. Nothing is wrong. Let him think that if he pushes past her, into the house, he will find Derek and Leo sitting at the dining room table, ready to eat the meat loaf she made for them, just after she scrubbed the bathroom floor on her hands and knees, whistling a little tune about the joys of housework.

"I sure will, ma'am." He smiles back.

"Anything else?"

"No, that's all I need from you today."

"Okay," she says. He seems to be waiting for her to say something else, so she adds, "I hope you find her soon."

He nods. "Me too, ma'am."

Diana bends down to the fountain so that he will understand she is finished with the conversation. She picks up the steel wool and begins to scrub. The pipe is unwieldy, slick with wet orange rust, heavy with whatever is wedged inside. For a moment, she worries that the officer will ask her something else, but when she looks up again, he is gone.

Diana has just come inside and pulled the screen door closed when she hears Leo behind her. "Did he want to talk to me?" he asks. His pale face floats in the late-afternoon darkness of the living room. She has the notion that if she opens the door again, he will be sucked outside and disappear in all that brightness.

"Were you sleeping again? It's almost four."

"I know. I mean—sorry. I wasn't sleeping."

She understands. Leo hasn't done anything wrong. Why should he talk to them? There is nothing to say. She says, "I think they're doing the last round of questions. I don't think they'll be back."

Leo's shoulders soften when she says this. He looks younger. His fingernails are rimmed in dirt, and she remembers the glistening letters he wrote with the garden hose.

He will not talk to her, but maybe he will help her with the fountain.

"I'm doing a project in the backyard. Fixing the fountain," she tries. "Want to help?"

When Leo was a little boy, maybe five years old, he insisted on having his own garden. It didn't matter that the dirt was basically dust, bad for everything except lettuce, which was so much work for so little reward, all those green worms nestling themselves like chameleons in the curling leaves. He loved it, and the strange miracle was that he could grow anything: lettuce, nasturtiums, beans, carrots that were somehow perfectly shaped and juicy. He planted patches of dill so he could watch swallowtail caterpillars munch their thin tendrils, the mashed lemony smell filling the air, then turn to a village of nubby green chrysalises, and then, at last, wet and slippery butterflies he held in his hands as he waited for their wings to dry.

It was weird. No other boys did this. Certainly not Gus Rowan. When he was little, Gus was sweet, quiet, but then suddenly Gus did nothing but what he wasn't supposed to: riding his bike down the sides of the concrete rain culverts in the field, catching field mice by their tails and throwing them at his sister to watch her squeal in disgust. Sneaking into the roller rink.

And now, hanging out in the field. The boys go in a pack every night after supper, or they did until a week ago: Gus and Leo and kids Diana doesn't know who swarm from their houses like ants. Leo comes home an hour or so after the streetlights come on, reeking of cigarette smoke and gum, and Diana pretends not to notice.

On the night the girl disappeared, she was working on her new idea. The arktoi are multifaceted, dimensional, and her idea about them does not fit into the shape of words, so instead she has been building maps. She cuts out tiny pieces of paper so that she can make layered diagrams, with flaps and narrow strips of Scotch tape. It is a more fluid language, a hybrid of words and pictures, a conjoining of fact and imagination, intuition. The channel the girls must have run beside can lead somewhere besides the ocean if she stabs the map with a toothpick and makes another paper layer to hover an inch above the first. The room they slept in might have other rooms, ones you can't see if you are looking at the definitive lines of a blueprint. If she gets it right, she thinks, the arktoi will speak to her, their voices high and clear over the yawning trench of the years. They will tell her about their year in the forest. They will tell her what she lost, when she changed from a girl to a wife, a mother. They will tell her how to find the wildness of girlhood again. She is sure of it.

So at first she didn't see anything at all outside, except Mary Rowan, sitting on her porch and staring at her like some kind of Peeping Tom. Poor Peeping Mary. Maybe Mary was watching Gus too, or maybe she was watching Leo. Diana understands Mary in this: sometimes it is easier to worry about the problems living across the street.

She remembers all of it. Gus was across the street, standing motionless next to a tree in his yard. The air conditioner hummed from the vents at Diana's feet. Its steady, mechanical noise turned the night outside her window into a silent movie, and she put her pencil down to watch. Mary Rowan was sitting on her porch, still as a rabbit in a field. Gus turned, once, to look back at his house, but he must not have seen his mother sitting there, and she didn't move.

To Diana, it felt like all three of them were caught in the same spell.

She never heard the door, but suddenly, Leo was at the tree too, wearing a backpack and crouching low. He put his hand on Gus's shoulder. When they reached the edge of the field and broke into a run, Diana felt her heart pound until they disappeared in the darkness next to the fence.

And then—something happened in the field. Diana doesn't know what it is, and even if she did, she would never tell the police. But the boys were there that night. She knows it, and Mary Rowan knows it too.

Leo nods toward the fountain. "I can help for a little," he says.

"Okay. It's kind of nasty, but I think I'm almost finished. I just need someone who isn't an idiot to help me."

"I'm the man for the job, then." Leo puts his hand out, pretending that they are making a deal. She reaches for him, playing along, but he pulls his hand away and laughs. His eyes are the color of sage, and they turn a shade darker as she holds his gaze. "Gotcha," he says as he turns to the door.

Diana watches him open the glass slider and step into the backyard. Oh, her Leo. He does not know what it feels like to watch your own flesh shape-shift, from inside your body to outside, from child to man. At first, the transformation feels natural, gradual. Babies are squishy and glossy, leaky, so helpless and needy that you strap them to your body like an extra limb. Then, before you know what has happened, they turn to muscle and hardened bone, bristling with hair and so far away from you that they will not even touch your hand, as if it were made of fire or acid. They are gone, even when they are right in front of you.

And once they are gone, they don't come back. Not in this world, anyway. But maybe there is another one, where Deecie Jeffries and the arktoi sprint deep into the forest. Crocuses sprout up in their path. The girls laugh and call each other's names.

Diana does not consider herself a sentimental woman. She is a scholar, with a scholar's sense of proportion and logic. But she can see this other world, now, as clearly as she sees her own backyard through the open door, as clearly as she sees Leo kneel next to the broken fountain's rim. This other world is here, so close, where the yard turns to a tangle of weeds.

Soon, soon, it will show itself to her. She will walk the road to the temple, and the arktoi will let her in.

Bee

Bee is packing. She has never traveled with Attie, so at first she thinks they will need two bags, an idea that quickly seems ridiculous when she looks at the tiny pile of clean baby clothes Charlie has left for her on the dresser. The diapers, Bee's clothes, Attie's clothes: all of it can fit in the same carry-on, as if the two of them are not quite separate beings yet.

Not like Bee and her own mother, who are so separate that it is impossible to imagine they ever weren't.

It has been three days, but she hasn't texted Leo again. It was a mistake to see him, to ask about Deecie Jeffries. She remembers that look sliding between Leo and Gus in the firelight. She remembers the sound of doors sliding open, windows sliding shut. Her whole body is crawling with unease.

There must be an explanation, though. Something simple. Harmless. Leo is probably trying to avoid dredging up the past. She should do the same. She would be happier that way, and so would Charlie. So would Attie, who is probably drinking Bee's restlessness in her breast milk.

She looks around at the room, its custom window shades, its carefully chosen Shaker-style furniture. After they bought the house, Bee picked out a Pottery Barn bedroom set, still amazed by the fact that she could afford something that felt absurdly extravagant. But before she could place the order, her new mother-in-law, Jane, brought over a catalog for an artisan woodworker from Bath—a wedding gift, she insisted, even though she had already paid for the rehearsal dinner and the honeymoon in Portugal. Now Bee has a hand-built, queen-size bed made of pickled white oak.

Everything Bee has is a better version of what she deserves. She imagines Gus with nothing, to cancel out her everything.

In the days since Bee saw Leo at the bar, she has searched for Deecie Jeffries (*Darlenia Jeffries + missing*; *Deecie Jeffries + suspect*; *Darlenia Cora Jeffries + footprints*) on Charlie's computer dozens of times. She is sure that he never checks the search history, but she deletes it, just in case. At this point, she has probably read more than twenty articles. She has read every piece in the *Austin American-Statesman* and in *The Dallas Morning News*. She has looked at photographs of Deecie standing in front of her house, photographs of the old field, photographs of the roller-skating rink and the Vaquero Drive-In. She even paid for the original police report, which doesn't say much but does list both her mother and Diana Nastasi as neighbors interviewed after the disappearance. There are checkboxes on the form for "runaway," "abduction," "abduction: family," and "at risk," but the box the police chose is simple: "lost." Underneath, in almost unreadable cursive, someone has added *circumstances unknown*.

She is thinking, maybe, when she is in Austin, she will go to the station. There must be something in the archives. She is picturing an air-conditioned basement, lined from floor to ceiling with cardboard boxes. They probably won't let her see anything, but still. At the very least she can walk the block from her house to the field, or where the field used to be, and try to picture what must have happened. Even though she never hung out in the field the way Gus and Leo did, it is still clear in her mind. She tried painting it from memory once, in college, but it ended up looking like a paint-by-numbers version of van Gogh's *Wheatfield with Crows*: a turquoise sky, a path like a brown river winding its way to the horizon line. Still. Maybe pretending to be there, pretending to be that age again, will open a door that the police never noticed.

Maybe it will open a door in her too.

She will check one more time, before she goes. Bee rests one hand on Attie's belly as she stretches and wiggles in the middle of the bed. She uses her other hand to type Deecie's name into the search bar on her phone. Something new comes up right away, an article about the backpack.

"Backpack Discovery Raises False Hope."

Attie stills, and Bee glances over at her. She is gazing at Bee calmly, as if to say, *Well?*

The missing backpack, it turns out, contained a Black Stallion book (the article doesn't say which one, although Bee is curious, and glad that Deecie wasn't one of the *Black Beauty* girls, who were prissy and puritanical), a fat ballpoint souvenir pen from Niagara Falls with ten different colors of ink, a snow globe trapping a mermaid in a sea of turquoise glitter, and a cheerleader's baton. There is a photograph of the items, laid out on a faux wood laminate table, probably in an office at the police station. The simple detritus of a girl's life. Every item, except the baton, is carefully sealed in its own ziplock bag.

The backpack also contained a note, from Deecie Jeffries herself, explaining that the backpack was a time capsule of her life as a ten-year-old in Austin, Texas, buried during October of the 1983–84 school year, years before she went missing.

```
Investigators have determined that the backpack
was buried in the field by Jeffries herself,
more than three years before her disappearance.
Her father, Arlo Jeffries, has confirmed that he
remembers the time capsule as a school project
from Deecie's time in the fifth grade at Webster
Elementary.
```

The newspaper hasn't printed the note. Bee scrolls all the way to the bottom of the article, but there is nothing there except advertisements for a special kind of shoe that will build calf muscle and a new kind of Similac. Maybe Deecie's family didn't want them to share it, although what could be so private about a fifth-grader's time capsule note? *Dear Future Deecie,* it would say. *Hi!!! It's me, ha, ha.* Or: *To Whoever Is Reading This Note: My name is Deecie Jeffries, and I am a fifth-grader at Webster Elementary. I love to play baton.*

Or something like that.

It wouldn't say what Bee's would if she wrote one today and packed it into the side pocket of her carry-on bag. *Dear Time Capsule: I am suffused with restlessness. At night, I sometimes want to drag my bed to the middle of my yard and stare at a sky made of dark blue paint, just to see if I might float.*

But Deecie was not awash in hormones when she made her time capsule. She was still a girl. Maybe she was one of the kids Bee used to watch with envy as they moved effortlessly through the halls, the center of a galaxy of friends. The baton is good evidence for this; girls who practiced baton in their yards after school were happy girls.

Bee can't remember anything about fifth grade except that they studied Texas history for the third year in a row and made cardboard Alamos out of shoeboxes. Everyone had to bring in their own box, no exceptions. Bee made hers using most of Gus's prized collection of G.I. Joe figurines. She never asked for his permission, though, so the night before they were supposed to bring them to school, he tore the soldiers out of Bee's shoebox and put them in his own. The glue Bee used to stick their gray plastic boots to the sides of the Alamo left long strips of torn paper all over the display, like a giant wild animal had come through instead of Santa Anna.

Bee looks at her suitcase, filling slowly with Attie's onesies and Bee's T-shirts and nursing bras and giant, elastic-waist pants. She should bring a pair of jeans, just in case her body shrinks miraculously in the presence of her mother's raised eyebrows.

If the plane goes down somewhere over Kentucky or Arkansas, the suitcase will be a time capsule of this morning, this moment. Someone will open it with wonder, stare at the ordinary items, grown disproportionately significant and poignant in their new context. Her deodorant will become an artifact. Attie's tiny socks, a relic.

The phone is on the bed, and when it buzzes it rotates just a fraction, a little dance. Leo's name appears on the banner, and Bee's heart lifts. Sings, practically, the way it used to, when they were kids and she saw his outline at the screen door, familiar and beloved. Or when they were older, and she thought sometimes that he might be giving her a sidelong glance across a mounded row of seedlings, his eyes flickering away from hers as quickly as a thought.

Stupid, but it can't be helped. Then, or now.

She ignores the message, a punishment for the goose bumps of joy tingling along her arms. She makes herself tuck her charger into the side pocket and slide her work laptop into a zippered compartment before she picks up the phone. Her face looks worried in the blank screen's reflection, then disappears in a gray glow.

I want to see you today, the message says. Can I?

When Bee was in college, there was one boy who used to say things like this to her, so bold and direct that she could not pretend to misunderstand his meaning. His mother was a florist, she remembers, because at the time it seemed like a romantic, simple job. He would show up at her door at strange times and get someone to let him in so he could leave enormous bouquets of ranunculus and freesias in her room. The flowers were ridiculous—exotic and delicate against the white cinder block walls—and her roommates would split the bouquets between them, arranging them in jelly jars on their dressers, leaving them there until the whole dorm smelled of something sweet and rotting.

But she was in college then, young enough to think that boy's desire for her was part of an endless lifetime supply. She wasn't married, with a baby who is lying on the bed in front of her, snatching at invisible fireflies while she sleeps. Bee sits next to her, gently, so that the motion of the mattress will not disturb her. She puts her hand back on Attie's warm belly, and the flailing limbs freeze in the air for a moment, then float gently to her sides.

The phone, still glowing, buzzes again.

Also, I wanted to say I'm sorry. I should have told you sooner that Gus and I talk sometimes.

There is a pause, the gray dots suspended as Leo types, somewhere far away. His farm is near Portsmouth, he said at the Spoke. Bee pictures a windswept farm, the ocean a narrow line of pewter in the distance, Leo sitting by a woodstove with his phone in his hands. The dots are moving quickly, and Bee waits for the message to appear. There is a long pause, and then, nothing.

Attie is scrunching up her face, as if she smells something horrible. Her arms and legs are churning again. Bee keeps her hand steady on Attie's taut belly, afraid for a moment that she will fall. She is so small, and the bed is large, but her movements are reckless and disproportionate. Sometimes, when Bee is holding her, she arches her back so suddenly and with such force that she nearly launches herself from Bee's arms. She is a fish on the end of a line, or a hawk beginning its dive.

Bee stares at the phone. Like magic, the dots appear again. They give her the feeling that she can see inside Leo's head. He is nervous. He hesitates. Dot, dot, dot.

But why? He has already told her his big news. Gus talks to Leo, not Bee. It's not news at all; it's the same as it's always been.

The taxi is coming in an hour to pick her up. The flight leaves Portland at one, lands in Austin at four. Charlie left for work before breakfast, while Bee was still in bed, after kissing her on the cheek so lightly that she put her hand to her own face to trap it there. He still does not want her to go—"Just wait until Christmas, Bee, and then I'll be able to help"—but for some reason the nonstop flight was the cheapest one, and the flight overlaps with one of Attie's possible nap times, and this kind of adult logic is unassailable.

Bee and Charlie are not fighting, not exactly. They have, in the past two days, reached a balance that feels sustainable.

Charlie doesn't want her to go, but he won't say so again. He seems to understand.

The suitcase bangs against the backs of Bee's legs as she pulls it down the stairs. She should not leave Attie on the bed alone, and Charlie offered to carry the suitcase for her this morning before he left, but she wasn't packed yet and she still needs to get the travel car seat out of the garage, and now Attie is asleep and this is, like the plane ticket, just one of the endless calculations that adulthood requires. When she reaches the bottom, she pauses in the quiet, listening.

There is a noise outside.

At first she thinks it is the taxi driver, standing silently on her front porch, although Bee did not hear a knock, and she has never known a taxi driver to come to the door. It could be Charlie, but he never forgets anything or leaves work unexpectedly.

The shape outside the frosted glass is not moving. Her heart begins to pound. She waits, staring, as if the figure is a deer and she will be invisible if she is motionless. Before she can decide whether or not she will open the door, the shape resolves itself into an outline that she knows, and her heart lifts for the second time this morning.

There is another message, now, on her phone, a short one.

Can I come in?

Now she understands. Her body prickles with electricity, her hands shake. Here it is again: her impossible, permanent, idiotic crush.

Here she is again: a girl.

Leo's smile when Bee opens the door is a question. "Hey," he says. "I'm sorry for coming by like this." It is cold, with snow still crusting the front walk, but he is wearing only a sweater.

Charlie's footprints are pointing away from the house, and Leo has walked over them, in the other direction.

"It's fine. Except—how did you find it?" This is not really the question Bee wants to ask, but it fills the air for the second it will take her to stop swaying unsteadily on her feet.

"Internet," he says, and his smile turns sheepish. "Wasn't too hard."

You could have found me years ago. "Oh," she says.

"So I texted you. I thought—"

"I get it." This sounds abrupter than she wants it to, and Leo flinches. Half of Bee wants to reach out, take the words out of the air.

The other half wants to hurt him again.

She says, "You're sorry. About Gus. Leo, it's fine. It's not even your problem."

Leo frowns and looks down at the tiled hallway where they stand. How is it that he is here, in her house, in Portland? She built a whole life that didn't include him at all. He doesn't belong here.

"I know. Bee, I know I should have told you everything sooner. But Gus—"

"Listen. Leo. I appreciate you telling me that you've talked to Gus. But isn't everything always about what he wants? He calls, and you jump. He suddenly decides that he's open to talking, so I have to make sense of that after not hearing from him for almost twenty years." She forces herself to breathe. "Whatever. It's good to know that he's upright. Alive. I'm glad. Obviously. But I don't need—"

Leo is staring at her. "Bee, you don't understand."

There is a sound coming from somewhere deep in Bee's ears. It is a roiling, dark sound, like a distant motorcycle. She does not want Leo to say whatever comes next.

Leo is standing so close to her now that she smells lemons and green grass. His sleeves are frayed but clean. He is wearing boots, and beneath them a puddle is widening onto the tiles, as if he is standing in an invisible lake that is slowly revealing itself as he talks.

He will sink, Bee thinks, absurdly, as she watches the puddle grow. She will have to pull him out.

"Bee, you need to talk to Gus. That's what I'm saying. Trying to say. I wish I could tell you the whole thing. He—you need to talk to him. Let me give you his number."

Bee is shaking. She does not know why, since she does not know more than she did a minute ago. But there is something about standing with Leo, all his attention on her, that makes her feel like she is too awake, too full of ions and electrolytes and blood, all of it zinging around inside her and making her woozy.

"Okay," she says, and Leo leans in. He tucks a strand of her hair behind her ear, and Bee shivers.

"Is Charlie home?" Leo looks calm, as if he would welcome the idea of seeing Charlie come around the corner, but he glances at the stairs.

If Charlie were here, he would somehow ignore the obvious. *Hello, hey, how are ya*, he would say. He would offer to make a pot of coffee.

The image makes Bee feel slightly unhinged. The text, the shape behind the glass, Leo standing in front of her, his fingers slowly tracing the edge of her ear, all of it is happening so quickly that it seems possible that it is another side effect of Attie's birth, like spouting milk and growing a shoe size. Maybe hallucinations are a side effect, too, one she hasn't read about yet.

But Leo is here. He is staring at her. He moves closer, bumps her shoulder. He is warm. His sweater is soft and smells a little like hay.

"No," she says. "He's not home." It is hard to tell if the feeling coursing through her is happiness or fear. She decides it is neither, and that she does not care. She wants to think only about Leo: his dark eyelashes, the sharp edges of his jaw, his waist with her hands around it.

His mouth.

He is hugging her hard now. One arm is around her waist, the other above her shoulder, so she can feel the whole length of him, surrounding her. He is strong. She can feel his heart. And then, in the next moment, she can feel the stubble of his cheek on hers, his lips, the knock of his teeth against hers. Everything is overlapping, all at once.

Suddenly, her senses unmix themselves. She is emerging from the bottom of a deep pond, her face touching the dry air, her eyes clearing of water. Leo's mouth is on her ear, her cheekbone.

"Leo," she whispers. She is wicked. "What are you doing?"

"I'm not sure," he says into her neck. "I'm sorry. Bee. I should go."

She has moved away now, her arms on his shoulders. He is not smiling, and he will not look at her. The air between them is warm from their bodies.

There is a muffled thud. A wail begins, weak at first, then gaining in volume and size.

Then Bee remembers. She left Attie upstairs, lying alone on the bed.

Mary

If a rubber band comes into the house, that rubber band should not leave the house until it has lived nine lives. It can end its time on this earth as a Christmas ornament hanger, or as a replacement for the hardened rubber stopper on the bottle of Youth Dew perfume on your vanity, or as a jar opener, but it must be yours until it dries out and snaps or your imagination does.

The same can apply to plastic bags, and garden hoses, and the flour that sticks to the counter when you knead your bread. The broken shards of a plate. All of it, every last bit, can be used again.

Waste not, want not. You have to take care of the things you have, tend them like a yard. The Rowan yard, Mary is proud to say, is a perfect square of dark green in a swathe of yellow straw. No one cares for their yard like the Rowans do.

The same goes for time. It slips away if you don't pay attention. Mary tells her children again and again that there are only so many minutes in an hour, and so many hours in a day, and so many days in a life, so they should use them the best they can. *Otherwise, you will end up stuck here, like me,* she wants to say, but of course she can't. Bee seems to understand her, or at least she doesn't contradict. But Gus shakes his head when she talks like this.

Gus, who wastes the most time, riding his bike aimlessly around with Leo, not reading or playing his guitar or making money like he should be, even though he is awake for more hours of the day than anyone. Mary hears the screen door slide so late sometimes that it becomes a part of her dreams: the scrape of a pirate's oar in its lock, the sound of a wing sprouting from her back.

The garage door is closed so the dust from the construction project outside will not sift its way onto Mary's storage boxes or Leroy's tools and his display of old football trophies. The wall of boxes makes Mary feel prepared, equipped. The twins' baby clothes are stored near the corner in boxes labeled by size. There are blocks and books. Everything she will need. Maybe they will move someday, if the street feels too busy after the road is expanded, and Mary will be halfway ready before she even begins to pack.

The play is less than a month away. When Leroy is at work, Mary likes to practice her lines in the garage because of the cool echo. It makes her words more resonant, more dramatic. Her director would say that it adds color to her tone, a comment that has always baffled her. She pictures her words popping out of her mouth like jelly beans, each one its own pastel shade.

It would be better with a mirror, like the one in her bedroom, but of course there is no mirror in the garage. There are oil stains on the concrete where Leroy parks his truck. When he is gone, Mary has no way to get to the store or to the bank, not unless she asks one of her neighbors for a ride, but more often than not the only person home is Diana Nastasi, Leo's mom, *practically a professor*, who seems to come and go as she pleases and who is strange and unpleasant and would probably say no anyway. The children have been friends for years, but Mary and Diana have never found a way to share so much as neighboring chairs at the town pool.

The woman is a snob. It matters less now than it did when the kids were younger, but even so, it is hard to see yourself so clearly in the eyes of another: frivolous, incompetent, vain. But Diana has never asked Mary a single question about herself, so how can she know? They have never sat together, in a kitchen, sharing a cup of coffee while the children play in the backyard. Diana probably thinks she is too busy for such things, even though she isn't a real teacher, like Laura next door, who drives herself to the high school at seven-thirty in the morning and returns to make dinner every night at five. Diana seems to follow no routine. More often than not, she is home when Leo is at school, gone when he is home, and considering that Leo always appears at the Rowan house when it is time for dinner, it doesn't seem like Diana can be bothered to feed him.

Consider the source, Mary would say to her children if they were to worry about someone looking down her nose at them. *You don't like everyone, and not everyone likes you.* It doesn't matter that Diana doesn't like her, or that she has never said a simple thank-you to Mary for feeding Leo and giving him Band-Aids and popsicles and Tang in the summer. It just means that Mary has one less person to talk to once the street empties for the workday.

Diana would never participate in community theater. She

would probably think it was beneath her, a silly waste of time for unsophisticated amateurs, that Mary should try seeing some real art for once, even if it's only at the university museum. She would laugh if she knew how Mary's heart rises when she sees Janine Hebert pulling the ropes for the stage curtain, her face pink and sweaty, as Mary stands waiting in the darkness to say her lines. And then—and then!—the deep *click* of the light switch. It might as well be a switch in her soul.

No, Diana would never understand.

There is a pile of sawdust in the corner behind Leroy's shop table, next to the shelves. No one has used the tools for years, not since Leroy and Gus spent weeks building a Pinewood Derby car for Cub Scouts when he was seven. More than half his lifetime ago, now. The brochure said, "Everyone knows the Pinewood Derby is all about FUN!" and at first that's what Mary hoped for, picturing the two of them bent over plans in the hot garage and trading the car between them as they sanded it smooth. Leroy told Mary and Bee that they were banned from the garage until the competition. "Let us have some father-son time," he would say at the dinner table, Gus quiet and blushing a little, as if he was pleased.

The car didn't win, though, and Gus threw it against the wall when they got home. There is still a dent and a faint stain of red enamel paint next to the front door, and although Mary knows that she should get out a piece of sandpaper and some spackle, she never has. Secretly, she wants the dent to remind him of his failure.

Not Gus's. It is Leroy's failure because he left Gus in that school gym after he lost. "I don't drive losers home," Leroy told Mary when he arrived, alone, in the driveway. Gus had to walk home by himself, and even though it wasn't far, just through the field, it was almost dark, and the distance was enough for Gus to turn into an animal instead of a boy, one who could only snarl when Bee asked him about the race. He was aiming for Bee when he threw the car, but she ducked. And now there's just the dent.

Other than the shop table, and the forlorn pile of sawdust, which really could be from anything, the garage is just like anyone else's. It has half-filled cans of paint and polyurethane, mismatched tires, and tools. It has a bike with no wheels and two deflated pool tubes.

Everything in here is broken, but just because something is broken doesn't mean that it has reached the end of its usefulness.

Mary's mother lived through the Depression, "on spit and grit," she liked to say. Christmas presents were socks and underwear, things Mary needed anyway, not the dolls she longed for. They baked bread, never cookies, and when Mary learned to read, her mother set her to work with *The Fannie Farmer Cookbook*. Still, Mary is convinced that there is something beyond the practical in her mother's lessons. Something magical about squeezing every last drop of life out of the objects in her purview. A ham can last for two weeks, in capable hands. A towel can become a dishcloth that can become a patch on an old pair of jeans.

An egg can split inside you and become an unfamiliar fruit, a child.

This new baby is like a brand-new, unbroken plate, hidden beneath a layer of newspaper. A surprise gift. It is nestled deep inside her, with no knowledge of the world outside, perfectly pristine and ready for Mary to give it all her love, all at once. When the twins were born, she felt divided all the time, one of them sleeping while the other one cried, then the other one crying while the first one slept, and there was no time to sit and stare at them in wonder as you are supposed to. Bee doesn't mind, as if she never expected anything else, but Gus acts like Mary owes him something. As if she should drop everything and pay attention to him, only him, for the rest of her life.

Maybe the new baby will give him what he needs. Undivided love. Whatever it is that Mary has failed to deliver. If she can figure out how to tell him he will be a big brother soon, how to tell him the right way, maybe everything will be fine.

She will practice how to say it right.

Mary bends down and rummages through a sagging cardboard box stashed in the far corner, behind a cluster of rakes. She is already wearing the only thing she owns that Elizabeth Proctor might wear, a brown wool cardigan that was once her mother's, but she needs a prop. There they are, the final two plates, peeking out from their newspaper wrapping like two cataract-covered, pale blue eyes. She grabs one and holds it above her head. It wobbles in her hands. What would Elizabeth Proctor do, if she were afraid to tell her family about the baby growing inside her? She would dig deep into her Puritan soul and turn her itchy woolen suffering into courage.

Mary Rowan is not a Puritan, though. She is not Marilyn Monroe or Diana Nastasi. Except for the fact that she is the mother of twins, she is *ordinary*. This is why she loves putting on her costumes, saying lines written by Mr. Arthur Miller while he sat in his white T-shirt, thinking thoughts so profound that they would never even occur to her.

She is not Elizabeth Proctor, and she is not suffering either. Not really. Her own mother would say that any woman who has a roof over her head and still complains is just asking for God to spit in her eye. And even though Leroy's face is puffy with drink, and he does not really talk to her anymore, or touch her on Saturday mornings the way he used to, there is still the roof, and the lawn, and the food that fills the trunk of the car on Saturdays like a cornucopia of carrots and Fig Newtons and Steak-umms and cheese.

Mary puts the plate on the workbench and uses the slats on the side as a ladder to climb to its surface. She likes standing up here because the height is almost the same as the stage at the Pips Playhouse, where the people in the front rows have to crane their necks to look up at her. It is good to replicate performance conditions as closely as possible, and although an empty garage isn't exactly a theater, it can be, with some imagination. Part of Mary wants to open the garage door so that Diana can see her. Would she notice Mary's creativity, her resourcefulness, or would she just think that she was cleaning the garage?

The workbench wobbles, a little, and something small and light falls from somewhere behind the bench to the floor. Mary takes a deep breath. Her director tells her that when she breathes in, she is Mary Rowan, and when she breathes out, she is Elizabeth Proctor. Into the clammy air of the garage, she whispers, "What keeps you so late? It's almost dark."

There is no response, of course. In her head, she recites John Proctor's line. *I were planting far out to the forest edge.* She is supposed to pretend to ladle soup, so she squats down and picks up the plate. "It hurt my heart to strip her, poor rabbit." She does not whisper this time, and her voice sounds absurdly loud, like she is using a megaphone.

She has forgotten something in the sequence. She tries to picture the script, lying on her bed upstairs. She knows she is on page 52, but there is a blank space in her memory where the words should be. She feels her heart clench with disappointment. Diana Nastasi is right. She is vain and delusional. She cannot even manage this small, insignificant role.

Blue Plate 5: You are a forgetful, cowardly woman.

The plate smashes to the floor. Mary did not mean to drop it, not really, but she feels better, more powerful, as if the sound has crowded out the doubt in her. The baby shifts and settles, as if in approval. *Gus, Bee,* Mary imagines herself saying. *I have a surprise for you.*

Mary has decided that the baby is a girl, and that she will name her Adelaide. Attie for short. Adelaide is the name of a city she once wanted to visit, in Australia, back when she thought she might ever go that far away from here. It is on the beach, and it was named after a queen. Leroy likes to joke that he drives through a tiny town in Georgia called Adelaide sometimes. *If you want to travel so bad, hop in the truck one of these days and I'll take you.*

If it is a boy, Leroy might try to insist on Carl again. It was his father's name. Because Carl is a horrible name, for a baby or a man, Mary hopes this will not come to pass.

The plate is broken into five uneven pieces, like a child's workbook lesson on fractions. Mary climbs down from the workbench so she can kick the shards into a pile that no one besides her will ever bother to sweep.

On the concrete floor, tipped up against the wall that it must have slid down when the workbench wobbled, is a small photograph. At first, she thinks it is a receipt or an oversize business card. Mary does not own a Polaroid camera, and she has seen only a few of these before. It is so out of place, here in the garage where she knows and owns everything, that her brain can't seem to add it to the register. She kneels to pick it up, then stares. She is an archaeologist, trying to piece together a relic from an unknown civilization. The square of film is greenish, and it is streaked with sawdust and grime. At first, she can't figure out which way is up, and she rotates it again and again until the blobby white shape makes sense.

She breathes in, sharply.

It is a boy. He is small, maybe eight or so, and he has no clothes on. He is not facing the camera, but his face is turning to the side, as if the person taking the photo has called his name. There is nothing wrong, not technically, except the nakedness, and Mary's sense that the boy is afraid, or that he is angry, or both.

Mary has taken whole rolls of pictures of the twins splashing at Lake Travis or at the park when they were babies, naked as the day they were born, and there's no harm in it. This is different.

The smell of sawdust, usually so soothing, has turned sour. Someone is inflating a huge balloon just below Mary's ribs. It is taking up all the room in her body, all the space she has for her own air and blood, not to mention the baby's.

What is the age when children become a self, with a body that holds and produces shame? Is it five? Six? The picture is both blurry and faded, so it is impossible to tell who the boy is, or where he is. There is only white skin, and black hair, and a green-gray background that could be inside or outside or anywhere.

There are fingerprints on it, dark smudges ringing the white edges, but she is careful not to add her own, and she is also careful to put it back just so, wedged between the workbench and the wall. The air in the garage turns to damp fog as nausea billows inside her.

There is one plate left in the box. Mary moves aside the newspaper and holds it to her chest. She is breathing so fast that she worries she will faint, here in the garage, with that Polaroid accusing her from its spot a few feet away.

How will she go back to the house?

Inside her, the apple splits its skin. Something wet trickles unevenly down her inner thigh.

Blue Plate 6 smashes to the ground, but Mary is frozen, staring at the stain that is darkening the front of her dress.

Blue Plate 6 is the final one, the answer to all the others. She hears it whisper to her, clear and calm in the coolness of the garage.

Oh, Mary, it says. *Oh, oh, oh.*

Bee

Portland, Maine
2011

Upstairs, Attie is on the floor, a look of astonishment on her face. She is not breathing. Bee is kneeling at her side before she knows how she has moved there so quickly, both hands under Attie's body, pulling her close. Something in her mind warns her she should not reposition her, something about spinal cords and backboards, but Bee can't help herself. She cradles Attie's round, soft head in her palms and stares at her, and then, without knowing exactly why, blows a quick breath into her face, hard.

There it is. The scrunching of the face, the rise of purple blood to her cheeks, her eyelids. The intake of breath before the cry, a sound so loud and welcome that Bee feels like it should be accompanied by a spray of silver confetti. Attie is angry, not hurt. She is making an accusation. If she could speak, she would be telling Bee that she does not deserve to be a mother to such wonder, such living, breathing, unbroken perfection.

Bee wraps both arms around Attie and stands up awkwardly from the floor. Her legs are deerlike, stiff and ungainly, as if she has been kneeling on the rose-covered rug for hours. She is crying, and when she sits down on the side of the bed, she pulls Attie's face to her neck, both of them sweaty and damp. Bee can feel Attie's wet mouth opening and her cheeks hardening as she screams. She can feel the tiny bones of Attie's spine beneath her probing fingers. "I'm so sorry," Bee whispers, over and over. "I'm so sorry."

"What happened?"

Bee looks up. Leo is standing in the doorway, both feet in the hall. She has the idea that he won't be able to enter this bedroom, as if there is a magical marriage spell that will keep him out despite what happened downstairs. Or, if he were to walk backward down the hall, down the stairs, and out the door, stepping in his own footprints in the snow, he might erase what they have done.

But he comes inside the room anyway. He looks stricken, and for a moment Bee is confused.

"She fell off the bed," she says. Her voice is shaky, but Attie is still crying, so Leo will not notice. Such a loud noise for such a small creature.

"Oh. Is she okay?" He reaches out, as if to pat Attie's back, but lets his hand drop. He is so close. That lemony, green smell. Bee's cheek still burns from the stubble of his chin.

"I think so. Yeah. She seems okay." Attie is quieter now, just tiny whimpers and hiccups. Bee does not want to bounce her in case she is hurt somewhere deep inside. Babies are so soft, but maybe their softness makes them strong, like a drunk hitting a dashboard with no expectation of pain. Bee hopes that Attie's cells are multiplying, growing, already in the process of forgetting this moment. She hopes that she will never learn to stiffen herself to the world. To expect pain.

"Good. That's good." Leo is still standing just inside the doorway. Bee wishes he would leave. There was a wall of glass surrounding this life of hers, keeping it safe and dear, and she has shattered it. Who was that woman downstairs, who let him kiss her, who kissed him back? He is frowning, as if he is asking the same question.

Then, in a quiet voice, he says, "Are you going on vacation or something?" Bee ignores him. She pats Attie's back, making a pattern, a secret knock that only the two of them will ever know. She takes her time.

"I'm going to see my mom." There is a pulse near Leo's jawline. "Just for a few days." She is not sure why she says it this way, as if she is trying to soften the news. She does not even know him, not anymore. He is not her husband. Charlie is the one she should be worrying about. She has been hurting his feelings for days now. For weeks, since Attie was born and she turned into whatever it is that she is now.

"She's beautiful," Leo says to the roses on the rug. He is rubbing his neck, avoiding the place where the scar winds up toward his hairline. He is not looking at her, or at Attie.

"What?" Suddenly, Bee is exhausted. None of this makes any sense. She wants to lie back on the bed, let it lift her into the sky above her own roof, Attie's warm body curling on her chest. But the Maine winter sky outside is a flat gray, not shades of blue and green, and she is not in an afternoon art class, staring at a painting. She is so heavy. If she sits here for much longer, her body will flatten the bed beneath her, until her hip bones reach the wooden frame, the floor planks, the kitchen below.

"I mean...I'm sorry." He looks up, searching her face. It is a staring contest of sorts, the kind they played as kids, but the stakes are unrecognizable. He takes a step away, back into the hall, like he is trying to convince her that he is harmless.

When he speaks again, his voice is a whisper. "Bee, I shouldn't have come here. I know that. But I needed to make sure that you understand."

"Understand what?"

Leo pauses. His eyes are wide, their green shifting from the dark green of a bottle to sage in the afternoon light. He says, "Bee, Gus has to tell you something. I told him I would try. I don't know where he is right now, or anything. I just know he wants to talk to you." He pulls out his phone. His face is searching hers.

Bee wants to knock the phone from his hands. "Leo," she says, one hand cradling Attie, the other gesturing to the room. She is angry now, and there is nothing to stop her from saying what she means. "Look at me. Look around you. I am *married*. This is my *baby*. I have no idea what you think you're doing."

Leo's eyes flicker over her shoulder to the bed behind her, but he doesn't say anything.

"I'm not going to drop everything just because Gus wants me to. Or because you do. Just—you should leave." Now that she has said it out loud, she feels lighter, more powerful. The legs of the bed hover an inch from the floor, and a gust of wind moves the crown of the tree outside the window. A leafless branch scrapes the glass. "I mean it. Go."

Leo's hands are shoved deep in his pockets. In two seconds, he will be at the top of the stairs. He will leave. The third step from the bottom will creak, because he is not Charlie and he will not know to skip it.

He will leave, and he won't come back.

Bee's heart is telescoping out of her chest. She is at the

doorway, Attie's head nestled in her neck. *I don't understand,* she is thinking. She is about to say it out loud when he turns and looks at her, as if he has heard her. His face is still, but there is movement everywhere, below the surface of his skin, below Bee's, in the last leaves outside the bedroom window, which are swirling in uneven circles in the wind.

He says, quietly, "We wanted you to be happy."

Attie begins to whimper, as if she senses Bee's confusion. "What do you mean? Leo? You and Gus didn't talk to me because you thought it would make me happy?"

Leo is turning away. He is at the top of the stairs now. Attie's face is wet and warm against Bee's skin.

"Leo. Wait. I am happy. I am. I promise."

Leo clears his throat. He turns to her. His scar is on the front, too, she sees now, like the path of a river that branches into creeks and channels. It must travel down onto his chest, which she will never see. She lets herself imagine what it would be like to lift his shirt, to follow that path with her mouth, her tongue.

"Take care of yourself, Bee. I missed you," he says.

Bee shuts her eyes. She doesn't open them again until she hears the front door close behind him.

Diana

Diana sits at her favorite table in the university library with a map of the ancient sanctuary at Brauron spread out in front of her and a map of the coast of contemporary Greece in her lap. It is her belief that maps always hold secrets. There is the world, drawn by a flawed and trembling and perhaps biased hand, and there are the details that are purposely hidden from view. Maps mark mountains and borders, but mostly, they record the limits of the human imagination, which is frustratingly linear and flat, the way the words in a sentence are poor substitutes for the worlds they describe. She wants something multidimensional, floating, that she can tip in the air with her wondering hands. Something like a map, but better.

She is looking for comparisons. Odd-angled correspondences that will reveal something no one else has seen. The solution to the mystery of the arktoi, hiding in plain sight.

She wants to know what kept them in the forest. What they found there. What they kept with them their whole lives.

What kind of women they became. Diana's life is falling apart around her, but her pursuit of the arktoi feels like a life buoy, one that might save her and Leo too. She has been reading about Brauron for weeks, and she has found almost nothing of interest, except this map and an article by a French historian who claims the myth is a simple exchange: for man's murder of wildness in the form of the hunt, he says, the girls must be wild for a short time, until they give it up.

This equation, to Diana, makes no sense. Where, then, does the wildness go?

The ancient sanctuary is designed like Diana's own ranch house. According to the blueprint, there are hallways and small rooms and what looks like a Jack and Jill bathroom on the western side. There is the Great Stoa, a rock-cut terrace, and a spring. The whole complex is nestled next to the rocky face of a small mountain, with its ledges and trees, and less than half a mile from the Aegean. Diana traces her finger along the map in her lap, following the line from the sea to the temple and back again. The river that once fed the spring and then the sea is gone now, its dry channel a groove of sunbaked dirt. The girls must have run from forest to ocean a hundred times, their legs growing sure and strong, their feet slowly losing the softness of their sandals. The sea must have spread out before them like a turquoise vein in a shard of quartz.

The map is rendered in shaky black ink, with numbers corresponding to neat labels that she is sure are wrong, insufficient. She needs to find more information, but there is next to nothing. Where would the girls go when they slept, their bronzed legs twined together at the ankles? Where did they eat together? Where did they hide to tell their secrets?

There is, on the southeast corner, a room inside a room

inside a room. A temple for Artemis. A secret-telling room. On the map, there are no doors anywhere, as if the girls are not flesh and bone but vapor. It is here, Diana knows, that the sacrifices were made: the spindles, the honey cakes, the clothing of women who died in childbirth. The goddess is irascible and ruthless. She takes everything, even unmentionable sorrows. Diana closes her eyes and imagines herself far above the map, watching a trail of weeping women winding their way to the temple from the town, carrying the blood-crusted clothes of a friend. She can see the little girls lined on the edges of the sanctuary in their yellow robes, pinching each other in their communal effort to keep from too much wiggling.

She folds the map. Diana hates parties where there are only women: baby showers, wedding showers, with their childish games and child-sized snacks. But Brauron would be something different. In a place like that, wedged between the mountains and the sea, in the innermost room of a goddess's temple, with only women and girls to hear, you could tell the truth. You could say, *My husband is leaving me*. And then, worse: *I'm glad to see him go.*

In the hall outside the library, she hears the overlapping, excited sounds of children. For a moment, she thinks that she is hallucinating, transported somehow to the marble halls of Brauron, but then she remembers that it is Thursday, the day the university summer day camp brings its campers through the library to see the archaeological museum. Diana has been the docent on these tours many times, and she wonders at the wisdom of bringing crowds of sweaty, hungry children to a museum that has no mummies, no dinosaurs. There isn't even any jewelry. Sometimes, you can get one of the serious ones excited about something—finding as many figures of Achilles as possible on the amphorae, maybe—but that's rare. Even Leo used to beg her to skip these visits.

Today is Mark's day to give the tour. Diana knows this because he already tried to get her to replace him, in a message taped to the side of her carrel. Diana flicked the note away, giving herself an excuse to pretend she did not see it, but if he spots her he will try to recruit her to take over, so she folds up her maps and slides them into their staticky plastic sleeves. If she hurries and leaves by the stairwell, she will be out of the library before he passes the door.

"I thought you would be here. Did you get my note?"

It is too late. Mark is standing beside her table, a little girl in the doorway behind him. His shirt is unbuttoned at the top, and Diana sees a tuft of grayish hair trapped in one of the buttonholes. He is always two inches closer than he should be, and now he is even closer, his hand pressing the table next to hers. When she stands, she can smell onions from his armpits and a distant whiff of tobacco, like a pipe smoked days ago.

"I just saw it. Sorry." She isn't, but the children are his responsibility now, so it doesn't matter if he can tell that she is dismissing him. From the doorway, the little girl says, "Mr. Mark, I need to pee. *Bad.*" Her name tag reads *Renée*, carefully written in purple marker. She has drawn a tiny heart instead of the accent.

Mark turns to Diana. "Can you take her?"

"Mark, I'm just packing up here. I need to head back." The girl is old enough to go to camp, so she is old enough to go to the bathroom by herself.

"It'll only take a minute. After that whole thing with the Jeffries girl, I don't want to be accused of anything."

"What?" Diana feels a chill at the girl's name. She pictures the officer standing at her door, Leo behind the tree. Why would Mark mention her here, now? Of course, she thinks, it's not really that strange—it's been in all the papers, every day, since it happened. The grainy photograph of dogs sniffing along the edges of the field, their handlers jogging behind them. Bucktoothed Deecie Jeffries, her face framed by even rows of text. The leads that point to Dallas and Waco and Houston and even Little Rock, then vanish, the way the girl herself has vanished, without even a sighting to go by.

Just her footprints in the mud, like the cheesy Jesus posters in the basement of Red Rock Methodist, where Derek insists on going for services every Christmas. *Insisted,* Diana reminds herself.

Mark's gut presses against the side of her carrel. "Once a girl goes missing, you know, every guy in a ten-mile radius is a suspect. Can't be too careful."

Diana has a cardigan in her bag, and she wants to pull it out now, drape it around her shoulders, or maybe her face, to disguise the shiver of disgust passing over her. Mark is an asshole, but he's not a kidnapper. Obviously. He is a classicist, for Pete's sake. He's spent his whole life studying people who are so long dead that their words might as well come from another planet. On most days, he drives from his air-conditioned house to his air-conditioned office and thinks about a world of cold marble and papyrus. He probably couldn't even wrestle a girl to the ground with his flabby, mole-covered arms. Deecie Jeffries would outrun him. She would speed into the trees like one of the arktoi, and he would not be able to find her.

She stands up and confines herself to saying, "I think it's pretty obvious that poor girl got kidnapped by some trucker. And I don't think the police plan to investigate every man who lives in Travis County."

Mark squints, as if she has insulted him. In the doorway, Renée is shifting from one foot to the other and twirling her braid in her hands. Mark says, "You're probably right. I just feel bad for the poor girl, you know? She was vulnerable. Girls need so much protection. You're lucky you have a boy." He wipes his hands on his wrinkled khakis, leaving a damp trail. "I worry about my daughter every single day."

"I guess so," she says. Mark has never talked to her like this. She did not even remember that he has a daughter. It makes him seem a tiny bit less disgusting, a tiny bit more human. Even though he's wrong to think Leo is not the source of all Diana's deepest fears, or that girls need more protection than any other child, she almost wants to say something gentle, to cement the slipshod connection he is trying to make.

Mark chuckles lightly and says, "Enough about all that. I'm glad I ran into you, actually. We'll schedule a formal meeting for next week, but I should let you know that I've discussed the direction of your research with the tenure committee and . . . well, the feeling is that you should pursue something with more source material, less speculation." In the hall, the student docent is waving at Mark, trying to hurry him along, but he ignores her. "Those arktoi—I hate to say it, but in my professional opinion, you're wasting your time."

Tiny half-moons of sweat appear beneath his breasts. She looks closely at his hands, still resting on the table. They are weak hands, pale and fat-fingered. She wants to smash them into a flat, peach-colored pulp.

Diana pauses to let the anger roll through her, heavy and slow. She is not wasting her time. Studying the arktoi makes her feel imaginative. Alive. She can't tear herself away from them. She won't.

Still, she needs time. She needs the cool shadow of the university to pay her bills, especially now that Derek is gone. So she will give Mark what he wants, and he will leave her alone.

She will lie.

"It's funny you should say that. I've actually been thinking about changing direction. I'll look forward to talking with the committee about it next week. Anyway, do you still want me to take Renée to the bathroom?"

"Sure, yeah. I mean—no, I can do it." He turns to the door. "Just a second, honey. What do you mean, change direction?"

"I don't know yet." She is glad the maps are already hidden in her bag. "I'm just thinking that there's not enough here. For a book-length argument. So, you know, I'll probably go back to my dissertation materials. The Comic Woman."

The tips of Diana's ears are hot, so she shakes her hair loose.

"That's perfect. Yes, much better." He appraises her. "You should wear your hair down more often." When Diana doesn't respond, Mark says, "We can talk about it on Monday. For now, Mademoiselle Renée, the bathroom awaits."

He turns away, smiling. Proud of himself. The Comic Woman was his idea, and the reason there is plenty of material is that it's been done already, by a hundred other scholars in a hundred simple, unimaginative ways. He believes he has beaten her, but Diana has no intention of giving up the arktoi. She is only giving them time. They will clamber up a grass-covered hill, the water gurgling to the sea behind them. They will go past the marble sanctuary, into the forest. Each small, yellow-robed girl will find a tree the very width of her body and stand behind it, hidden. Breathing.

She watches as Mark takes Renée's hand and leads her down the hall.

"Leo?" Diana calls once she's inside the house. The hall is dark, which means that Leo isn't home and hasn't been for hours. He turns on the lights in every room he enters, even in the middle of the day, and he never turns them off again. You can trace his path through the house by following the lights: on in the kitchen, so he must have made a sandwich; off in his room, so he didn't do his homework. But today there is nothing. She walks through the cave of the living room and slides open the patio door, marveling at the change in temperature. The outside air, which she just left a moment ago, feels ten degrees hotter and wetter in the backyard, as if a front has come through while she was inside.

The fountain looks worse than it did when she started. Not the fountain itself, maybe, but the ground around it, which is raw dirt and bits of rock that Diana and Leo could not figure out how to fit into the jigsaw puzzle of the design when they worked on the fountain together a few days ago. The sod is so cheap that it rolls away in dusty strips, years after its installation. *That is the way with all landscapes, all work*, Diana thinks. *All marriages.* You pull everything away, and you can see the grubs and rusting pipes underneath.

You have to make a mess so you are required to fix it.

Put that on a bumper sticker, Diana. She shakes her head as she kneels next to the fountain. Leo scrubbed everything clean, and the crumbling bricks they were able to refit look sturdy enough, thanks to a long and confusing conversation with the old man at Foster's Hardware. Diana wants to finish the pipes. They are laid out beside her in order of length, like a rusty xylophone. She imagines turning on the repaired fountain when Leo walks out into the yard, the way his face will light up at their success, and she picks up the longest piece of pipe from the ground beside her.

This is the piece she was working on a few days ago, the day the police officer came to her house for the second time. It's the center of the problem, clogged with muck, and she hopes that she will not have to replace it. It's a couple of inches wide and more than a foot long. Diana has tried shaking it, poking it with one of her tomato stakes, but whatever is inside will not budge.

And the smell. She thinks of Mark, the onion and tobacco. This is something vegetal and damp.

The garden hose is coiled like a snake at the corner of the house, next to Leo's herb garden. Diana finds the nozzle and unfurls it; she will not bother to wind it back when she is finished, as she makes it a principle not to do tasks that will only have to be redone. It does not matter if the hose is coiled or piled. As she begins to drag it away, a single yellow swallowtail lifts away from the fringes of Leo's patch of dill.

Diana fits the hose into the opening of the clogged pipe. The water backs up at first, but then starts to dribble through the other side, along with wet clods of something Diana can't identify at first. The smell is worse now, but also less like something rotting. The clods are snot-colored, gummy and gray.

It is newspaper. Diana gets the tomato stake again and pokes it down into the pipe. Whatever is stuck there is freer now, moving a little as she jabs at it. More newspaper comes loose, wads of it, coming out in larger chunks now, some of it still dry, as if it hasn't been there for very long. She is pretending to herself that she is only excited to get the fountain working again, but her heart is thudding loudly, unevenly.

Diana can see words now. It's the *Statesman*. She knows this, even though the ink of the masthead is smeared, because of the flourish at the foot of each letter. A little whimsy before you begin the business of the day.

And then, on the next dryish clump, the corner of a photograph she's seen before. A dog, sniffing the edge of a field she knows. The dog is a black blur of ink, its tail scything the grass.

Diana scrambles to turn off the water. She lays the driest pieces in front of her, on the lip of the fountain. "Girl Goes Missing from Austin Suburb," she reads.

Diana is calm now. She is a scholar, piecing together the artifacts of an ancient rite. She is following the fragments, looking for the thread that will tie them all together. "Then from that reeking sewer of my life / I might haul up a bucket of spring water," the ancient poet Sappho said, or is said to have said, herself a fragment.

There is still something in the pipe. Diana's stomach turns.

The newspaper has to be a coincidence. Maybe Leo was trying to clean out the pipe and used the old newspaper stacked in the garage, and it got stuck. Or at worst, it is a joke, the kind that kids might play. Maybe Gus Rowan did it, on one of his nightly expeditions from that stultifying house, so that the fountain would be permanently broken and Leo would be free from this chore.

Diana jabs the tomato stake into the pipe. Whatever is stuck in there is not only newspaper. It is hard, and it breaks the wooden tip of the stake as she tries to force it through to the other side. Whoever put it here must have labored at the task, pulling the pipe from the back of the fountain, shoving this newspaper and this thing inside it, and then putting it back. Whoever did it must have known that Diana would find it here.

She goes back inside to get the yardstick from its spot next to the pantry door. With her new tool, the thing begins to move, a slow path through the pipe that makes Diana think of Leo's birth, the excruciating impossibility of it, the callous laughter of the nurses when they told her that he was sunny-side up— "Sorry, honey, this might take a while," they said—and Diana's fierce refusal to acknowledge how much it hurt.

Leo, always flipped a little bit the wrong way, always harder than he needs to be.

The thing plops to the dirt at her feet. For a moment, Diana can't tell what it is. It's covered with the black slime of the inside of the pipe and still wrapped in a last sheet of newspaper. Carefully, she lifts off another layer, holding it like a page of a rare book between two fingers, some small voice in the back of her mind telling her something about evidence, crime scenes, fingerprints.

It's a shoe. A flip-flop, actually. It's probably the same size as one of Diana's, a seven or so, but it's not hers, nothing she has ever owned or even seen before. It's pale pink, a color she avoids. And it's not Bee's either, because Mrs. Rowan makes the twins wear sneakers to shield them from tetanus and glass shards and rattlesnakes and "who knows what all," as Leo likes to imitate her saying. So it isn't Bee's.

Diana stands and takes a step backward. The scene in front of her is so odd, so nonsensical, that she feels like she is just seeing it for the first time. There are the pipes, still laid out in neat rows. The dirt, the fountain. The clods of newspaper laid out on its edge like the beginnings of a child's papier-mâché project for school.

The sewer of my life.

There is a sound behind her. Diana turns, and in one of the

holes in the fence next to Leo's garden, she sees one dark eye, blinking. Brown, or maybe black. Not Leo, but one of the twins.

"Hey," she calls out. She can't think of what to say next. It doesn't matter though, because whoever was there, watching her, is gone.

Diana is standing in the kitchen, holding the pink flip-flop and considering whether or not she should rinse it in the sink, when the doorbell rings. No rinsing, then. She puts it carefully behind a row of cereal boxes in the pantry, which might look bad if someone were to find it, but who would be looking for a pink flip-flop? And why here? Diana hears Mark's smug voice—*"When you hear hoofbeats, Diana, think horses, not unicorns"*—and decides that, in this case, he is right.

The police will not search her house.

She is almost to the foyer when she hears a soft thump against the door. One of the kids from the neighborhood, maybe, playing a joke. Egging the car, toilet-papering the trees, as they have done a dozen times since the Nastasis moved here. Or, worse, tossing a bag of dog shit at her door. Never when Derek's truck is in the driveway, though. They are bold enough to commit petty crimes, but not when a man is home.

By the time Diana is at the door, she is angry, ready to run after the fleeing kids who have tossed something rotten or disgusting at her home. At her Leo. Her hands fumble on the knob, and she wishes she had washed the dirt from her nails. She probably has dirt on her face too. It doesn't matter. She will look as wild and reckless as she feels.

But the twisting, moaning body curled up on her porch is not a kid at all. In a brown cardigan that is too warm for this late-summer day is Mary Rowan, her neighbor, and she is mumbling, whimpering, saying something Diana can't understand.

"Mary." Diana does not remember kneeling, but she is next to Mary now, her hands cradling the woman's damp, tangled hair. A sour, metallic smell surrounds her, and Diana looks around frantically for its source.

Beneath Mary, a pool of blood is spreading, pushing the dust of the concrete porch ahead of its path.

"I don't know what to do," Mary whispers. "Diana."

The street is empty. The only cars Diana can see are her own and the Moynihans' rusted truck.

"*Diana*," Mary says again, louder this time. The blood is thickening even as it spreads. "Please. Leroy has the truck. I need you to help." She is turning pale, but her eyes are steady on Diana's. "The baby. I need you to drive me to the hospital." She says this part slowly, as if Diana is foreign, or stupid.

"I know," Diana answers. "I mean, of course. Yes. I'm sorry." The words are tumbling in a confused mixture of reassurance and apology. She had no idea that Mary Rowan was pregnant. "I'll get . . . my keys. And a towel. Stay here." She is standing now, horrified to see that the blood is on her, too, a slick of red coating the side of her leg, so bright it looks fake.

"Okay," Mary whimpers. She is still curled up, but her chest is heaving, and Diana pictures the baby inside her, gasping for air.

She runs. To the linen closet in the hall, where there are pool towels and bath towels and extra tampons and a first aid kit. It is her plan to grab all of it, take as much as she can in her arms to the car, then lift or drag Mary to the back seat so that she can lie down on the way to the hospital.

The towels are stacked in piles of three, and Diana pulls

one out, then another. She is about to turn away when something catches her eye. Something pink, wedged in the back of the closet. She would never have seen it if she did not pull the towels away all at once. She stops for a moment, her heart on pause. Then she leans in and sees what she knows she will: a small pink flip-flop, a clean one, duct-taped to the bottom of the lowest shelf.

She shuts the closet door. The knob is darkened with fingerprints and now, a thin streak of blood, already browning as it dries. She will have to clean it later, when all of this is over.

"Diana!" Mary is shouting, with more volume than Diana would have thought possible. "Diana, come now. I can't." Her voice is the shriek of a creature in pain.

Diana finds her still at the door, the pool of blood beneath her spreading on all sides now, so that she is the center of a blooming red flower. She is sitting up, but her skin is white.

"This is my fault," Mary whispers. "I'm so sorry."

Diana hesitates. Her fault? Mary isn't making sense, which means they need to get to the hospital as soon as possible. But Diana does not want to touch Mary again. Her leg is still covered in the woman's blood and who knows what else, and Mary's begging desperation makes Diana want to jump into her car alone and drive away alone.

She doesn't. She pulls Mary up by the elbows and crosses her arms in front of her chest to hold her steady. Beneath the brown sweater Mary's breasts are damp and soft, two balls of raw dough, and beneath them her heart pounds. For a moment, the women wobble, embracing.

Then Mary finds her feet, and Diana drags her to the garage and drives her to St. David's, where she sits on a sweaty plastic chair in the waiting room for three hours until the doctor comes out to tell her that Mary's baby is gone. Leroy is out on the highway and won't be there for hours. There is no one else. The doctor leaves, and Diana leans over her knees, weeping for the child who will never be her neighbor.

At Brauron, women would offer the clothes of women who died in childbirth to Artemis, the goddess of change and wilderness. They also offered the clothing of women who lived, as if the outcome made no difference. It didn't matter to Artemis whether the empty garments belonged to ghost or woman. Driving home from the hospital, the evening light turning from gold to brown on the other side of her windshield, Diana wonders if there is also a goddess for unhappy mothers, the kind who suffer for their wayward and lonely children.

Would the goddess take a closet full of chlorine-scented towels as a sacrificial offering?

A small, pale pink flip-flop?

A lie?

Bee

Outside the plane window, the clouds are the kind a child would draw, piles of gray-and-white cotton balls. Attie is still, the tiny hairs of her eyebrows thin as pencil markings, her ears two pink shells. The drink cart has come and gone. Everyone is silent, settled into their own private worlds.

Deecie Jeffries is sticking to Bee's skin. Sticking there, and then attaching to pathways of her lungs like tar. Bee is supposed to be worrying about her brother, or her new baby, or the hole she just recklessly punctured in her marriage, but all she can think about is the girl. There is a twisting ache in Bee's chest, as if Deecie's absence is new. As if it belongs to her somehow.

Maybe thinking about Deecie will help Bee pretend that the moment the wheels of the plane lifted, she traveled to another world, one where Leo does not exist and where she is not the kind of woman who would kiss him hungrily in the front hall of the house she shares with her husband. She is just a woman, any woman, sitting on a plane filled with strangers. She is on her way to visit her mother, like any daughter.

"Take care of yourself, Bee. I missed you."

Attie is snuffling, rooting for Bee's breast like a moist, frantic rodent. The prickling begins, starting deep in her armpits and moving like electricity to her nipples. It is disturbingly similar to the sensation that Leo caused when he took her earlobe in his teeth and inhaled a deep breath as they kissed.

Bee closes her eyes and tries to picture herself hurtling through the air in a metal tube, which is both possible and impossible. She is the woman floating in Chagall's suspended bed, who is more sensation than person. She is thirty-two thousand feet in the sky. *Behold, Bee Rowan is flying.*

It is *The Dream* again. With her eyes still closed, Bee tries to picture all of it, like she is giving herself an art history test. The perfect score will bring her back to a darkened room, and she will sleep there, endlessly, on an old-fashioned wooden bed. She will be nineteen again, and Leo will be her brother's best friend, a pipe dream, and she will have forgotten the girl who once disappeared from her neighborhood. There are the pointed rooftops, the angel that looks like a moth. There is the floating, oversize rooster and the vase of white flowers.

She remembers now that there is another figure in the bed too. The woman is not alone. She is being grasped by someone else, a lover, and their foreheads touch. The lover's face is painted in shades of orange and pink, as bright as a child's crayon. His coat is dark blue. The two of them are suspended peacefully in their imaginary, rose-tinted world, but the rest of the painting is sad. Or it feels sad.

This is the trick with paintings, and with dreams, Bee thinks: they are only what we think they are, or what we feel they are. The idea is disorienting, but the logic feels transferable.

Leo is only a dream. She can paint over him, in a wash of dark blue oil.

Bee's phone is shoved deep into her diaper bag, but her desire to check it is as unrelenting as an itch, so she turns it on as soon as the drink cart passes. No Charlie, and no Leo. She checks Leo's Facebook page, which still has the same two photos.

The news is frozen on the opening page and will not scroll. Marco Rubio, something about Steve Jobs, a Miami cop accused of driving more than 120 miles per hour while he was off duty. South Sudan, an attack in Kabul. The world is impossibly huge.

Still, the girls who disappear today get plastered all over CNN. If they are blond, they become an episode on *Dateline*, where the anchors speak in hushed tones about their love for babysitting and soccer. Their ordinariness is a virtue. If they are teenagers, they leave behind a flashing trail of photographs and likes and comments. Google Maps will tell you where they entered the woods, how many steps they took, if they paused or sent a desperate message into the darkness before they vanished.

Even Gus, who does not want to be found, appears now and again, in the online police blotters of small-town papers. He can't disappear, not totally. No one can, anymore.

But a girl who disappeared in the late summer of 1987 leaves only a handful of archived articles behind a paywall. No Instagram, and probably no DNA. She is an empty house with rooms covered in dust, a single cardboard box in the basement of a police station, its lid taped shut. How would anyone find her?

It is somehow true that the cells of a baby live on in a mother's body for months, even years, after birth. Attie, snuggling now in Bee's lap, her slick pink lips opening and closing as she dreams, is somewhere inside her still. This makes sense.

What would happen, though, if the child herself disappeared? A baby, with no online profile to track? A girl, decades ago? You should be able to use those cells as some kind of homing device, like biological Bluetooth, a genetic road map. Otherwise, what are they for? Deecie's mother, if she's alive, must still feel those cells, throbbing like a forehead vein as she . . . what? Waits tables? Sings onstage? Sorts mail?

Bee's mother must miss Gus too. She knows all of his smells and edges, his needs, the way Bee knows Attie. And even if he's gone by choice, he's still gone.

Suddenly, Bee is sweating. There is an idea scratching at her with restless fingers, so clear and insistent that she sits up straight. She takes a magazine from the seat pocket and unhooks the tray table. It doesn't quite fit over Attie, so it rests on her shoulder and tilts toward the seat pocket, but Bee leaves it there. In the margins of the crossword page, she begins to sketch.

She is imagining something beautiful. Simple. A white computer screen with a single gold frame, surrounding only space. It is the frame of a stolen painting, the kind left behind when the robbers slice out the canvas and stuff the rolled Rembrandts and Klimts under their shirts. *A Lady and Gentleman in Black*, 1633. *Portrait of a Lady*, 1916. And in the white space inside the frame, you could type anything about any missing girl in the world. You could say, This girl cooked a mean omelet or This girl liked to climb the catalpa tree in my yard.

You could say, I used to know this girl.

Anything you typed would be anonymous, and as long as you added the name of a missing girl, the entries would be collected together, into a kind of album—no, a gallery—and anyone could look at the collection, so that every girl would have a hundred people looking for her, or a thousand.

Not just one.

Every voice would count, and so would every girl. There must be a thousand stories about Deecie that only her family knows, the little ways that she was just herself. A favorite scratch-and-sniff sticker. Something she used to say to her mom before bed. The way she walked with her left foot splayed slightly. She would be remembered. And if people knew her, they would look harder. They would never give up. They would feel the way Bee does.

Attie is starting to fuss with hunger, and Bee can tell that she is about to squall. Well, her seatmate will have to deal. Bee sneaks a look at him—he is pale, no more than twenty-five, a tattoo of a serpent crawling up his strangely hairless, scrawny arm—and decides he is more barista than bully. She refastens the tray table, angles herself away from him, hangs a burp cloth over her breast and Attie's face, and begins.

Attie has been slurping away for a minute or so when her neighbor mutters, "Oh, Jesus." On his tray, his Coke quivers.

How does he think his own mother fed him? Through a straw?

"I'm sorry, is this bothering you?" Bee regrets this right away. Feeding her baby does not require his permission.

"You're good," the man grunts. He unbuckles his seat belt and angles himself away from her, toward the window. A ripe, sour smell comes between them as he lifts his arm to pull down the shade.

Normally, Bee would let this one go. She hates conflict. But isn't that what is going wrong with Charlie? Isn't that what makes her Sunday calls with her mother feel like she is playing a part? Isn't all of it just Bee refusing to say how she feels, just in case she hurts someone?

And isn't that what has made her reckless? All those feelings from the past, pushed below one surface and popping up, miles away, like Leo appearing at her door, snow caught in the curls of his hair.

She can practice. Here, with this stranger, she can pretend to be bold. She thinks of her mother, performing in her community theater productions, Bee and Gus squirming in the itchy folding seats as they watched *Bye Bye Birdie* and *Godspell* and three separate productions of *Our Town*. Her mother was stiff onstage, and their father made fun of her every time she tried out for a new role, but she loved that theater, as if it were a container to hold all her whimsy.

Bee can be an actress. She can turn on the spotlight above her seat. She can play the role of the Confident Mother and tell this man where to put his misogyny and his antiquated ideas about nursing. She will remind him that the choice is between feeding her baby and letting her scream for the three hours they still have before they get to Austin. She takes a deep breath and runs her finger around the suction cup of Attie's mouth. Milk dribbles down her chin, and she looks slightly confused at the interruption, but Bee tips her up and pats her back. When Attie sees the man, her eyes close and she burps.

"Ahhh," she says, opening her eyes wide, and her hands seem to reach for him. She is too young to know what she's doing, of course, but Bee is still delighted. Mr. Tattoo looks down, as if he is unsure what to do, and then—oh, this world and its small miracles—he takes one tiny hand and shakes it.

"I guess she likes you." The words do not come out as sarcastically as Bee intends them to, but still, she is proud. She and her daughter are a team. Bee is as stoic as the *Migrant Mother*, as glowing as the *Pietà*.

The man doesn't even respond. He is cooing now, all his absurdities turned to gentle, good manners in the face of Attie's cheeks, her shining eyes. The armpit smell that was so repellent a few moments ago now seems familiar and comforting, a yeasty bread dough rising in the air between them.

Good girl, Bee thinks. She smiles to match her daughter.

Under her smile, a small part of her is angry that they've interrupted her. Her idea is churning. Whining. Loud and relentless as an engine.

Even though the last few texts to her mother have gone unanswered, Bee still expects to see her waiting at the baggage claim. She lets the conveyor belt go around once, twice, her own suitcase at her feet, before she admits that she will have to find her way from the airport alone.

No, not alone: with Attie, who is angry now, her charm dissolved like so many spit bubbles. There is a burnt-orange stain peeking up from her pink elastic waistband, even though Bee changed her in the airport bathroom just ten minutes ago and put her in the best onesie she owns, a white one with tiny blue flowers around the neckline and the leg holes, to match the pants that are made to look like a tiny pair of skinny jeans. Nevertheless, or maybe as a result, she is screaming.

Mr. Tattoo is long gone, striding out the automatic doors without slowing down to toss a word or a look in her direction. There is a cluster of older women standing nearby. Bee can feel the weight of their stares, but she will not give them the satisfaction of meeting their gaze. They long to step in, soothe this shuddering, maniacal baby with their home remedies and old-fashioned lullabies. Their desire is palpable, like the current of lust between strangers.

Well, they will have to restrain themselves.

Tsk, tsk, nod, nod.

Bee sighs, pulls up the plastic handle of her suitcase, and follows the path Mr. Tattoo took, Attie's car seat thudding against her left kneecap with every other step, her desperate screams halting in surprise when the automatic doors open to the Texas heat. Sweat beads pop out on Bee's forehead, cartoon-style.

This was a stupid idea, all of it. Now that she is two thousand miles away from Charlie, suddenly she wants to see his face, his brown eyes drooping slightly at the corners, his wry smile. He would take the car seat from her hands, without a word, without complaint.

He was right. She is not ready.

And she is nervous. She has not seen her mother since her wedding, almost four years ago. If you added up all the minutes they have spoken on the phone since then, it might not even equate to a day. The heat is making her woozy. Her skin is clammy.

Attie's expression is calm and distant. Soon she will be asleep. Maybe it will be okay. Bee yawns and heads for the taxi stand. She is already picturing her childhood bedroom, its pale purple walls, the Madonna posters taped to the closet door. She is imagining her old bed, the polka-dot sheets washed to silk, the mattress that will still fit the form of her body perfectly. She will sleep in her old bedroom with the popcorn ceiling. Her mother will gasp and cry at the sight of Attie. She will be moved, undone. Her mouth will crumple when she says the name of her lost baby aloud, in Attie's presence, for the first time. She will ask Bee about nursing and pooping and growing, the way she has been doing for the past two months on the phone, and Bee will answer. There will be three days of this, which will be long enough for Bee to start her project. It will be long enough for her to learn to miss Charlie and forget Leo.

It will be fine. Bee will sleep, and the churning waters inside her will settle, smooth, until they are as flat and unbroken as a morning lake.

Bee was never proud of the way her mother kept the house nicer than all the other ones in the neighborhood. When she was little, it made her feel uncomfortable, especially next to Leo's, which her mother complained was a neighborhood fire hazard and did seem, maybe, like it could spontaneously combust, filled as it was with papers and books and old Bob Dylan records. In the Rowan house, everything was assigned and labeled. Knives on the right side of the cutlery drawer, sharp edges pointing left. Socks rolled in neat pairs. Everything extra was in the garage, packed away in neatly labeled boxes, white ones with lids that fit perfectly. *Toys to Save. Christmas Decorations 1. Christmas Decorations 2. Easter. Wedding Dishes.*

But it was the lawn that made their house stand out like an oasis in a desert. All the houses on the street looked like they had dropped from the sky from a passing cargo plane, fully assembled and identical, and they must have all started with a somewhat decent lawn, new turf unrolled in long green strips, but the Rowan house was the only one that maintained it. Dark green blades of grass grew thick as holiday ribbon in the shade of the live oaks, while every other house on the street had lawns that panted for water and broke out in brown, crusting sores. Mary woke up early to water, and in the evenings when the sun was low, she would put on a pair of white tennis shoes with holes in the toes and push the mower up and down, making lines as perfectly patterned as a baseball field. The lawn was the marker of the Rowan family's ability to maintain itself, even if nothing else felt quite right, like a flag flying outside a wartime embassy, rubble all around.

When the taxi pulls up to Stillwood Lane from the airport, it is the lawn that makes Bee realize that something has changed since she was last here, a month before her wedding to Charlie, when she brought him here to meet her mother. On that visit, Bee was so absorbed in Charlie, in the strangeness of being in Texas without Leo and Gus, that she didn't notice the lawn or the house. But now she can see that the change is so fundamental that it makes her own home, the house she lived in for the first eighteen years of her life, look like a stranger's. There are leggy weeds everywhere, and around the trees, the neat circles of mulch have turned into necklaces of crabgrass. The lawn is covered in scorched patches and brown anthills. And the woman who is waving now from the front door, her hair streaked with gray that Bee doesn't remember seeing before, can't be her mother because her face is too pale and thin.

"I can't believe you're here." Bee's mom is reaching for her now, and for a moment they are tangled together awkwardly, Attie smooshed between them.

There is nothing to say to this because she has delayed this moment for too long, so Bee just smiles. "It was an easy flight," she says. Her heart is pounding, but she tries to look calm as she rotates Attie to face outward and wipes a slick of drool from her chin. "I should do it more often."

Bee expects her mom to perk up at this idea, but she doesn't even seem to hear her. And she doesn't ask to hold Attie, who is arching her back recklessly and flapping her arms as Bee tries to make her way into the house, scraping her knuckles on the doorjamb as she uses one arm to hoist the suitcase and then the car seat into the hall.

"You can put your things in your old room. There's a stationary bike in there, but other than that, nothing's changed."

Bee is mostly baffled, but she is starting to feel annoyed too.

Why isn't her mother asking to hold the baby? She has only seen pictures, and every Sunday, she says that she wants to see Attie in person. And here they are, after traveling for the whole day, and she is treating Attie like a suitcase she isn't even offering to carry.

"Mom, do you want to meet Attie?"

"Oh. Oh—Attie." She pauses on the name. Bee feels a stab of panic, like she has made the wrong choice in naming Attie after that long-ago lost baby. But her mom seems more distracted than upset. She swallows and pats the front pocket of her shirt, as if she is looking for her keys, and says, "Of course I do. Of course. I'm just . . . I—"

"Mom, it's fine. I'll put everything in my room. I'm sure she's hungry. Just give me a few minutes. I'll feed her, and then I'll come back out." It has been five minutes, and already Bee has turned into a leaking, exhausted version of her fifteen-year-old self, too eager to please, too quick to smooth everything over. It was stupid to think that her mother would magically transform from someone Bee talked to once a week into a real grandmother.

"No. Wait," her mom says, standing in front of Bee, feet wide, as if she plans to block her from entering the living room. Her hands are jittering back and forth between her front pocket and the small silver barrette that is fastened precariously in her hair. "I should tell you something, Bee. You're going to be upset. I understand if you are. It's just—"

Bee's mom turns and looks behind her, into the darkness of the living room. There are no lamps on, and the walls are the same orangish faux wood from childhood. Bee thinks she sees a pile of dishes on the coffee table, neatly stacked but crusted with food. Just beyond, through the sliding door, the backyard looks like a framed, overexposed photo. Bee follows her mother's gaze and sees a flash of movement outside. At first, she thinks it might be a stray animal, but then she sees that it's a man, sitting on one of the patio chairs.

Has her mom found a lover? This would be amazing. It has been more than twenty years since Bee's father died. And this would be just the thing to distract Bee's mom from giving advice about Attie and Charlie and organic leafy greens and breast milk and everything else. And it would distract her from worrying about Gus, whose absence must dominate her every thought.

Bee is smiling now, and her mom smiles too, relief and the dim light of the foyer erasing the lines on her forehead. She is beautiful. It is easy to see how any man would think so.

"You found someone?" Bee asks.

Her mom's forehead creases in confusion. "How did you know?"

"Mom, I'm glad! It's fine with me. Really, Mom. It's good." Bee feels generous. She is a queen commuting a death sentence. Her father has been dead for so long now that Bee is not even sure she could draw him from memory. He has slowly become the picture that she keeps by her bedside, polishing the silver frame every now and again when it tarnishes. In the photo, he is smiling, jaunty almost, in a way she does not remember from her childhood, one arm around her mom and the other gripping the side mirror of his Frito-Lay truck. Her mother is stiff, lips closed around her teeth.

"Oh," her mother says. "Okay. I didn't think—oh. I'm surprised." Her mom is almost squirming, and Bee remembers how rigid she was onstage, how the other neighborhood parents were transformed by pancake makeup and the glaring lights of Pips Playhouse, but her mom was always just her mom wearing a costume and wobbly eyeliner. Such a small life. Why should she not enjoy it?

"No, I mean it. Amazing!"

The figure on the patio turns his head, but he does not stand.

Bee stares when she sees his face. In the deepest channels of her ears, she hears her mother say, "Gus. Your sister's here. Come help her with her bags."

Mary

Austin, Texas
1987

It wasn't the lawn, or the costumes, or the preening, Mary thinks as she lies in the dark, the machines glowing green beside her. Those are faults, of course, but they are not dire enough to require this steep price. Vanity is an ordinary sin.

When she had the twins, she felt like she had been touched by a magic wand. There they were, two minuscule humans grown in two separate sacs, inside her single uterus, like the miniature green peppers you sometimes find crouching inside one that looks perfectly normal from the outside. One born one day, one the next; one free of her amniotic sac and screaming, the other billowing out of her like a silent bubble. The doctors told her they had never seen anything like it. They told her she was lucky.

But Mary hasn't protected the children she has, not enough, so she was not allowed to keep the child who felt to her like a breeze blowing through an open window.

Adelaide Rowan. Mary was not quite four months along, so

of course the baby did not survive. The baby grew long enough inside her to be a person, with a small, perfect nose and fingernails the size of pinheads, but not long enough to be a person who can live in the world. She didn't even live long enough for anyone to notice she was here.

Everyone will know, soon enough, that she lost the baby.

Not "the baby": Adelaide. A girl. No middle name. Attie, she would have been, if she had breathed long enough to acquire a nickname. Some babies change from William to Billy, Elizabeth to Lizzy, while they are being wiped down by the delivery nurse. Bee and Gus were still wrapped in their striped hospital blankets when they swapped Beatrice and Augustus for the more efficient, playful versions of themselves.

This was out of desperation, though. Leroy thought the names were affected, and he would not call them Augustus and Beatrice, no matter how Mary pleaded. "I like the one-syllable name. Two, maybe. Three is just putting on airs. Asking for trouble." So Mary conceded, because those were the days when a simple concession was enough to keep him happy. She gave Gus a plain, ordinary version of his name, just like Leroy wanted. But she gave Bee something special, something a little unexpected, an extra *e* instead of an *a*, in hopes that it would always remind her to be more eccentric and braver than her mother managed to be. *She's my little bumblebee,* she would have told Leroy, if he had asked her about the spelling, which he never did. She would have said, *Isn't that darling?*

She didn't want the name to be cute, though. She wanted it to be a hidden command. *Be.*

The doctors have told her that her milk might come in even though there is no baby to feed. *How can that be?* Mary asked, or maybe just thought.

How can that be? That her body would not know?

How could a mother not know?

But it is only the one Polaroid. Just one, and it could be anyone. It looks like Gus, because of the dark hair, but the boy in the picture isn't facing the camera, and the lighting is a foggy, dim green, as if it came from these hospital machines. It is probably from the family who lived in this house before they bought it; Mary found it shoved between the workbench and the wall, and no one in the house has a camera like that.

In her mind, Mary has an inventory of every object in her house, even the hidden ones. Bee has a sheet of Leo's English homework under a flap of carpet in her room, a simple sheet of grammar exercises that the poor girl must have saved from school. Gus has a tiny baggie of weed in his drawer behind his socks, not even hidden, not really. Mary thought it was oregano from her spice rack at first. In her bedroom, there is a loaded gun, Leroy's of course, a fat black metal beetle sandwiched beneath the mattress and the box spring.

If there were an expensive camera in the house, Mary would know about it.

It isn't Gus. It can't be.

There is another woman in the bed across from her, staring out the window with tears trailing down her face. If Mary could get up, she would pull the woman's curtain for her, and then her own. They would be invisible to each other, then, as they are both pretending to be now. Each woman starring in her own play.

The show must go on, she thinks, and then she giggles. The doctors have given her something for the pain, or for her mind; she is not sure.

If this were a scene in *The Crucible*, Elizabeth Proctor would have something plain and brave to say at this moment. She would beg for forgiveness, maybe, or she would praise God in his infinite wisdom. When is the performance at the Pips Playhouse? For some reason, Mary can't remember. Will it be this week? Next month?

Will she be ready?

In the morning, if Leroy comes to visit, she will tell him to call Janine Hebert to let her know that Mary will miss rehearsals for a few days. Her part is not that important, not like some of the others, so it will not matter. Bee could replace her, in a pinch; she is the same height, and she has that small touch of whimsy that will make her shine on the stage. She is smart too. She can learn the lines in a moment.

Leroy is not likely to come to the hospital, though. He is busy, with the truck, with the business of driving away from her, day after day, a flask sitting in his shirt pocket, over his heart.

The play will go on without her. No one will mind.

She will tell Bee to sweep up the broken plates in the garage. She can't ask Leroy, of course. There might be some blood, and he has to go to work. And she can't ask Gus. He won't go into the garage, not since the Pinewood Derby, not unless he has to. It is as if it has a force field around it. Mary has noticed this, but she has not asked him about it. He would not answer anyway; he has a force field around him, too, like that caul that covered him when he was born. There he was, so curled up and peaceful, a baby inside a jellyfish, until the doctor pulled it away, and then, suddenly, he was turning dark pink and screaming, already angry at the interruption. He was so small, smaller than Bee by half, and so he needed twice as much of everything: more milk, more burping, more sleep.

More love.

After the twins were born, Mary stood in the hot shower at the hospital, watching the blood turn pale pink as it trickled to the floor and poking her puffy stomach with wonder. Just ten hours before, it had been hard as a rock, and now the babies were in the nursery, two flushing, squalling humans. On the inside, they were as invisible as an idea, and on the outside, they were full of practical requirements: air, food, water, warmth.

But this baby never needed anything from her. Baby Attie. She was safe until she wasn't, which is no different from any other life. She is somewhere in the hospital, still and silent. She passed from invisible to invisible, idea to idea. She is stuck in a loop that will never open into a path.

The woman in the bed across from her has lost a baby too. She must be thinking the same thoughts. *The show must go on,* Mary wants to tell her, but this would not be kind, and she does not believe it herself, so she stays silent. There are no more blue plates left in the box. Mary is out of chances. This loss is a sign that she has not been good enough, or grateful enough.

She has not kept her babies safe.

She will clean up the broken plates and put them back in the box. She will go home, cook dinner, make sure the kids are ready for the day ahead. And after some unknown amount of time has passed, this day will look like any other.

"Why do you keep saying this is your fault?" Diana Nastasi asked her in the car on the way to the hospital, as if she could hear Mary's thoughts. Her fingernails were rimmed with dirt, Mary noticed, and her knuckles were white on the steering wheel as she drove. "And where is Leroy? Isn't he home? It's Saturday." As if Mary didn't know what day it was. As if she didn't know how strange and shabby she looked, stumbling across the street to her neighbor's house, grabbing fistfuls of hair in her panic. As if she could answer. She had the best excuse in the world for her lack of explanation, though, moaning at each bump in the road, ruining Diana's towels and probably the car seat with all that was coming out of her body.

Diana was the only one who could help. If Leroy had been home, instead of out on the road on a Saturday, ignoring Mary, ignoring the twins, he wouldn't have known what to do. And Bee shouldn't have to see her mother like that, clenched over in agony, clutching the space between her legs as if she could stop the baby from coming. Mothers should be towers of calm. They should be dignified, with their hair set and their clothes ironed and stylish. They should know, automatically, how to run a house. Even if their own mothers were cold and removed, they should know how to make their children feel warm. The house should smell of cookies. There should be flowers.

Mary wants the doctor to come again, to bring her another tiny white paper cup filled with pills so that the boy in the photograph will disappear. He has the same hair as Gus, and the same build, but without seeing his face, who is to know? He is someone's child, certainly, and the photograph is not what anyone would call appropriate. She should do something.

But now, with Attie lying alone in the darkness of the hospital basement, Mary wonders if the universe, in its terrible grinding machinery, has exacted its punishment. She wonders if it has seen something that she has not.

Diana Nastasi was surprisingly gentle. Women can be like this, when the veil of difference is lifted and they become animals together, making babies and bleeding inexplicably all over each other's car seats. But then the veil plummets down again, as final as the curtain at the end of a play. The End. You were a character, and now you are just yourself.

They will not be friends, not even after this. So there is no one to tell. Mary will pay this price, and then it will be over.

The Jeffries mother must have done something horrible too. To have her baby girl disappear, just like that. The woman in the next bed too. The universe, charging its fee. Mothers are supposed to be selfless. They are supposed to watch their children grow, to see only part of their children's lives, not the whole thing, start to finish. They are not supposed to see a sky full of maroon balloons, floating away over an elementary school playground.

There are no more plates, but Mary has saved all the shards. She will make something for the baby's grave. Not the gravestone, of course, which will be square, with all the proper details of that tiny life. A name, a single date. But flat on the ground in front of the stone, there will be a mosaic of sky-blue milk glass. She can make it in the shape of a balloon, or a flower. She can turn the broken plates into something beautiful. A first and final gift for her daughter.

In *The Crucible*, a whole village makes almost every woman into a witch, one way or another. Poor boring Elizabeth, too, is accused, though she is the one who has been wronged so deeply, by her husband and her maid alike. It is an injustice, one that the audience resists, one that makes her character noble and important, Mary's director has told her, his face earnest and close to hers, the smell of lime and mint in his warm breath. "Mary, we are all on the side of the underdog, of fairness." Elizabeth is saved by the baby she is carrying. No one seems to realize that making a baby is the most witchlike trick of all.

Always, in a play, there is irony, her director says. It is the actor's job to decide how much of it to reveal to the audience.

Such a strange interest, for Mr. Arthur Miller. Salem, Puritans, women being dunked in ponds or burned at the stake. Or maybe he was on a mission of exploration. What turned Norma Jeane into Marilyn? Wasn't that some kind of alchemy? Afterward, didn't she ooze magic, with every breathy, sequined, inimitable shimmy?

Did her mother miss her, or was she proud of this new creature her little girl had somehow become?

Next to Mary, the monitor beeps slowly. The door to her room is ajar, and she can hear the doctors murmuring about discharge times and charts. Soon Leroy will come in his truck to take her home, and she will have to explain to Gus and Bee that there was a baby, that Mary lost her.

It is not useful to think of yourself as an underdog, no matter what the audience decides. Self-pity never brought any applause. But the tears roll down Mary's cheeks, all the same.

Bee

Gus is on the back patio, sitting calmly on a plastic chair. He did not move at his mom's command, and he does not stand when Bee stumbles onto the patio, clutching Attie. His long arms splay across the armrests, the joints bony and bent in a way that makes Bee think of the spiders they used to find in the dusty corners of their shared bathroom. Gus would pull their threadlike legs off, one by one, until all that was left was a brown jelly bean, staring at them with baleful eyes from the folds of his open palm. "Here," he would say. "Take it. I dare you."

"Beatrice," he says, eyebrows raised. When they were kids, he used her real name when he wanted to tease her or embarrass her in front of Leo. Now it sounds formal, like he has somehow forgotten her nickname, or he doesn't feel like he's allowed to use it. "It's good to see you." He does not smile.

Bee has lost control over her face, her tongue, her limbs. She wraps Attie tighter in her trembling arms. She has practiced this moment, in the mirror, in the shower, but now that it is here, she is not ready.

"Gus," she says. Her heart is beginning to stutter and gasp. She knows she should say something more. *Where have you been?* Or *Are you okay?* Or *Why haven't you called me?*

Why did you call Leo, and not me?

Instead, she says, "You too."

Gus brushes his hand through his hair, gathers a handful, and tugs, the same way he did as a kid. His wrists are sticks, scarred with purple slashes and strange, uneven circles. "So. Big news." Gus points at Attie. He is smiling now, a wry half effort, but his eyes are guarded.

"Mom," Bee says, ignoring Gus and turning back to the house, where her mother is waiting by the sliding door, as stiff and anonymous as a waitress. Attie grumbles. "Mom," Bee says again, hating the plaintive tone in her voice. "What's going on? You didn't tell me that Gus would be here."

Mary doesn't answer. Bee shifts Attie from one shoulder to the other. Attie is so light, but Bee's arms are wobbly from the effort of holding her. She needs to sit down, but she does not want to take the patio chair next to Gus. She wants to go back to the front curb. Maybe her taxi is still there, the driver eating a granola bar in the front seat. Maybe he will take her back to the airport, and she can reverse this whole trip, like playing an old VCR tape backward. Doing, undoing.

"Bee, it's okay," Gus says. "I'm not here to upset anyone. I'm just here—"

He shoots a look at their mother, who is watching, listening, her face unreadable. "I told you this was a bad idea," he says to her.

Suddenly, Bee is shaking. She knows this feeling. She has felt it a thousand times, when she was a kid, when she was on the farm with Gus and Leo. It is what she felt at the Spoke when Leo said Gus's name.

She is always the one left out, left behind. She does everything she is supposed to, and everyone loves Gus more.

"A bad idea? Did she *ask* you to come here?" Bee is swaying now. She shifts Attie again, suddenly worried that she might drop her.

Gus stands abruptly. His spidery limbs resolve themselves into human form. His eyes are bloodshot, Bee sees now, and the circles under his eyes are dark, unfaded bruises. Even in the heat, he is wearing blue jeans, too loose and baggy to see if he's anything more than skin and bones beneath.

"Gus. Bee," Mary says suddenly, as if they are ten again, squabbling over some simple injustice. Her voice is a whispery croak. "Don't fight. Please."

"Mom, it's okay. Don't worry. We're not fighting, okay?" Gus is interrupting, just the way he used to, but somehow his words are gentle. They land softly in the room. An invisible net holds the moment suspended, until Attie burps, small white curds covering her chin and rolling down into the creases of Bee's neck. She kneels, fishing for wipes in the side pocket of the diaper bag.

There is a split second when she thinks Gus might reach for Attie. He takes a step toward her, so small that it seems unconscious, but makes no other movement. Bee squeezes Attie tighter. Would he be cruel, somehow, pulling Attie's plump little arms like a spider's? She doesn't know what he might do. She doesn't know him at all. She thinks of the baby formula he stole, how that might mean he has a baby of his own, or at least that he was trying to take care of someone else's.

"I'll go get you a wet paper towel," Bee's mother says, nodding at Attie. The patio door slides closed behind her, leaving Bee and Gus alone. The afternoon heat pulses around them.

Gus rubs his forehead and says, "Bee, don't worry. I won't stay."

"Why are you even here?"

"Like you said, Mom asked me to come. I've been doing better, Bee. She thought we should—I don't know."

"Has it been like this the whole time? You talk to her, and she doesn't tell me?" Bee's eyes fill. She turns to the patio door, pretending to peer inside, so that Gus will not see her cry. "I haven't had any clue where you've been for seventeen years, Gus, but you and Mom have, what, been eating Sunday dinner?"

"It's not like that."

"What is it like, then? She didn't even come to see me when I had a baby. She doesn't really talk to me on the phone. She says the same thing, over and over, or she tells me some story about people I don't even know. But she never says anything, not one word, about you."

Bee is angry. She means to wound Gus. But she is unprepared for the look on his face, some combination of resignation and sadness.

"I thought it would be better for you if I stayed away. For everyone. But then she asked me to come here. She's . . ." He brushes a hand across his forehead. "Bee," he says into the silence. "Have you noticed anything strange about Mom?"

Bee thinks of the stack of dishes. The lawn.

"No," she lies. "Gus, I've been here for about ten minutes. I don't really talk to her. What do you mean?"

"I don't know. She called me, Bee. She asked me to come here. I haven't talked to her in so long. Years. But then she told me about the baby, and she told me you were coming, and I wanted to see you."

A surge of hope rises in Bee. Gus is here, and they are adults now. Maybe Charlie is wrong—maybe people can change. Attie could have an uncle; Bee could have her brother back.

She says, cautiously, "You wanted to see me. You wanted to see me after all this time."

Gus continues as if he hasn't heard her. "And then I get here yesterday, and it's—the house is, you know, like this, and there are boxes everywhere, and there's no food." He gestures at the house. Inside, Bee's mom is singing. A familiar line drifts in, something about the moon, her mom's voice as high and clear as a girl's. Bee has only ever heard her sing songs from musicals—*Godspell*, *Carousel*, *My Fair Lady*—anything that the community theater performed all those years ago. *Camelot* is her favorite: the grouchy old king with the soft heart, the wide-eyed queen. "I mean, look at it."

Bee stares at the house. Now that she is following his eyes, she sees it: not just the lawn, but the tattered kitchen shade, the weeds sprouting up between the patio tiles.

"Do you think she called because she needs help?"

Gus grimaces. "I'm not sure I'm the best person to ask for help."

A noise behind him makes them turn. It's their mother, standing in the doorway of the kitchen, holding a roll of paper towels and peering out at them. Attie squirms in Bee's arms. There is still a slick of milk curds coating her cheeks and chest.

"Later," Gus says. It is almost a whisper. Then, in a voice Bee has never heard before, an imitation of another version of Gus, he reaches out his arms. "Hey. Can I hold her?"

Bee hesitates. She does not want Gus to hold Attie. He is too shaky and thin. She can hear Charlie's voice in her head, telling her that she should not trust him. Then, before she registers what she is doing, she passes Attie to Gus and says, "Okay. Just make sure that you put your hand behind her head. See? Like that." Her voice is patient, measured, as if she is trying to

175

soothe him. Her heart has turned to a hummingbird's.

They stand there, the four of them, not quite touching. Gus gazes into the backyard, his eyes empty, his body still. One hand splays behind Attie's downy head. She squirms a little, but she does not make a sound.

There is nothing except saltines and grape jelly in the house, so Gus rides his old bicycle to the Dewberry Market and then Bee makes dinner. She washes the pile of plates from the coffee table and throws away three empty cereal boxes from the pantry. The air in the house smells like cabbage. Bee finds a dust-covered vanilla candle under the sink, opens all the windows, and turns on the house fan. As she moves around the kitchen, she tries to catch Gus's eye. She is waiting for him to invite her to sit on the back patio or take a walk around the old neighborhood so that they can talk, but he is silent and will not look at her directly.

"Later," he said, as if he were picturing days together. As if he had never vanished in the first place.

Dinner is a live version of the Sunday script between Bee and her mother. Gus has no lines in this play. How can there be so little to say aloud when there is a torrent of words gushing beneath the surface? Bee is grateful for Attie's presence at the table, her gurgles and grunts, so that they have some neutral ground. She watches Mary carefully, but other than the fact that she sprinkles pepper on her spaghetti when she means to use the salt, and the fact that Mary watches Gus instead of Attie, there is nothing amiss.

After dinner, Bee uses Attie's sleep schedule as an excuse to settle herself in her old room for the night. Gus retreats too, to his room on the other side of her wall. She can hear the hiss of the curtains when he closes them, the soft rustling sounds of his body and the creak of the mattress as he settles into bed. She thinks, maybe, she hears him murmur something to himself before he turns out the light.

She hopes there are no drugs in his bag.

Her mom has changed her room, after all. She has painted it a grayish-pink color that makes Bee think of Band-Aids stuck to the floor of an elementary school bathroom. Towels dry on the exercise bike like cartoon ghosts. Bee folds them and stacks them on the seat. There is a framed Monet poster on the wall by the door, but otherwise the walls are empty. The bedspread is new, too, and the polka-dot sheets are gone.

She is not tired. She is replaying her conversation with Gus. Does the dust coating the picture frames in the living room mean that something is wrong with their mother or that nothing is? Couldn't the weeds and the empty pantry and the dirty plates just mean that she is getting older, maybe that she needs to hire a cleaning company?

Attie is asleep in the far corner of the room, outside of the pool of light from the bedside lamp, and she is breathing deeply, oblivious to Bee's rattled nerves. Bee hopes all this time in her car seat will not be long enough to flatten the back of her skull, the way the pamphlets she gets at the pediatrician warn her. She hopes she will sleep until at least two o'clock before she is hungry again.

Bee does not want to call Charlie and explain to him that Gus is here, under the same roof as Attie, just the way he feared. She does not want Gus to hear her through the thin walls. If she goes into the living room, her mother will eavesdrop. She types Charlie a message instead: Long day. Sorry. Will find a window tomorrow so we can talk. When they flew down to Texas before the wedding, they stayed in a hotel downtown, so Charlie has never slept here, but he has his own mother. He will understand.

Almost asleep already! Love you. Talk tomorrow. The reply is instant, as if Charlie is sitting on the other end of the line, waiting for her. She hopes he isn't.

The bookshelf in front of her is the only part of the room her mother has left unchanged. There is the collection of tiny glass animals Bee loved when she was small: a fawn the size of a glossy thumbnail, an orange fox with eyes made of tiny black blobs that look like beads. There is her jar full of unfinished friendship bracelets. She scans the spines of the books, trying to imagine a day when Attie will be old enough to want to read these stories. *Bridge to Terabithia*, which Bee is pretty sure is too grim for a child. All the Ramona books. *Charlotte's Web*. Judy Blume. *Misty of Chincoteague. Island of the Blue Dolphins*. Bee remembers riding her bike to the pool with a new book at the bottom of her towel bag, resting against her spine like a warm hand.

All the books on her shelf are about girls, or being a girl, or being young. Nothing about what it might be like to be a mother, with a life that doesn't seem to belong to you. So far, Bee has read only one book to Attie, *The Wind in the Willows*, a page or two at a time while she nurses. In Bee's opinion, it is a perfect book. It has taken a whole month to read it out loud, mostly because Bee falls asleep while she is reading, but also because she sometimes skips from the end of a paragraph back to the beginning if she likes it.

"Here I am, footsore and hungry, tramping away from it, tramping southward, following the old call, back to the old life, the life which is mine and which will not let me go."

And then, again, like a refrain: "Here I am, footsore and hungry, tramping away from it, tramping southward, following the old call, back to the old life, the life which is mine and which will not let me go."

Maybe that's what happened to Deecie. Maybe she took one look down at these books, and up at the road ahead, and just thought, *No*. Maybe she read about Huck Finn and lit out for the territories, or maybe she just packed a bag and ran away, the way Bee is doing, right now, in her feeble and half-hearted way. The way she could have done, when she was fifteen, heartbroken over Leo, if she had been less obedient. More imaginative.

Braver.

On the lowest shelf, there is a section of books so battered that their spines are unreadable. Here, then, are the Black Stallions she used to collect when she was little, ten years old maybe, or twelve, the long line of them like trophies on her shelf, before she realized that she was bored with horses or that she never really liked them anyway. She pictures the three of them as kids, escaping the heat on a summer day, lying on their stomachs on the dark yellow carpet in Bee's room. Bee, her brown curls jumbled, flattens the spine of the book she is reading. Gus, wiggling in the middle, reaches over and closes it to make her mad. On the end, Leo, utterly still, turns the page slowly before the others have even begun. His brow is furrowed. He tugs on one ear as he concentrates.

Bee glances over at Attie. Still asleep. She picks the closest book, *The Black Stallion*, careful not to tear the thin cardboard further. When she opens it to the first page, her heart quickens.

"Chapter 1: Homeward Bound."

Holding it in her hands makes Bee feel like she can transport herself back in time, the way she wants to, before she kissed Leo, before she knocked on her mother's door with one hand on the suitcase and the other holding Attie. That's all she really wants: to go back to the time before Gus became so unhappy, or at least, the moment she let him go.

Bee checks her phone again. There is nothing else from Charlie. And there is nothing from Leo. Not that there would be. She has dive-bombed her marriage, and for what? Kissing Leo wasn't some star-crossed fulfillment of a childhood inevitability. For him, it was just the impulse of a dramatic moment. He's not married, or a father. He has nothing to lose.

And yet. What was it that he said, just before he left her standing in her own bedroom, that lemon balm smell of him on her hands, and her life a pulsing heart, open, split in two?

"I missed you." Not: *Gus is waiting for you at your mom's house.*

He said, *"We wanted you to be happy."*

Bee is still holding *The Black Stallion* in her lap. She pages through it, idly, while she thinks. Her life has shifted into a new, unrecognizable shape. It doesn't feel gradual, like growing a baby, but headlong, impossible to comprehend. Bee wants to find a pattern in the fragments. She tries to put the story together in her mind.

Leo asked to see her, and she went to the Spoke to meet him.

She was looking for Gus online, the way she always does, and found a story about a missing girl instead.

Leo kissed her. She kissed Leo, maybe.

Now she is here, away from her life, and so is Gus, like they have landed together on some other planet, and it is only the girl who is missing.

She slides the book back onto the bookshelf and picks out another. A coating of dust makes the cover feel gritty, but otherwise the book seems brand new. *The Black Stallion and the Girl*, she reads, and grimaces. She does not remember reading this one, which seems to be about a girl jockey and a chaste preteen crush. Its stiff formality would have made her laugh, even at twelve, even when she had a chaste preteen crush of her own.

Once, she stole a sheet of Leo's graded homework from the trash after English class and hid it under a flap of carpet in her bedroom. It was nothing important, just grammar exercises, but it had his name on it, and in the bottom left corner, there was a pencil drawing of a small animal, a mouse or maybe a rabbit, wearing a tiny crown. For Bee, it was a holy relic, a talisman.

She had forgotten all about it until this moment, in this room, where her mother has changed everything except the bookcase.

And the carpet.

Bee has to move Attie's car seat to reach the loose edge she is looking for, so she hooks her arm carefully around the handle and holds her breath as she transfers her to the side of the bed. Attie squints in her sleep when her face hits the lamplight, but she doesn't wake up.

Bee kneels, lifts the carpet, and there it is. Or there is a piece of paper, almost the same as the one she remembers. The piece of notebook paper is folded and dusty, just like the one she put there, but the lines are a brighter blue.

Bee's hands have turned into two heavy leather mitts. She carefully pulls out the paper and unfolds it on her lap. She sits back on her heels to hold it into the light.

The note is not in pencil, and there is no drawing. The ink

is dark green for the first two lines, then it switches to purple, then to pink. It is written across the lines rather than along them, and then folded, as if it is part of a book. The letters are plump, with short lines that make the words look only half formed.

She knows before she even begins that this is not Leo's grammar homework. She has never seen this note in her life.

> To the boy in the field,
>   I know you probably have never noticed me. You did wave one time but that was a while ago. I don't know why I keep thinking that you'll come over and talk to me. But I also feel like you're different from the other one, the tall one with black hair, and the one who is always laughing too loud. You are quieter, and also nicer. I can tell.
>   Anyway, maybe one time you could come over to my side of the field. We could walk to the Dewberry or something. If you want.
>   I hope you find this note. If you find it, wave to me.
>   My name is Deecie, by the way.

Bee's blood is racing. Deecie Jeffries, writing to Leo. It has to be. The one with the black hair is Gus, the other one is their old neighbor Patrick Moynihan. She is talking about seeing them in the field. About Leo waving to her.

Bee and Deecie are in love with the same boy. They were. They are. The verb tense seesaws, struggling to keep up with the moment, with the unknown, the way time does when you are sitting alone in your childhood room, holding a relic in your hands. Deecie is connected to her by more than a gut feeling, a whim.

Bee lifts the rug until she hears it rip, flips through the pages of every book on the shelf, but there is nothing else. How did this note get here, to her own room? Bee never knew Deecie Jeffries, even if they did both love Leo. And she has not been home in years.

All of it is a jumble, a twisted heap of yarn that is riddled with impossible knots.

Leo at its dark, tangled center.

Attie is still quiet. Bee has watched enough detective shows to know what she should do. She should make sure not to touch this paper any more than she already has. She should pick up the note with metal salad tongs and drop it into a plastic bag. She should call the police.

Bee lies on the bed, breathing fast. Above her, there is a beige water stain in the popcorn ceiling, its edges dark and meandering. Bee follows its path, willing her heart to slow. She counts to three, forward and backward, until she can breathe again.

She is being ridiculous, she decides, once her breathing slows. The note is a coincidence. It must be. It is impossible to imagine that Leo had anything to do with Deecie's disappearance.

But there is a note from Deecie Jeffries hidden in Bee's room. *You did wave one time,* she wrote.

And there were the fires. The one in the bottom of the locker at school, the one in the field after Deecie disappeared. Setting a fire is reckless. Destructive. She has never tried to reconcile the two parts of Leo because they don't fit. He is calm and kind, but arson is an act of anger.

And this note, hidden away in such a strange place, means he might know something about—might have something to do with—Deecie's disappearance.

Tomorrow. She will bring it to the police tomorrow, or she

will wake up, and she will turn on the light, and the note will have vanished from her bedside table. Leo's homework will return to its spot under the flap of carpet. All of this will be a dream.

She is tired. She is still recovering. Charlie is right: she needs to take better care of herself, to stop obsessing over something that has nothing to do with her. Get her mind right.

The lamp clicks off with a loud, metallic strum that lingers in the darkness. Attie shifts in her seat above the loose flap of carpet, and Gus's body brushes gently against the other side of the wall. Mary is in her bedroom, on the other side of the living room, lying alone in a bed built for two.

Bee lies still, eyes open, waiting for one of them to call for her.

Diana

The last sources Diana requested from the university librarian have finally arrived, three days too late. On the shelf of her carrel are piles of xeroxed articles in manila envelopes with return addresses as far away as Boston and Oxford and New Zealand.

In the bag at her feet are Deecie Jeffries's pink flip-flops, one dirty, one clean.

Diana knows they are Deecie's, as surely as she knows her own name. They are Deecie's, and Leo hid one in the fountain, one in the house, because he has done something terrible, something worse than a fire in a locker at school, just like the principal said he would. They are hidden again now, in an empty envelope that once held the thick but useless article by H. Mannigan Struthers, sent to her from the Saxo Institute of the University of Copenhagen and now stacked neatly along with the others on the shelf in front of her.

Diana rubs her eyes. She hasn't slept since she found the flip-flops, since Mary Rowan appeared on her doorstep like an ancient omen. Three days ago, Diana still thought she would forge new ground with the arktoi. She knew she might not get tenure, but she believed she would discover something more important. She would unfold the true meaning of the arktoi, and they would tell her the secret to motherhood, womanhood, wildness, all of it.

Now, none of it matters. Diana wills the sheets of paper to furl themselves into columns and roofs, fold themselves into origami marble blocks so that she can feel their magic again. "The small mixing bowls found at the site provide ample evidence for the ritual," she reads. "The Athenian girls wore *krokotos*, yellow robes dyed in saffron." Each sentence seems unconnected to the next, or maybe her eyes are jumping around the page. "The death of the bear provoked the anger of Artemis."

Is it her logic that is failing her, or is it that logic no longer applies?

She flips the pages. Her stomach rolls with hunger. There is a fly bumbling high in the corner of the windowsill. She has been reading for hours, but there is nothing here, not anymore.

And then, like she has let loose a notched arrow, she knows what she has to do. She will ask Mary Rowan what she saw, the night the boys went to the field, and Mary will tell Diana that it was nothing, nothing at all. The answer is so clear, so simple, that Diana nearly sobs with relief.

Bee Rowan answers the front door when Diana knocks. She is barefoot, and her dark curls are gathered in two unruly attempts at braids. She looks surprised to see Diana standing there. Can it be true that Diana has never knocked on this door just opposite her own, not even for a cup of sugar or a box of matches?

"Is your mother here?" Diana asks the girl. It has been only a day since she saw Mary shuffle from Leroy's truck to the house, still in her hospital gown, nothing in her hands.

Bee nods, slowly. Behind her, the house is cool and quiet, a dark cave with Bee standing guard at its mouth. "Yes, but—"

"I know. I'm not going to bother her. I just have something to ask her." The misshapen manila envelope is poking out from her bag, and Diana realizes suddenly that she should have wrapped it in some kind of colorful paper so it looked like the present she should have brought. Well, it is too late. It is also too late to add "I'm sorry about what happened," but she does so, lamely, and Bee looks at her with a flash of distrust.

Still, she lets Diana in. She doesn't call for her mother, who must be lying in bed, but leads Diana through the kitchen to the master bedroom, which is in the same place as Diana's. The mirrored blueprint of her own house makes her want to turn around. If she opens Mary's door, will she find the swim coach there, tangled up in Derek's hairy legs?

No, of course not. It will be Mary, sitting on a giant maxi pad, looking at a magazine.

"Diana. Hello." Mary looks surprised, but not embarrassed or annoyed. And why should she be? They are closer than neighbors now. They are closer than friends. There should be another word to describe their connection. Maybe there is one in ancient Greek. There are words for the various shades of love—*storge, pragma, agape*—and Diana has sometimes wondered if a feeling is lost when you don't have the word for it. What is the word for the love for one who has bled out her own baby in your arms?

Diana takes a step inside the room. "Are you feeling okay? Is Leroy taking care of you?" she asks. She knows she should offer to bring Mary a meal or sit with her on the porch, but she doesn't. Her question is pressing against her lungs, demanding to be spoken aloud in place of this small talk. Diana wants to ask it quickly and then leave. The bond between them does not require that they spend time together, or even that they like each other.

It only requires that Mary tells her the truth.

"Of course." Mary is serene, propped up on her pillows like a movie star, her hair dark on the lace throw pillow behind her. Her skin is pale. She must be on something, Diana realizes when she sees her pupils, glittery and large as dimes. She is wearing a yellow nightgown with pale blue ties, and Diana can see the edges of her full breasts. She thinks of the way her own small breasts filled when Leo was born, milk ducts sprouting painfully along her armpits and reaching their tendrils to her back. Nothing about nursing made her feel more connected to herself or to him, so she stopped after a few weeks and gave him formula. Derek said he was happy to have her back, all to himself.

"Good." There is a long silence, so Diana begins. "Mary. I need to ask you something. I know this isn't a good time. But the other day—"

Mary sighs, but she says nothing.

"The other day, before you came to the door, I was—I found something. In my yard. And inside too. And I know this probably sounds wrong, and strange, but I feel like you know something about it. I need—"

"Is it a photograph?" Mary whispers. When Diana walked into the room, Mary was almost serene. Now she is sweating, her face covered in dew. Diana is worried that Mary might faint.

"A photograph? No."

Mary seems delirious. She is clutching her nightgown, the same way she clutched Diana's hand on the way to the hospital, an animal's desperate strength turning her fingers to claws.

She says, "What is it, then?"

Diana pauses. "It's hard to explain."

"Just tell me. Diana, I appreciate what you did for me. I really do. But I'm so tired, and I have to tell Bee what to fix for dinner before Leroy gets home, and . . ." Mary's words slur and her voice fades. Slowly, she pats the mattress next to her. Diana perches on the edge of the bed. The closeness of Mary's body, its warmth and small movements, makes Diana queasy.

Now that the moment is here, Diana isn't sure what to say. How will she explain to this neighbor, this housewife, what she needs? Putting it into words seems impossible. *Mary, I know you have watched the boys head into the field at night. I know you saw them go the night that girl disappeared. I need you to tell me that girl's disappearance had nothing to do with Leo. It can be Gus's fault. It can be Patrick Moynihan's, or your husband's, or mine. But it can't be Leo's.*

If it was my Leo, I will not be able to live.

Was it him?

No. It will not work. Mary will not remember. It is ridiculous to ask. It is, Diana sees with sudden clarity as she looks at Mary's sweating face, pointless. Besides, Diana is a failing tenure candidate, not a detective. Still, she asks, "Have you noticed anything going on with the boys?"

Mary does not answer right away. She stares out the window, where the afternoon sun is dappling the leaves of the oak in her side yard. A tiny green lizard is sunning itself on the white brick windowsill, its tail curled like a fiddlehead. The pause lengthens, seems to stretch into the length of an afternoon, an evening, a whole day, a year.

"In the garage," she says finally. "Leroy's not home. You'll find it there, between the workbench and the wall."

Diana's heart is pounding. "A photograph? Of what? Mary, of what? Of Deecie?"

Then she remembers what Mary said, over and over, as they drove to the hospital, her voice keening. *"My fault. My fault. My fault."* It made no sense, three days ago. Losing a baby is no one's fault. Of course not. But now, Mary's words sound like something more.

A clue. A confession.

"Deecie Jeffries? The missing girl? Of course not. No. Why would you say that?" Mary turns back to Diana so quickly that the pad beneath her crinkles. Her cheeks redden, two splashes of pink that spread slowly as she stares. Diana can see a dried trickle of brown blood on the pad beneath Mary's left thigh.

Mary's chest is rising, falling, moving faster than it should. Tears are hovering in the corners of her eyes. "You asked about the boys. The photo. It's a boy. I found it, and I—" She pauses and puts both hands over her eyes. "Diana. You don't understand. It's all my fault."

Then she is sobbing, and Diana is hugging her, trying not to wipe away the tears that feel like warm glue on her neck, grotesque and sticky and permanent.

Bee

The Cherry Creek Library opens at eight, and Bee is there before the librarian unlocks the doors. She waits outside, swaying back and forth as if Attie were resting in her arms. But Attie is back at the house, propped up in her car seat on the kitchen counter and watching her grandmother, who is holding the dishes from breakfast like wobbly steering wheels as she wipes them down. Gus is still asleep.

Bee feels like she has lost ten pounds. Part of her is worried about leaving Attie with Mary, and part of her is telling herself that she's being ridiculous, that her mother is fine and Gus doesn't know what he's talking about. An hour of work—just an hour—will be good for her.

Still, Bee keeps patting her pockets, as if Attie will be in there, a tiny bobblehead doll with a shockingly strong suck reflex.

Behind the glass windows, the librarian is arranging chairs and spritzing the leaves of the fig tree behind the desk. Bee glances at her watch. Her impatience courses through her like electricity. This is not enough time to do everything that she has planned, but it will have to be. When the librarian finally unlocks the doors, Bee brushes past her without saying anything.

Bee hasn't been here since she was a child. There is new carpet and a new circulation desk that looks like it came from a Star Wars set. The smell is the same, though: mold battling its way through Pine-Sol and something that reminds Bee of wet felt.

Workstation 3 feels lucky. Bee signs up for it, even though there are at least ten others farther away from the children's section, which is filling with a steady trickle of mothers and strollers and babies. A few feet away, a toddler is frowning in concentration as he attempts to open a board book with pudgy, slobbery hands. His mother is sitting at a child-sized table near the water fountains, scrolling on her phone.

The computer is already on when she sits down—another sign. Bee lets the air-conditioning cool the sweat on her back. She takes a deep breath.

She should have enough time to build a passable version of her project, her airplane sketch. Not the whole thing, but a start. Something she can bring back to Portland with her, something that will give her days a shape beyond walks and sleep schedules. Something important, even.

Early this morning, when she saw the note still sitting on her bedside table, she shoved it into her backpack and decided to drive straight to the police station. She was almost there when she found herself making a U-turn on Burnet Road and heading for the library instead. The note was under that carpet for years. Decades. There is nothing that proves it is about Leo. Maybe Gus wrote it, some long-ago prank. Maybe Bee wrote it herself in a fit of imagination and just forgot. One girl's handwriting is the same as another's. Maybe Bee put the note underneath the carpet and it vanished from her memory, as easily as a coin slipping through a slit in a pocket. As easily as a brother vanishes, or a girl.

One more day won't make a difference. She has to figure out what it means before she decides what to do about it. While she is thinking, she will do the next best thing, which is to start working on this site. She can't control Gus, or her mother, or anything else, but she can do that. She can offer this small act of service to Deecie, to girls like Deecie.

For a moment she can't remember the password to her work account, but then she is in, the interface loading choppily on the library's weak internet. She has not designed anything in months, and she gets trapped at first, toggling between one screen and the next and clicking frantically at the menus. The program has become more complicated since she went on leave, and she curses herself for ignoring her work email.

She is wasting valuable time.

Tilting her chair just slightly away from the rug, she taps her pen on the notepad next to the keyboard. This is how she designs: not just on the screen, but always on paper, too, the slow drag of a felt-tip pen across the grain of the page allowing her mind to slow, to deliberate. Her layout is, thankfully, simple: she grabs an image from the Gardner Museum's website, the giant frame with the famous missing Rembrandt, and erases the nameplate and the unfaded green silk wallpaper in Photoshop. The empty gold frame hovers in the middle of the screen, and she places a cursor in the upper left corner, then trades it for a pencil. She could call it *Portraits of Loss*, maybe, or *A Gallery of Love*. The font will be something like handwriting, to remind people that these are girls from a time before the internet. A time before anyone could walk into a library and design a web page that would reach its electric arms through the windows and the walls and into the world.

Drawthemback.com. That's the name. Each girl will have her own frame, her own outline to fill, with details about the books she read, the giraffe T-shirt she always wore for picture day at school. The small details that make us important. Not just a memorial, but a portrait. The site will draw the girls onto the page, and maybe, just maybe, it will draw them out of their hiding places.

At Grapevine, her best site was one that she designed entirely on paper before she made it digital, a website for an Italian restaurant in Boston. The background was a still life from Caravaggio, and the font was one she made from a book she found about Renaissance handwriting. The site won an award, some industry thing, but she never bothered to mention it to Charlie. The whole thing seemed so unimportant compared to saving lives every day.

This site could be important, though, if it works. It could help a grieving family. It could even save lives, if any missing girl is found—not just Deecie. Here, with the frame and its cursor floating on the white screen in front of her, she feels like she has floated from a patch of white water into a wide-open expanse of blue. Her brain is filled with cogs and greased wheels that spin and hum.

This website might be nothing, but it might work. It might be the thing that calls Deecie Jeffries back to the world, or at least uncovers something about where she might have gone.

It might do the same for Bee.

The mother on the other side of the room has stopped scrolling and is staring at her, unabashedly. Bee realizes that she is mumbling to herself, making little hissing noises of excitement at the page she is creating. Her fingertips are filled with a restless, watery energy, like plasma. She has forgotten about Leo, about her mother, about Gus.

She refreshes the home page. Nothing. She will add something of her own, just to make sure that the site works. In the gold frame, she types, Deecie Jeffries grew up in my neighborhood. I remember that she had maroon balloons at her memorial.

She presses Return. The entry populates a new frame in the gallery view, and the nameplate reads "Deecie Jeffries."

It works. Bee raises her eyebrows in delight. She sets Google Alerts for the frame she's designed so that any new articles from the web will appear there too. She hesitates for a moment, then uploads a link to her Facebook page.

It's enough for today. The site isn't perfect, but the basic idea is there. Bee hasn't felt a sense of accomplishment like this in a long time. She leans back, smiling to herself. Every detail of the room feels suffused with import: the fig tree draping its leaves over the circulation desk, the librarian and her salad. The dust motes floating by the high windows. The murmuring mothers and their children.

She can come back tomorrow, or she can try to find a café where she can use her work laptop. Bee is pushing her chair away from the computer table when she looks up at the clock.

Her heart drops.

It's been three hours.

She looks again, sure that there must be some mistake.

But now she sees that the automatic shades in the lobby have slowly lowered against the noon light, and the room has turned a glowing lemon yellow. Fear surges through her. She feels the prickle of milk coming from deep in her armpits.

Attie. She is hungry. Bee should never have left her for this long.

She is frantically stuffing her drawing notepad into her bag, milk seeping through her bra, when she hears a soft bell that she thinks at first might be coming from one of the toys stored in the plastic bins on the bottom shelves.

It's the computer. But her website has been live for only a few minutes, and Bee is not completely sure it is working properly. It can't have gotten to more than one or two people. It probably has broken links and corrupt files. There is a glitch.

And then there is another sound, like someone has hidden a tiny xylophone inside the computer, and the words begin to scroll. Bee freezes, half standing, car keys in her fist. The digital pencil wobbles and pauses, as if there is an invisible person sitting at the desk, considering, composing.

I was at a party once and a girl
drove away. I heard

a splash of water but I never said
anything

The lines stack themselves like a poem, then they vanish. Bee looks around. Is it someone in the library? Someone who looked over her shoulder when she was focused on her project, and thought they might play a prank on her?

The soft bell rings again, once and then three times in a row.

Once I saw him smash the locker right next to her head and
then he pushed her in the library, but everyone thought she
was being dramatic when her chair fell

Julie was my best friend and she loved

The last entry hovers in its frame, unfinished. None of the
entries has a name attached, except for the last one, so they
should go to the empty gallery, one that Bee has decorated with
digital dark blue velvet ropes to show that it is under construction. It would be too much to expect that any of these clues
might be attached to Deecie's case, but still. They are attached
to someone, somewhere.

Bee pulls her bag onto her shoulder. The note is there, a
corner of lined paper sticking out from the side pocket as if
it is a harmless grocery list. She knows what she should do.
She should add another entry, in case the police ever look at
this site. She should type, Deecie Jeffries left a note about a boy
she saw in the field. She should go to the police herself and tell
them that Leo knew Deecie Jeffries, or she knew him, because
finding this note means that Leo knows something about what
happened to her, something dangerous, something that would
get him in trouble if anyone were to discover it.

Kissing him was a grievous, terrible error, one that will
probably take away the life that Bee already knows she does
not deserve. But he is the gentlest person Bee knows. He grows
flowers. He smells of fresh, blooming plants and overturned
soil.

His bottom lip is as soft as Attie's shoulder, a petal.

She does not want to hurt him. She can't.

She has to go. Attie needs her. Before she can think about

what she is doing, she stuffs Deecie's note into her pocket and goes to the bathroom, where she tears it into tiny pieces that she drops into the toilet and lets soften to a white and pale blue slurry. Then she kicks the handle and flushes it all away.

Mary

It is September. The heat is a living thing now, with impulses and noises and a personality that seems to Mary to be demanding, cruel. Soon, though, the air will be bearable, even at noon, and Bee and Gus will go back to school. *The Crucible* will go on, as planned, on the eighteenth. Next spring, the bluebonnets will fill the field again, and the cicadas will sing to each other in lazy, half-hearted refrains, and Mary and Leroy and the twins will go on, the way they always have.

Diana is walking silently beside her at the edge of the field, a manila envelope in her hands. Her footsteps in the dry brush sound like someone chewing saltines. She hasn't even looked at Mary, much less explained why they are walking into the middle of the field together in the middle of the day.

After Mary told what she found in the garage—stupid, so stupid!—Diana just stared at her, head tipped, as if Mary had handed her a key she did not recognize. Then she said that they should meet at noon the next day at the end of Diana's driveway, when the construction workers would be gone for lunch. Mary should not tell anyone, she said. Not Bee, not Gus. Not Leroy.

But she should bring the photograph.

The twins are at the pool, and Leroy is not at home, anyway. It is Wednesday, which is supposed to be his day to catch a ride with Jim Moynihan to the depot, but today they both called in sick to go to Brady and bet on the horse races. Mary is therefore free to do as she pleases, which is not to walk in the noonday heat with Diana, her thighs chafing, her armpits dripping with sweat.

She should be in her air-conditioned bedroom, sitting on her giant maxi pad, mourning the baby girl who slipped out of her like a seal, bluish gray, eyes open.

Attie. Mary's belly throbs, and her breasts answer, like an echo across a mountain range. Her milk is coming, indignant and pointless.

When they reach the end of Stillwood Lane, Mary sees the row of bulldozers, backed up against the toppled fence like they are waiting to begin a race. They are giant, yellow, the kind you see in the Richard Scarry books she read to the twins when they were small, before they began to squirm away from her and close their bedroom doors at night. She half expects a fox driver, an elephant with overalls. Dear Mr. Frumble getting stuck on a newly tarred road.

Somehow she has forgotten about the new road. As if her memory has seeped out of her along with the baby. The field will not fill with flowers in the spring. The animals will need to find new homes, maybe in burrows underneath her own home, where Leroy will set out traps or poison, or in Diana Nastasi's tangled backyard. By spring, everything here will be gone, plowed under, paved over. Forgotten.

The manila envelope that Diana is holding has something bulky inside it. Diana will not show her what it is. Now it also contains a Polaroid of a small boy, his body pale white against the darkness of what Mary now understands, now admits to herself, is her own garage. Her own sweet boy. His black hair a black hole. There, in the top left corner, is the box marked *Christmas Decorations 1*—it's too blurry to make out the words, but the shape, the placement of the letters, are enough—and there, on the lowest shelf, is the box that once held six blue milk glass plates. At the edge of the field, before they started to walk, she handed Diana the photograph upside down, the black square on the back facing the sky, which means that the boy was facing the sky also but was allowed to keep his dignity. Diana's eyes widened, but she did not ask her to turn it over.

Maybe she has already seen it, Mary realizes. Maybe, after Mary told her where to look, Diana left her in the bedroom and went to the garage. Maybe Diana understood, before Mary did, what it is. Who. The mother across the street who can't even make dinner for her own child, seeing it, getting it, while Mary preened and practiced her lines and did nothing.

"Here," Diana says, stopping, and her voice sounds to Mary like it is coming from the other end of a long tube. They are in the middle of the field, at a spot where the animal paths seem to converge, like the center of a flower. Mary has never been curious enough about the field to come this far. To her, it has been only a single line of brown, or sometimes blue, the way a child would draw it, with yellow scribbles for the tall brush. Up close, though, she can see that it is full of movement. Each blade of grass has its own choreography, and the dirt teems with small creatures. She is the largest living thing in the field, but it ignores her entirely.

She says, "Here? Diana, I don't understand what we're doing."

Diana doesn't explain. She turns away from Mary and bends down. When she turns back, Mary can see that she is holding a dry tuft of grass. Small seeds stick to her dark blue shirt, a tiny constellation. She drops the bundle on the ground between them, then turns away again. "Gather as much as you can," she says, over her shoulder. "We're building a fire."

Diana never said anything about a fire. She said only that they would meet here, at noon, when the whole street is at work and the construction workers have gone to eat their lunches at the Vaquero.

"What? It's too dry. It'll burn everything. We can't." Mary hates that her voice is shrill. But she should not even be outside. Her steps are as small as a child's. It is too hot, too quiet. Even the birds are hidden deep in the brush, panting and fluttering their wings.

Diana stops at Mary's words. Slowly, she turns back to her. "We can," she says, a second tuft of grass dangling from her fist. She has left the manila envelope behind, at Mary's feet, and she stares down at it. "Mary. We have to."

Mary thinks of the boy in the photograph, standing in her own garage. She thinks of the edges of the photograph curling, bending in the flames, until the boy melts away. But burning the photograph, burning whatever it is that Diana has in the envelope, won't make his sorrow disappear.

The photograph is the only evidence she has against Leroy.

"It won't help," she says. Her voice is plaintive and small.

Diana steps closer to her now, and for a moment Mary is afraid that she will lean in, rest her head on Mary's shoulder. But she only puts a hand beneath Mary's elbow, as if she is trying to prop her up. "It will," she says. "Trust me."

Mary looks at Diana's face, pink with heat, a stray strand of hair plastered to her sweating cheek. She remembers the way Diana hooked her hands beneath her shoulders and pulled her into her car, the way she tucked a bath towel around her lap, the way she drove with one hand on the wheel while the other smoothed the back of Mary's damp head. *We aren't friends,* she thinks. *Why would I trust you?*

But she does.

There aren't many sticks in the center of the field because there aren't any trees. Mary tries the area by the fence, but the branches there are all cypress and won't burn easily. What would people think if they looked out of their houses and saw her now, in the heat of the day, gathering kindling and arranging it according to Diana's instructions? Walking in circles on one side of the field while Diana walks on the other. Both of them bringing their piles of twigs and brown grass back to the center, like a pair of ants collecting crumbs for the nest. It is ridiculous. Mary hopes everyone on the street is gone, at work, at the pool, at the store, everyone with somewhere to go except her. And, somehow, Diana.

Diana points to a spot to Mary's left. "Put that pile there," she says. "Spread it out into a line." The pile of twigs joins to another, and Mary sees, suddenly, a letter forming in the mound at her feet. It is not a letter she knows, not in English. It is oval, with a line crossing its center.

Mary did not go to college, but her childhood neighbor Leora did, and when she came home from TCU that first Thanksgiving, all she could talk about was rushing for Pi Phi, which Mary heard as Pie Fi and decided was a club for lovers of pastry before she finally figured that the curving letters on Leora's sweater stood for those unfamiliar sounds.

The letters they are building in the field are Greek, then. She does not know what they mean. She does not even know if she is looking at them upside down or backward. Why is Diana making her do this? If she wants to mock Mary's lack of education, she could pick an easier way.

And if she wants to help her with the photograph, writing a Greek word with sticks will not be enough.

They are almost finished. The last letter looks like the infinity sign, chopped in half, or like a fish a child would draw. The letters are large, maybe five feet from top to bottom, so Mary does not realize at first that they are working on the same line, heading toward each other around a loop. Diana is two feet away on her knees, patting a pile of twigs together.

Mary is bending over at the waist because she is not sure what will happen between her legs if she tries to squat. She is still in her nightgown. When Diana met her at the edge of the field, she didn't seem to notice. She just took the photograph from Mary's outstretched hand, dropped it into the envelope, and started to walk.

They are only a foot or so apart now. Mary is afraid that she smells worse than she thinks she does. Her hair has not been washed in days, and the cloth of her gown is thick and sour. Its bottom hem is ringed with dark brown dust.

Diana stands and brushes the dirt and twigs from her knees. "What does it mean?"

Diana looks up in surprise. A smile plays at the corner of her mouth. "It says '*thysia*.'" To Mary, the word sounds like "the sea-ya." She thinks of the ocean. Or "the see-ya." A farewell.

"Oh," she says. She does not want to give Diana the

satisfaction of asking for a definition. A line from *The Crucible* appears, as clearly as a thought bubble hovering over their two sweating heads. She recites, "It is rare for people to be asked the question which puts them squarely in front of themselves."

She does not stutter or speak too quickly. It is John Proctor's line, not hers, but it doesn't matter. A cicada calls, then another interrupts. Diana stares at her, mouth open. She is swaying slightly.

"Yes," she says. She places the manila envelope in the center of the first letter. She takes a lighter out of her bag, a small leather pouch with embroidered straps and tassels, and lights the corner of the envelope. It flares, turns dark brown, and dies. She tries again, on the other side. This time, the flame takes.

"And what would your question be?" she asks. She is serious now. She is taking Mary seriously too.

It is because of this, and because of the heat, which has painted them both the same shade of pale pink, and because of the fire, which has spread to the swirling piles of brush and is turning the envelope into a knot of bright orange flame, that Mary decides to answer truthfully. She looks down at the field, which will soon be aflame with a mysterious Greek word, and then back at Diana. She hears herself whisper, "I would ask: *What did I do wrong?*"

Diana reaches toward her. She puts her hand on Mary's shoulder, where it rests, heavy and calming. Mary has to stop herself from rubbing her cheek against it like a dog. Diana does not hug her, and she does not look away. She says, "Nothing. Mary. You did nothing wrong. It's Leroy. He's the one who did something wrong."

The fire is licking the lines of the letters and straying into the dirt, where it finds small bits of fuel. The word will be gone soon, and no one will see the strange spinning letters that flared for a moment in an empty field. For now, the smoke could pass for the thick haze of a September afternoon, but the heat is prickling the hairs on Mary's leg. It will light the edges of her nightgown if she does not move. Sweat runs so thickly down her face that she almost confuses it for tears.

"*Thysia*," Diana says. In her mouth, the word is guttural. It sounds ancient, magical, like it has traveled from another planet. There is no twang. Not a single syllable is familiar. "It means immolation. A sacrifice." She looks at Mary, eyes narrowed. She is trying to tell her something. "It means offering."

Mary nods, slowly. She understands. It is like *The Crucible*: the life of a woman in exchange for the sins of a town.

The flames are growing taller. Soon they will start to wander down the paths, to the fence, to Stillwood Lane, if no one comes.

But Diana has her other hand on Mary's shoulder now. She is pulling now, pulling Mary away from the field. They are standing on the hot asphalt in front of Mary's driveway before Mary registers that they were running.

Diana takes Mary's hands. There is dirt beneath her nails, and beneath Mary's too. Their fingers twine together so tightly. They are holding Mary upright.

Diana says, "I don't have time to explain everything. The police will be here soon. When they come, I want you to tell them that you just saw your husband burn a pair of pink flip-flops in the field. I want you to tell them that you just remembered you saw your husband in the field the night Deecie Jeffries disappeared."

There is a whine of sirens in the distance. Mary feels like she might faint. The firetrucks are screeching at the end of the street, but Diana's words are an announcement, a spell that keeps her upright.

"Mary," Diana says. "That photograph wasn't enough to bring you the justice you need. It's gone now. You never have to look at it again. But now you need to do something more." She is pointing to the trucks. Their lights are painting the smoky air pale pink as they flash. "He's home today, isn't he? I didn't see his truck leave this morning." Mary can feel fear swell in her stomach as she begins to understand what Diana is saying. "Are you ready? There isn't much time. Listen to me. It has to be now."

She gestures behind her, at the blanket of smoke lifting into the air, at the carpet of fire in the field. A police car is speeding down the street, its siren growing louder as it comes.

"Mary, this fire is your only chance. Leroy has to pay for what he did. Now go."

Bee

Bee turns the air-conditioning in the car to high, but by the time she gets back to Stillwood Lane, sweat and leaking milk have turned her pale yellow T-shirt a shade darker. The drive has melted her resolve. When she watched the letter from Deecie Jeffries swirl in the bowl of the library toilet, then disappear into the pipes, she was sure that she understood what she was doing. She ran to that bathroom without thinking, but when the note turned to mush, she felt calm, purposeful, as if protecting Leo were not decided but predestined.

Now, though, she isn't sure. Outside of the library bathroom, her actions seem desperate, impulsive. She should have at least found a way to show it to the Jeffries family, who would frame it, cherish it, as something touched by the hands of their lost daughter. She should have at least copied it to her website.

But what can she do now? *I found a note from a missing girl in my bedroom. Then I flushed it at the library.* The proof is gone now, sliding down the pipes to be filtered away forever.

If she went to the police, she'd only get herself in trouble for destroying a potential clue in Deecie's case.

She should have been home, feeding Attie, not pretending to be a sleuth in her childhood library. Standing in the driveway of her mother's house, Bee locks the car doors three times before she goes inside. *Attie, Attie, Attie,* she thinks. As if that were enough witchery to erase what she has done.

Inside, Attie is thrashing in Mary's arms. She is sweaty and irate. Bee bounces her for a moment or two, trying to get her to stop screaming, then lifts her shirt in the middle of the living room, not caring if Mary or even Gus sees her. Attie bangs her face against Bee's dripping breast in desperation before she finally latches on, making little gasping sounds as she sucks. Mary insists that she just started crying, that she slept for most of the morning, but Bee isn't convinced.

As Attie's sounds turn from gasps to sighs, Bee feels herself relax. Attie is fine. Bee is here now, and the note is gone, and the site is working. She has accomplished something. She should call Charlie. Or text. He is at work, probably so deep into mysterious vomiting and stitches and Narcan that he has not even wondered how her day is going.

She pulls out her phone. Hey, she writes. She considers a bit, then adds a heart.

Morning, he answers, right away. Another heart. How are my girls?

Part of her wants to tell him about her idea. But it can wait until she calls, later this afternoon. Or it can wait until she is back in Portland. It is so hard to explain, and he will probably think that she has come even further unhinged, and he will ask her if she really needs to spend time on that when Attie is so young and Bee is still on maternity leave. He will tell her she should "take care of herself" the way the other mothers do: taking yoga class, going for walks with friends. But now that she has started her site, she does not want to give it up. She wants to have everything: Attie, Charlie, her project.

Her family.

Through the window, she can see Gus kneeling in the backyard, yanking up some kind of ivy that has attached itself into the grass. He pulls it out in hairlike, stringy tendrils that he drops in a pile at his side. Bee watches him work until Attie's sucking slows and her lids close. When she is asleep, Bee lowers her into the car seat and goes outside.

Gus's skin is a sickly beige color, and when Bee gets closer, she smells deli meat and cigarettes. She puts the car seat down between them and pulls down the shade to cover Attie.

"You're still here," she says. He looks up and squints into the sunlight. Sweat is running in rivulets down the veins of his arms and dripping unevenly into the grass.

He turns away and yanks at the ivy. "This stuff is choking the grass," he mumbles to himself. A bird lands on the tangle of honeysuckle on the back fence. Staring at it, he says, "You couldn't wait to run out of the house either, huh? Must be a twin thing."

That isn't true, Bee wants to protest. *We are nothing alike.*

Instead, she shrugs and kneels down next to him. The grass is sharp beneath her knees, and there are tiny volcanoes of fire ant nests dotting the lawn, but she is determined not to complain. She grabs a dried-out tendril of ivy and begins to tug. It stretches against her weight, the leaves turning to a green slime on her hands. Gus isn't as weak as he looks.

"What are you doing?" he asks, frowning.

"Helping."

He looks down at her, then shifts a little to block the sunlight from her face.

"Okay," he says. For a minute or so, they work side by side. Gus has deep wrinkles around his eyes, Bee notices, as if he is outside all the time. He seems calm. Maybe working outside is good for him. Maybe that's what he's been doing all this time, in between stealing unattended packages and baby formula. Bee wraps a vine around her fist and allows herself a fantasy: Gus stays here to take care of their mom. Leo moves back to Texas, away from Bee. Leo and Gus buy a piece of land together, raise wheat or melons or cattle, and Bee visits once a year. Once every two years, maybe.

"Forget it," he says, as if he is dismissing her idea. "I'm done. Let's walk to the drive-in. There's nothing in the house. We can grab—I don't know. Whatever."

"Week-old boiled hot dogs? Icees?" There is no real food at the Vaquero. "I can't, anyway. I have to stay here with Attie." She gestures at the car seat and shrugs. "I was gone for way too long this morning, I think."

Gus stands, rests his hands on his lower back and leans into them. "No. I mean, yeah, you should stay with her. But—I don't know. Would you want to go for a walk or something? We could bring her?"

"Sure." Bee tries to sound casual, but suddenly, she is nervous. Gus hasn't asked her to go anywhere with him since they were ten years old. It feels unnatural. Did Leo tell Gus about the kiss? Is that why Gus is looking at her, head tipped, his eyes dark as a catbird's?

The thought of Leo, the kiss, the note, makes Bee reckless.

Before she can stop herself, she says, "I just saw Leo, did you know that? In Portland." Bee checks for a reaction, but there is nothing. "He said you wanted to talk to me."

Gus nods, slowly. "Yeah, he told me that." Bee's heart flutters, but she's the one who started this conversation. Now that it is rolling forward, it is too lumbering and heavy to stop.

She takes a deep breath and says, "Gus, did Leo know Deecie Jeffries?"

The question slices the air between them. Gus stares at her, his mouth opening and closing. No words come out.

She will wait. Her desire to know the answer is in equal balance with her fear of it.

Gus's body settles, his mouth stills. "Bee. Why are you asking me that?" He turns away, toward the side of the yard, and begins to walk.

Bee picks up Attie and follows. She can't let it go. "I found this note—"

"What note?"

"In my room. A love letter, kind of. From Deecie, to Leo. It was under the carpet in my room. But I didn't put it there."

Gus's face is white. "In your room?" He takes a step away, his lips moving like he is reciting a prayer. When he turns back, he asks, "What did you do with it?"

"I flushed it. At the library." She feels self-conscious, as though admitting this reveals how much she loves Leo, what she would do to protect him.

The muscles around Gus's mouth loosen. "Okay," he says, mostly to himself. "Okay. Okay."

"Is it? Okay? I don't think it is. You're here, at Mom's house, out of nowhere, after you haven't talked to me in fifteen years. There's this weird fucking note in my room. And now I get the feeling that you know something about Deecie that you won't tell me."

"Bee, you don't get it. I've been—I've been trying to stay away. From you, from everyone. I'm only here now because Mom asked me to come. She wanted us to see each other. I don't blame you for not wanting to see me, but lately, I don't know. I've been a little better. Maybe I can do something for her. She isn't right." He seems exhausted from the effort of so many words. "I wanted to see you too, Bee. I felt—ready. That's what I wanted Leo to tell you. I swear, I have no idea why that note was in your room."

When Gus and Bee were kids, Bee realized that he had a tell. If he was lying, he widened his eyes, just slightly, a cartoon version of sincerity. He does it now, but Bee can't decide what he's lying about.

"I don't believe you," she says.

"Fine. Whatever. You can believe anything you want. But I'm telling you that Leo doesn't—Leo didn't do anything wrong. He doesn't have anything to do with it."

If this were a detective show, Bee would have a bulletin board with colored string connecting one pushpin to the other. Slowly but surely, the pieces would unravel, and a handsome, battle-worn detective would stand in front of the room and explain how it all fit together. But she is not a detective. She is not anything. In her mind, the story is a rotating strand of DNA, a child's model of the galaxy. She can't figure it out. It is just beyond her understanding, rotating slowly in a liquid darkness.

They are somehow at the end of the street now, at the old opening to the field. Bee can't even picture the way it used to look. It is as if these new houses have always been here. Only someone who lived here decades ago would know that once there was a field here, or a missing girl.

"We can talk tonight," Gus says. He is speaking quietly, but his voice is reedy and strained. "After dinner."

Attie squeaks, and when Bee peeks under the shade, Attie's eyes are open, as if she has been eavesdropping. Bee hopes that her mom isn't looking outside, watching this scene. At least she won't be able to hear them over the air-conditioning. Bee thinks of the note, on its long path through the city's pipes. She thinks of Leo, standing in the doorway of her bedroom in Portland.

She thinks of her website, its row of empty frames. She thinks of Attie, her old woman's face pinched with hunger or smoothed with joy. She thinks of Charlie, patting a plaster cast on someone's broken leg with wet, gentle hands. Of Leo, the way he tucked the hair behind her ear before he bent down to kiss her. And, somehow here is Gus, who wanted to see her, who has returned to her and is standing on Stillwood Lane, sweat running down his face like tears. All of them connected, even now.

She thinks, *Behold, Bee Rowan, you have been touched by something you don't deserve.*

She doesn't understand what Gus wants. But suddenly she knows what to say.

"Gus." She takes his hand. She tries to be gentle so that he will understand she does not want to fight. His hand is cool and dry in hers. She says, quietly, "I missed you."

He bows his head, as if he is considering her words. When he looks up, he is frowning, but his eyes are glassy and clear. The gold flecks in his irises glint as he looks at her.

"Same, Beatrice," he says, and his forehead smooths. "Same."

Mary

Mary kneels beneath Leroy's truck, trying to find the cable she needs. Outside, beyond the trio of windows, the field is crawling with men and hoses. The fire multiplies the heat tenfold, a hundredfold, until the neighborhood glows with an eerie midday sunset.

Inside the garage, it is as cool and dark as a cave. Her nightgown is filthy, from the field and the fire, and now this. She will not be able to get the oil stains out of the white cloth, so she will have to throw this nightgown away, somehow, so that no one will find it.

Is it the long cable that runs the length of the truck's body? Or is it the one that attaches the two front wheels together? Mary is not sure. She decides that it doesn't matter and takes the nail file from her pocket. It scrapes across the cable with a promising rasping sound. Five minutes pass, and her arms are throbbing, but it is as if she is not even here. She has hardly made a mark.

She needs something else. She shimmies out from under the truck and peeks out of the corner window. The firemen are tiny black ants, their hoses searching antennae. The whole city is busy, just at her doorstep. They do not know that she is here.

She did not tell the police that she saw Leroy in the field, the way Diana asked her to. She is not a liar.

He will be home soon. He will burst into the house like a bull, dropping his filthy coat, tracking his dirt everywhere, undoing all that Mary has done to keep the house for him. He will sit in his brown corduroy chair in front of the television, the beers lining up on the floor around him, until Mary brings him dinner or he falls asleep.

Mary stands and stretches. Her arms are pulsing from the effort of filing. The garage is filled with a faint haze of smoke. It must be seeping underneath the door. The twins will be back from the pool at four, and she will need to feed them. They will be hungry, thirsty, tired. They will need her.

"There isn't much time," Diana said.

In the far corner of the garage, near the dent in the wall, is the small station of wood and tools where Leroy and Gus built that Pinewood Derby car. Mary roots in the box for what she needs. It is a small saw, its blade built for wire and cable. Back underneath Leroy's truck, she starts again.

Scrape, scrape. Saw, saw.

She will cut the cable only partway. Maybe it is the wrong one. Maybe it will be weeks before it snaps. Maybe the truck won't crash after all, just coast to a stop on someone's lawn, the tires tearing two brown tracks through the grass.

Maybe she will have to think of something else. But all she can think of now, as she lies beneath the truck with her head

throbbing and her heart a skittish mouse, the air slowly darkening with smoke from the field, is Gus. His own heart breaking. His fear.

Bee

Austin, Texas
2011

The kitchen counter where Attie's car seat perches is sticky and makes a clicking sound as Bee rocks her. Attie is frowning a little, the way she does when she is about to fall asleep. Gus is in the living room, looking at his phone. It is only five o'clock, but Bee is so hungry that her eyelids are throbbing.

"I can help you with dinner, if you want," Bee says, her voice sudden and strangely loud. Her mother is frying chicken in a cast-iron pan. There is only one small piece, a bony thigh, pink and slimy. The grease spatters and pops. Outside the window, a van rolls by, and Bee watches it as she chops the ends off a pile of limp green beans.

The spring Bee turned eight, a man in a white van roamed their neighborhood for weeks. Their parents warned them that he would try to trick them, steal them, do something mysterious to them that they had no words for. "He'll ask you to help him find his lost puppy," they said. "He'll offer to take you to Pizza Hut so that he can buy you an extra-large pie, all for yourself." The kids called him the "Van Man" and bragged about how they would laugh at him if they ever saw him, right in his face; the danger he represented was as remote to them as the tornado drills that made them crawl under their desks once every few months at school, or the "inflation" their parents talked about in hushed voices before dinner. In other words, he was harmless.

Once, though, he pulled up to the side of the schoolyard, next to a break in the chain-link fence. There was a kickball game on the concrete slab by the double doors, but Bee wasn't playing. She didn't feel like it, or she hadn't been invited. It didn't matter. There he was, the Van Man, and she was the only one there to see him. He was smaller than Bee expected, like a leprechaun leaning out of the window, his face red and mottled under a wispy beard.

He called Bee over. Heat rose from the idling engine and blurred the air around it, as if he were under a spell, or casting one. She turned sideways to fit through the fence, let him hand her a candy bar from a box on the passenger seat. A Hershey's bar, already drooping in the heat. The Van Man's hands when they brushed against hers were dry, almost scabby, and he panted, slightly, when he handed it through the lowered window. He didn't say anything. Bee thanked him and watched him drive away. That was that. No pizza, no puppies. The man didn't seem to know that he was supposed to do anything else.

She hasn't thought about this moment since it happened, but as she gazes out the window, the green beans ignored in front of her, it comes back to her: not the man himself, whose features have dissolved with time, but the way she sought out the danger. The way it turned into something flimsy, laughable, the closer she got to the lowered window of the van. None of the neighborhood kids thought he was a real threat. But they didn't think anything was, until Deecie.

Tonight, during dinner, Bee will tell her mother and Gus about Drawthemback.com. She will show them the website, and Gus will understand that she is not trying to blame Leo for anything. She is just trying to give people a place to share what they remember about the people they have lost, and maybe help find the missing girl from their neighborhood.

Maybe their mom knows how that note got under Bee's carpet. Maybe she saw it when she redecorated the bedroom.

The note is probably nothing.

Suddenly, a spatter of grease flies from the pan and lands on Attie's yellow duck blanket, two feet away. It sizzles there as the fibers melt into a hard knot that darkens as Bee stares at it.

"Bee!" In one hand, Mary holds the spatula upright, like a flyswatter. Bee hasn't even moved, and Mary has already grabbed the handle of Attie's car seat to pull it to safety. Bee realizes for the first time in her life that her name is a command. It hangs in the air between them.

Mother to daughter: *Be!*

But be what? *Finish your sentence,* she wants to say. Be a website designer? Probably not the answer. Be a wife? A mother? Be better?

And her mother's name too: *Marry!*

Be, marry, or don't. Either way, you will find yourself back where you started, in your mother's house, your careless error turned to her command in your ears. The grease drop didn't burn Attie, but it could have, and it would have been Bee's fault. She is the one who put her car seat too close to the stove. You can never be half-good, half–paying attention, when you are a mother. The world threatens. There are strange men driving in white vans around your neighborhood, their laps full of candy, ready to take your daughters. She thinks of adding this to Drawthemback.com:

There used to be a man in a white van who would offer us food.

"Sorry," she says, to Attie, to the air. Bee's mother turns away, as if she hasn't even heard.

Gus sets the table. He folds each napkin precisely, places the forks just so. Bee wonders if his slow, careful movements are meant to preserve the truce they fashioned between them outside, which feels flimsy and impermanent, like a single skein of spiderweb. Pound for pound, spiderwebs are stronger than steel, but this is one of those facts that feels impossible, like a feather falling at the same speed as a stone, or worker bees dying after they sting.

Attie is curled on Bee's chest, having refused to sleep in her car seat again, her hand a pale pink shell coiled around a curl of Bee's hair. Bee does not want to hold her while she eats one-handed, but the near burn means that she should pay some kind of penance to erase her lack of attention. She settles herself in her seat and wedges Attie's body in the crook of her elbow.

Bee watches Gus's face when their mother slides the platter of chicken and green beans onto the table, but he gives nothing away. For a long moment, Bee and Gus chew silently, knives squeaking against the china. Bee's mother is smiling to herself, humming a little as she saws her chicken into smaller and smaller pieces without putting any into her mouth.

"I wanted to tell you," Bee begins. Gus and Mary look up in unison. Bee's breath is fluttering, as if she is about to give a speech to a room full of investors, not just her family, sitting at the same kitchen table where they have eaten a thousand meals, although not like this, just the three of them, or not that Bee can remember. They must have, but the years after her father died are a blur.

"I'm making a website," she says.

"Oh yeah?" Gus says, carefully.

Bee hesitates. She wishes she had a glass of wine, but she has already looked, and there is nothing in the cabinets, not even cooking wine. But there is nothing to be afraid of, she tells herself. Why shouldn't she tell them about her idea? It is just a little project. She doesn't have to mention the note again, which will shred the spiderweb she and Gus are spinning to tatters. She doesn't have to say Leo's name.

"Mmm. It's—well, it would be easier to show you. But it's for missing girls. A place to collect anything anyone knew about them. What they were like, or how they went missing. I had the idea . . . I thought maybe it could help find some of them." Even talking about it fills her with a wiry thread of alertness. She does not mention Deecie. "I got kind of fixated on the idea, for some reason."

Suddenly, her mom is leaning forward so far that her chest is brushing the tablecloth.

"Missing girls? Let me see," she says, and her fork clatters to the table. In the overhead light, her eyes look cartoonishly large, like an insect's.

"Okay," Bee says. "Sure. Hang on a second." She has not tried to look at the site on her phone, but it should work. Her mother raises her eyebrows as she waits. Bee can't remember ever showing her mother her work. Even when she was a child, Gus's drawings hung on the refrigerator, his tiny clay ashtrays on the bookshelf, but nothing from Bee. She wishes she were unveiling something more finished, more polished, so her mother could see what she was capable of. "I'm not sure if it will load on my phone. It's really rough, sorry."

Her phone is on the coffee table in the living room, so she heads to get it, Attie squirming on her chest. A single strand of Bee's dark hair has wrapped itself around one of the creases in Attie's wrist. Bee perches on the arm of the sofa and unwinds it carefully, giving herself time. She can see Gus's face, lit up like a spotlight in the bright light of the kitchen. Bee wants to tell him that she will not mention the note, that she understands that they just need a little more time to weave the thin strands of their connection into something more like steel. That she wants to keep it too.

The phone glows blue in her hand. She loads the site and looks back to Gus and her mom, waiting silently. Gus's mouth is set in a thin line and his leg is shuddering beneath the table. The water is wobbling in his glass, as if there is a tiny, imperceptible earthquake rattling Stillwood Lane, one only the two of them can feel.

"Hey," he says. His eyes are locked on the phone. "Let's just finish dinner, okay?"

Bee sets the phone back on the table.

"Yeah, it's not working anyway," she lies, and heads back to the table to finish her chicken in silence.

An hour later, Bee and Gus are sitting in a cramped booth at the Golden Lion on Guadalupe. Their mom went to her bedroom right after dinner, insisting that she would clean up later, or in the morning, and Bee and Gus played cards and watched an episode of *American Idol* before they decided to go out for more food, laughing like coconspirators as they pulled away from the house, Attie in the back seat like a chaperone.

Bee is drinking a glass of wine. She knows she shouldn't, because of the catch in Gus's voice when he asks for a Coke, but she wants the wine to dampen the clanging of her nerves. She is looking down at the menu, absentmindedly patting Attie, when Gus says, "So. Are you going to show me that website you made?"

"You really want to see it?"

"Why wouldn't I?"

"It didn't seem like you wanted to, before."

Gus stares at her for a moment, then says, "No, I wanted to. I just didn't want to upset Mom."

Bee roots around in her bag. All she finds is three diapers, a ziplock bag full of wipes, two absurdly long CVS receipts, and some lip balm. "Shoot. I must have left my phone at the house."

"You could load it on mine," Gus says, passing it across the table. He seems calm. There is no movement in his legs, no twitching, just the occasional tug on his hair. Bee is worried anyway. Maybe he is setting her up, planning to tease her, the way he used to. Maybe he will be angry with her for digging up something that is none of her business.

He is watching her, his hands outstretched, waiting. She loads the site and hands the phone back to him, holding her breath while he looks at it.

He doesn't tease her, though. He scrolls through, pressing buttons, without a word. Then he looks at her, eyebrows raised, and says, "You did this?"

"Yeah. The other day. It's—anyway. It was just an idea I had on the plane. I thought it could help because I'm sure there are little things that people remember, nothing you would tell the police or anything, but details that only a family member or friend or close neighbor would know . . ." She drifts off, realizing that she is thinking not of Deecie but of Gus, the way she has searched for him using the smallest of details, with nowhere to put the little breadcrumbs she finds.

"Bee, this is really great. I didn't know—I didn't know you were creative like that. I mean, I should have. You were always drawing and everything. But I didn't know you could make something like this."

"I'm not." This is a lie. She is, but she hasn't done anything important with it, not until now. Unless you count making a human, which any fool can do, even though it seems impossible, miraculous.

"No, this is amazing. I mean it." Gus takes a long drink of water. His throat moves visibly beneath his skin. Attie shifts her warm body on Bee's chest. She lets out a giant, full-body sigh, and Bee's nerves loosen.

The rareness of the moment strikes Bee like a sign. She has come all this way, and so has Gus, and they are somehow together, sitting in a restaurant like ordinary siblings reuniting after a long parting. But Deecie Jeffries's note is still hanging in the air between them.

She decides to be bold. She asks, "Gus, how did that note get to my room? I don't understand. It's—it doesn't make sense. Did you put it there?"

She is hoping he will leap to explain, to preserve the connection between them the way she wants him to. To preserve Leo, somehow. Instead, he slides his water glass a few inches to the left and rubs his forehead. There is a crash of glass from the restaurant kitchen, and he jumps. When he finally speaks, his voice is so low and quiet that she has to lean forward. Attie whimpers in her lap.

He says, "Okay. You're leaving tomorrow. What difference does it make?" He sounds like he is talking to himself, or to his water glass, not to her.

"What do you mean?"

"It's just . . . I've never . . . but now you're here, and I guess you think . . ." He picks up his water glass. The liquid sloshes over the rim, and he puts it down again.

He says, "Bee, I'm sorry." His voice is cracking, the way it used to when he was angry or upset. It is part of the spell that is making the past reappear and ooze its way into this room, covering it with a mustardy fog that coats everything and makes it impossible to see. "I know I should have told you. A long time ago. And now it's—"

"Gus. I know you're sick. I can see that. I'm not blind." Bee does not want to hear this story. She already knows it. "You've been making yourself sick for years. I wish you would—I'm sorry. But I don't know what to do about it. You won't ask for help. And you don't . . ."

While she is talking, Gus grabs her hand. When they were kids, he might have pushed her as she walked down the hall to her bedroom, making her stumble. Or he might have dunked her in the deep end of the pool, his hands clamped like two metal vises on her shoulders. But he has not touched her with tenderness, not that she can remember, until this moment.

"Bee, no. That's not it." He is looking at her hand as if it is a precious artifact he has removed from behind glass. She looks, too, to see what he might find there, but all she sees is jagged fingernails and deep wrinkles that she has always been afraid to learn more about: the heart line, the head line, deep and feathery. "It's not good," he says quietly.

Tears spring to Bee's eyes. Whatever is wrong, whatever Leo has done, she should know it by now. She should have seen it coming, a headlight on a train track in the middle of the night. She should have gotten out of the way.

"I know," she says. "I'm sorry. But Gus, we're here, together, like you said. It might not happen again, not for a long time. Can you just . . ." She lets the sentence hang in the air between them.

"Tell you. Okay." He coughs, wipes his mouth on the paper napkin crumpled next to his water glass. The waitress arrives with two burgers, and Gus goes silent as she leans over the table with the plates, the ketchup, the extra glasses of water.

As soon as she is gone, he starts to talk. He does not look at Bee.

"On the night that girl disappeared, we were planning to run away. Leo and me. We were packed and everything. We were going to steal a car, and just go. West, north, anywhere. We were going to be farmworkers, picking fruit or whatever. Leo wanted to see California."

Gus's eyes are shining. He is lost in his story. Bee can tell he has not spoken it aloud to anyone, ever, and even though her heart is racing, and even though she wants to know why he was running away at fifteen years old, why he took Leo and not her, she is determined not to ruin it by asking questions.

He stops, breathing hard. He picks up a french fry and puts it down again, but he doesn't continue.

"Okay," Bee finally prompts. "You were running away. What happened?"

Gus frowns at her, and Bee wishes she hadn't spoken. He says, "When we got outside, Leo saw—he saw something in the field, and he got spooked."

"Saw what?" she asks. "What did Leo see?" Her heart is thundering uncontrollably.

She knows what Leo saw, but she needs Gus to say it.

Leo saw Deecie Jeffries. That must be what Gus is trying to tell her. Leo must have known Deecie, somehow. And that night in the field, something happened, something so terrible that he had to hide it, and Gus did too, and now it will finally, finally be here, in the open, and Bee will have to tell everyone—her mother, and Charlie, and the police—and everything she thought she knew about her own life will disappear, or float away like a balloon, and there will be nothing, no one, to anchor her to the earth.

Gus flexes his hands on the table, steadying himself on its surface. "Bee, I never wanted you to know this."

"I'm an adult, Gus. I can handle whatever you have to say." She hopes that's true. She braces herself. Leo saw Deecie in the field.

Say it, say it, say it, she commands him. *Say that Leo saw Deecie in the field.*

"Dad. Bee, he saw Dad. In the field." A small wheeze escapes Gus, and he whispers. "He was there, in the field. He knew we were running away. He knew why. And he was—" Gus stops. "He was coming for me."

For running away? Bee is confused. "To bring you home?" she asks. She doesn't understand, but she can feel the pieces of the story lining up in her mind. She closes her eyes, and the light hanging over the booth makes the inside of her lids a kaleidoscope of orange and blue. Something is coming, some glimmer of understanding, the low growl of a beast around a corner, and she wants to push it away. "Why were you running?"

She does not want to hear the answer, but Gus says it anyway.

"I had to, Bee," she hears. His hand is on hers. It is light and warm. "Don't make me say it. I had to get away from Dad. But then he was there, and he had his gun, and it didn't work."

Bee does not know how long they sit there in the booth, their food cold and uneaten. Attie is still asleep on Bee's lap. Someone has scraped out Bee's insides like a pumpkin, leaving nothing but a ghoulish, empty shell. She wants to sit next to Gus in the booth, take his head in her lap. Soothe him, like a mother.

Gus's hands are in his lap now. He is twisting them around each other, his fingers tense and white at the knuckles. He is panting, slightly, and there is a little color in his cheeks. The waitress walks toward the table with the check in her hands, but Bee waves her away.

"It's okay, Bee," Gus says, quietly, watching her. "It was a long time ago. Just—you understand now, right? I don't know what that note is. But that girl had nothing to do with Leo. He was only there that night for me. To help me get away. He was my best friend."

Attie is breathing quickly, the little gasps that mean she is about to wake up. Bee stares down at the fringe of her eyelashes, fluttering on her round cheeks. Bee knows everything about her. Every smell, every look, every movement of fluid through her small, perfect body.

How could it be that something horrible would happen to your baby and you wouldn't know? Even if your baby was a boy, tall, strong. How could you not know?

"Did Mom know?" Bee is gasping, gulping huge mouthfuls of air so that she does not cry. "Did you tell her?"

Gus reaches across the table and takes her hand again. "No.

Jesus, Bee. No. Of course not. Leo said I should tell her. He tried so hard to get me to tell her. And he tried to tell his mom, but she didn't—" Gus takes a deep breath. "She didn't understand what he was trying to say. And then there was the accident, and Dad was dead, so there wasn't any point. Right?"

Bee has never seen the expression on Gus's face, pleading and self-loathing at the same time. He must have wished for that truck to twist itself around a tree a thousand times. He must have felt the Rowan sorrow as a twisted kind of joy.

"Why didn't you tell me, then? All this time? Gus, I thought you were just—I don't know what I thought. But I had no idea."

Gus's mouth is open. He is breathing hard. "I didn't tell you for the same reason I've never told Mom. I didn't want you to be unhappy. I wanted you to be able to think—"

"Think what?"

"I don't know. That your life was normal, maybe. That you had a normal childhood, with normal parents. That it was just me that was wrong."

"You should tell her now."

Gus shakes his head. "Why? You've seen her. She wouldn't be able to take it. Not now."

The light in the restaurant is pulsing somewhere behind Bee's eyes. She can hear her blood hurtling through her veins, trackless and heavy. How had her mother missed something so massive, so evil, under her own roof?

Gus swallows. "We did go back, though."

"What?" Bee's voice croaks, as if she hasn't spoken in days. She doesn't know what he means.

"The next night, after we realized that girl was gone." He points, and Bee follows the imaginary line of his arm through the restaurant window and over the highway and Shoal Creek to a pale orange house with a clay-tiled roof, sitting where the edge of the field would have been, all those years ago. "It was Leo's idea. He found something the night before, he said, and he wanted to check. To make sure there was nothing else. We went just before dinner, maybe four-thirty or so, before Dad got home from work. I told him it was a bad idea, that the police were looking everywhere. But he said we had to."

"I thought you said he saw . . . He saw Dad in the field, not Deecie." Gus flinches. "What was he looking for?" Bee adds quickly.

"I guess he saw them both." Leo, with those scars curling up his arms, poking up from his collar. Those hands, which made her feel like she was floating. "I don't know what he was looking for. Leo doesn't talk much. And he never asked for anything, you know? So I went with him. I wanted to get out of the house." Gus smiles ruefully. "Same as now. We walked along the edge, outside the police tape. It had rained the day before, and everything was still wet. I remember being worried that my shoes would be muddy, that I would make a mess and have to explain it to Mom. Anyway, we walked until we had gone all the way around, to the other side. It felt peaceful, kind of. Just walking with Leo like that."

Gus's forehead is smooth. This is the most he has ever talked to her.

"Did you ask him what he found? Was it the note?" Bee asks.

Gus shakes his head. "No, I told you. I don't know anything about the note. All he said was that he found a pair of shoes. Stuck in the fence, where we always hung out."

None of the newspaper articles mentioned anything about shoes. There were footprints in the mud, and that was it. Nothing about missing shoes. Bee's palms are slick with sweat.

"Pink flip-flops, he said. I told him he should give them to the police. I thought they might be evidence, or something. But he didn't listen. He said he had to keep them because we were in the field that night, and he was sure we'd get blamed for that girl going missing. And then he said he knew what to do with them."

"But you must have thought . . . You must have—"

"Bee, all I knew was she was missing, and he was scared. I trusted Leo." He pauses. "I trust him now. You should too."

Trust Leo? Bee can't even trust her own lungs to work properly. Her world is collapsing, falling, its beams pancaking to the ground as the earthquake rumbles underfoot.

The field burned, just a couple of weeks after Deecie Jeffries disappeared. That could be something, nothing. But she was barefoot when she disappeared, and Leo, gentle Leo, is the one who had her shoes.

Mary

Austin, Texas
2011

Mary has not slept through the night since the fire in the field. This was more than two decades ago now, and if she thinks about it that way, she feels the heaviness during the day, like she is swimming through sludge. She is so thick, so weighty, that she cannot mow the lawn, or write the Christmas cards, or wipe the slime from the crevices behind the kitchen faucet, the way she should. At night she wears her exhaustion like a shirt of lead.

She sponged the counter with Windex tonight, after dinner, and that will have to be enough.

She heard the twins murmuring to each other in the living room before they left the house. She still thinks of them like that—*the twins*—even though they do not see each other, have not seen each other for many years now. They have broken apart, the yolk from the white in their separate bowls. But tonight, they left the house together, and they will return together, in a way they never even did as children, not that she remembers, or not that she knew.

Gus, her Gus, has finally come home to her. He is not the same—how could he be?—but he is here.

Bee is here, too, and she is strong now, stronger than she thinks.

Can you be blamed for loving your son too much? Even if it was too late? Even if it was not enough? Mary did not know, before the fire, before she crawled beneath Leroy's truck with a saw in her hands, that she could love that much. Diana Nastasi was a different kind of woman, all action and nerve, but now she has moved away, to Greece, a faraway, foreign country where she will likely never see her boy again, which is a different kind of crime, and maybe a worse one. Who is to say? Mary has Gus, even if he is not the same. He is alive. Bee is a mother now. And Mary herself is still here, in the house on Stillwood Lane, which she now owns, all of it, even its unweeded lawn and its squeaking refrigerator door.

Only Leroy is gone.

There is something to be said for endurance.

Mary sits up from the bed slowly so that the mattress will not creak and sips the last water from the glass on the bedside table. They are nothing alike, her children, not even in small ways. But they are connected across a distance, like electrical wires or a suspension bridge, and she is here, too, a pole holding them aloft. Mary grips the glass and closes her eyes. What do they talk about when she is not there to pull on the cord that connects them? What are they talking about now?

She tiptoes across the carpet and opens the bedroom door. In the living room, she presses her forehead to the glass of the front window and rolls her cheeks against its cool surface, one and then the other. Across the street, its windows dark, is the old Nastasi house. She still calls it that, in her mind, even though Diana has been gone for years, and there have been new owners and renters since she left, young couples and old, one of them with a rangy dog who dug a small ravine in the side yard and barked all day long. None of them with children, though. Nothing worth watching.

When the twins come home from wherever they have gone, Mary will see the headlights from the top of Stillwood Lane. She will scurry back to bed, lie down, and pretend to sleep.

The silence in the living room seems heavier now that they are gone. It is dark, furry, like a sleeping bear in a cave. Dangerous.

She leans against the glass. The side of her face is moist against the windowpane, and there is a faint rushing sound deep in her ear. From the coffee table, she hears a small noise, as if there is a cricket caught in the wooden joints. Bee has left her phone behind. There on the screen is part of a message from Charlie, something about flight times. What would be the harm, just to look? It's not snooping if you don't know what you're looking for, the saying could go. Mary tries typing Bee's birthday, then her own. Nothing. She tries 1-1-1-1 and then 0-0-0-0. Only one more chance, the screen tells her.

She tries Gus's birthday, a day after Bee's. The screen opens, and a pulse begins to flutter in Mary's throat. She resists the urge to read Bee's messages, but the site Bee told them she was making at dinner is open. It works, then, after all. It's called Drawthemback.com. *Copyright Bee Rowan, 2011.*

The empty gold frame appears slowly, as if someone is pulling up an invisible white curtain. Mary doesn't understand. What does an empty museum frame have to do with missing girls? She clicks the menu at the top, and then she is on another page, somehow, with a row of frames. The instructions on the top say that you can write in anything you want about any missing girl, and that all the details will be collected and sorted. "Each detail will be a piece of a portrait," the text says, "and when we gather enough together, these missing girls will be drawn back."

Her Bee did this? She can hardly believe it, that her daughter could bring something like this to life, and so quickly. Mary sees countless frames, each one of them filled with small details, photographs, maps. She clicks on one and sees a photo of a girl with a shell necklace, her eyes sparkling with delight. Next to her in the frame, someone has written, My baby sister used to have a pet rabbit named Mona.

It is the anonymity of the thing that pleases. Anonymity and intimacy are perfect lovers, like an actor and an audience. There are two girls Mary has never seen before, a blond named Molly and a bright-eyed little girl named Katherine. She keeps scrolling, clicking. Why is Bee so interested in these girls?

Then, on the fourth page she opens, there is a face Mary recognizes, a face she hasn't seen in years. It is Deecie Jeffries, the girl from across the field, staring out of her school photo. Her collar is worn, slightly, as if her mother did not bother to remind her that it was picture day at school.

Her teeth are crooked, like Mary's.

Under the frame, there are dozens of links. Mary clicks on an article about Deecie Jeffries's backpack, found buried underneath a sidewalk just a week ago. Then the next article, which says it had nothing to do with her disappearance. Mary's heart is rushing. This whole time, there was a backpack, hiding under the same layer of dirt that must still hold a pair of melted rubber flip-flops and the ashes of a burned photograph. She pores over the articles, trying to find something more.

Mary clicks back to the picture of Deecie Jeffries. On the night she disappeared, Mary was so young. As young as Bee is now. Mary sat on her porch, her baby curled inside her, alive, and watched those boys run into the field like it was a lark. She did not know that it was the end of the living part of her life, or that their childhoods were long gone.

She knows it now.

An idea is forming, swirling in her gut like an undertow. She has been resisting it for years, but she is tired, so tired. She wants to lie back, let it drag her under.

"There isn't much time," Diana Nastasi said to her, a long time ago, as the lights from the fire trucks painted the smoke coral and pink.

Thysia, Mary remembers. She looked up the word, once, at the library, months after the fire, after Leroy was gone. It means "offering," just like Diana said. "Sacrifice."

It also means "victim," as if the words are all the same.

It is time, at last. She has been a fool. A coward. The fire was nothing, like a match flaring in the middle of a dark forest and sputtering out. Leroy is dead, which is also nothing. The police told her that he was drunk, that he wrapped his truck around that tree by accident. "Sorry, ma'am, so sorry, sorry to be the one to tell you." The bottles rolling at his feet meant that they never bothered to look beneath the car, where they would have found that cable, sawed halfway through, and then frayed and snapped, finally, finally. They never asked Mary if he was home the night Deecie disappeared, if she could be absolutely sure, so Mary never said a word. She never spoke to Diana Nastasi again.

But Deecie Jeffries had a family too. They deserve to know everything that Mary knows. They should know about the sliding door she heard that night, and who it was. They should know that it couldn't have been Gus because she saw him crawl through his own bedroom window, and she could practically hear his poor heart hammering in the dark.

They should know that Mary could have stopped everything if she'd just stood up to check.

The sliding door was Leroy, leaving this living room, slinking to the field, to frighten Gus. To the garage, to hurt him.

What would stop a man like that? When Deecie disappeared, Mary told everyone, told herself, that it had to be an animal that took that girl, and she believed it. She could see it in her mind, padding up behind the girl, sinking its teeth into her soft, freckled shoulder and dragging her away.

Maybe she was right, in a way. Leroy was an animal. That was true. He was an animal, worse than she could have imagined, a monster, and now she has to tell someone, so that poor girl isn't lost forever. If she has to leave this house, if the police circle the house like a wagon train, closing closer and closer until they reach the door, knock, tell her that Leroy Rowan was a kidnapper, a murderer, a beast, if she melts into a heap on her own front porch, well, then, so be it. It will be her last performance.

She cups the phone in her left hand and begins to type with her pointer finger in the frame. The words come slowly, which is good because she has to make sure that she remembers the line. She can still feel the jealousy that smoldered in her when Irene was cast as Abigail, while Mary had to settle for Elizabeth, who had hardly any lines. And her disappointment, when she didn't get to play her part anyway, because Leroy was dead and the director said it was too soon for her to go onstage.

All that practice, for nothing.

The line she is typing is deleted from the play now. It is Abigail's line, from the end. Mr. Arthur Miller must have changed his mind, even though Mary's director said that it was the key to the entire play, which hurt her feelings at the time—so foolish—but now seems perfectly, exactly right.

Oh, how hard it is when pretense falls! But it falls, it falls!

Mary presses Return.

Mary looks at Deecie Jeffries's frame, but her words have vanished. She must have made a mistake. She opens a new frame and types, They never interviewed all the truckers. The one they should have asked died in a car crash before they ever asked him anything. At the end, she adds, Deecie Jeffries. The line is there, now, underneath Deecie's smiling face like a caption.

Even though Leroy is long gone, he will not be able to get away with this too.

Bee is so smart. She will be able to see what it means, without Mary saying a word. And she will be able to see, too, that each one of these hundreds of missing girls, thousands, is a wonder, but there is not one of them as wonderful as Bee herself, who has made something that will make a difference in this world, who is not content to stay quiet, bide her time. Her own Bee. Her own beloved girl.

There is a flash of headlights at the window. Mary clicks the side button of the phone and puts it back on the coffee table. They are back. Bee will pick up her phone, read the message on her website, and she will know what Mary has done. She will tell Gus. They will decide together what to do.

The lamp in the living room is dim, but it lights up the tips of Mary's slippers under the curtain. She will have to stay entirely still so they do not notice her. It is a little like being backstage, with the lights from the scene washing over her as she waits for her cue. But there will be no cue this time, because she has no role in this play. She has already tried her best.

Some people will say that she should have done more. They will be right, of course. But they are not the ones who lived here, with Leroy, in this house.

They are not the ones who had to map a new road through a burning field.

Bee

In the car on the way back from the Golden Lion, Gus drives slowly, like he can't quite remember how. The inside of their mother's car is spotless and smells faintly of cigarette smoke and mints. Bee tries to make a joke about their mother smoking, but Gus doesn't smile. He just says, "It's weird. I don't remember her ever driving anywhere when we were kids."

The kitchen counter is streaked with Windex. The house is quiet, as if Bee and Gus are its only inhabitants. Bee walks to the front window and leans her forehead against the glass, which is strangely warm beneath her skin. The streetlights must be broken; there is no light outside, and Leo's old house is invisible. If Bee didn't know better, she would be able to convince herself that the old field was still out there, the night breeze churning the tall grasses in the dark.

She tries to put everything she knows in order. Something horrible happened in this house, the one she grew up in. The one she has avoided for years, for reasons she thought she understood. Leo hid evidence, which can only mean that Leo knows what happened.

Or that he is responsible. Fear pulses through Bee's body as she rocks Attie's car seat with her foot, and then a long shiver of disgust. Everything is wrong. Her own father, some kind of horrible monster. And Leo. How could she have let him kiss her? Now she can never convince herself that it never happened, or that it is only a small transgression, one that can be explained by exhaustion or nostalgia. Whatever he is, he is not the boy she thought she knew, all those years ago.

Bee settles Attie in a corner by the sofa and tucks her blanket beneath her shoulders. The melted grease spot is hard, like a calcified scar. Attie stirs under her hands and lets out a wet burp. She is getting bigger by the day, by the hour. Bee is amazed by the rate: it is vegetal, exponential. When they get back to Portland, when the wheels of the plane touch down, Attie will have grown a millimeter here, there, and she will have new synapses, a new sliver of fingernail. She will be different.

Bee will be unrecognizable.

Gus is opening a cabinet in the kitchen, turning on a faucet. He is trying to be quiet, but the glass clinks against the metal. Bee can see him through the doorway. He does not make her think of a spider now, but an abandoned bird, something small, bony, in need of sustenance and protection.

"What should I do?" a muffled voice says. For a second Bee thinks it is Gus, but the voice is too high, too hushed, and it is coming from behind her, where the curtains hang to the carpet. Gus freezes, his hand hovering just above the faucet.

"What should I do, Diana?"

Bee and Gus stare at each other. Bee turns to the window. The fabric shifts, just a little, and as she watches, an arm reaches out and pulls the curtain aside. Mary is not asleep.

She is walking, in small steps, into the living room.

"Oh, you're here. Gus. Bee. Your father is gone now." The muffled, whispery voice has turned suddenly cheery, and Mary's face is flushed. She is looking at Gus, as if she is asking him a simple question, what he wants for dinner, what time his dentist appointment is next week.

Bee is paralyzed. This isn't simple confusion. Something is horribly wrong.

Before she can gather her thoughts and decide what to do, Gus rushes across the room to Mary's side and holds her elbow. Bee thinks again, *He is a father now, maybe. He knows how to be gentle to a small, precious thing.*

"It's okay, Mom," he says. "You're sleepwalking. Go back to bed." He is steering her to the bedroom. The door is cracked, and inside the room the light is golden.

Mary stops by the coffee table, looking up at Gus like they have just met and she is making conversation. Her eyes are heavy. Bee wonders if she is asleep, or drugged, or both.

"No," she says. "I'm awake. Do you ever feel so awake, at this time of night? Even after you've gone to sleep?"

Her voice is small, doll-like. She weaves her arm through Gus's and rests her head on his shoulder. They make a single figure, a *Pietà* in reverse, with Gus turned into the doting mother, his blue button-down a lapis lazuli robe, their mother's nightgown a marble white drape.

Mary is sick. Bee sees this now, so clearly that she can't believe it has taken her this long to understand it fully. She should have known, when she pulled up to the house in her taxi and saw the lawn. When she saw the dust, the clutter, the unwashed forks in the kitchen drawer.

Maybe this moment is the only chance they'll have to hear the truth.

Bee's words tumble out, a wall of water, full of sharp sticks and refrigerators full of rot and downed power lines.

"Mom," she says. Her voice is louder than she intended. "Did you know?"

"Bee, stop," Gus says, his voice sharp. "It's okay. *I'm* okay. Look at her. She's tired. She doesn't need to have this conversation."

He means that he doesn't want to have it. Bee knows this, and for a moment she hesitates. He is right. It is his story, only his. But there is Attie, tucked under her blanket, one hand tugging her own ear in her sleep. Mary should have to explain, even now, leaning against Gus like a tired child, her hair plastered on the cloth of his shirt, its strands clinging and unruly. She should have to apologize, to Gus, to Bee. If their father is not here to do it, she is the next best thing.

"No, Gus. She should talk to you. She should apologize. *Someone* should apologize to you."

She waits, but her mother says nothing, just unweaves her arm from Gus's elbow and lets it dangle by her side, as if it is broken.

"I did," her mother says. She is looking at the carpet, but her body is angled to Gus. "I did."

"Apologize?" Bee swallows a lump, scratchy and huge as a tumbleweed.

Gus is shaking his head. "No, Mom, it's fine. You don't need to say anything." He takes Mary's dangling hand in his. He is pleading. Bee realizes suddenly that she has made a mistake. Gus is telling himself a story about the past, one that makes sense of it, so that he will not dissolve into sorrow. He is telling himself the version of the story that he has learned to live with. He is adding, deleting. If he hears more, if the story expands, it will destroy him for good. He will never come back from wherever he goes.

Bee is about to take it back when her mother says, "I did. Something." She points to Bee's phone, then lifts her head to stare directly at Bee. "Like you. You did something, with your website. I did something too. Diana Nastasi and I."

Bee looks at Gus, whose mouth has turned to stone, then back at her mother. "What? What did you do?" she asks.

"It's there," her mother says. She points again to Bee's phone, which is glowing blue. Bee can see messages from Charlie, and one notification from Drawthemback.com. "Read it," she says.

Bee picks up her phone and loads the website. Deecie Jeffries's photo is there, with a new caption underneath. They never interviewed all the truckers, she reads. The one they should have asked . . .

In the mornings, when she was small, Bee used to wake at the sound of her father's keys. He left before anyone was awake, and she believed she was keeping him safe on the roads, just by opening her eyes at the jingle. Austin to Dallas to Oklahoma City and back again.

A trucker. A trucker who would do something horrible to his own child.

For a moment, the story rotates on its axis. Bee glimpses new planets, a strange sun.

Into the silence, her mother says, "Oh, but sometimes I don't remember my lines." She is shaking her head, rolling it in a circle as if she is warming up for the Pips Playhouse. "Elizabeth Proctor was a liar, you know. But they forgave her. Do you remember that play?"

"I do. Of course I do," Gus says. "Let's get you to bed."

Gus turns to lead Mary to her bedroom, and Bee slides the

phone into her pocket. Beneath the fabric, the words glow. They are burning in the air between them.

"What does it say?" he asks. He is still holding Mary's arm.

Bee knows she should tell him. But her mother's eyes are two sequins, flashing as they follow Bee.

There is no reason to believe anything she says.

And there is no reason for Gus to read that entry. Not tonight, and not ever. If he sees it, he will think that Deecie Jeffries is his fault, that it could have been prevented by him telling someone about what his father did. But nothing is Gus's fault. Bee takes the phone out of her pocket and pretends to load the site again, but she is pressing Delete. Her mother's post disappears, letter by letter at first, then whole words popping like bubbles as Bee holds down the button.

"Oh. Weird," she says. "It's gone."

She can tell that Gus does not believe her. His skin has turned to pewter. He shoots her a look of appeal. *You already know everything,* she wants to tell him. *You know enough.*

"They forgave her, didn't they?" her mother says, suddenly. She is standing upright now. Her hair is a staticky crown around her head, as if the air in the room has been electrified.

"Who? For what?" Gus asks.

Mary turns to him and rests both palms on his cheeks. Bee remembers her doing this, when Gus was small and frantic, when she needed him to pause and pay attention to her.

"For forgetting," she says. Her voice is clear. She is awake, just like she said.

"They did," Gus says, cautiously. There is a hitch in his voice. He wraps his hands around her wrists and lowers them slowly to her sides. "Of course they did."

Bee knows that she should stand up from the arm of the sofa, where she has been balancing, the arm digging into her pelvic bones. She should help, but her muscles are disobedient, heavy.

She can't move, so she watches as Gus puts his arm around their mother, lets her rest her head on his chest, then bends down and carries Mary to her room.

When they are gone, Bee kneels next to Attie in the corner by the window. She pats her gently on her stomach and feels her rabbit heart, her steady breathing. She hears Gus murmuring behind Mary's door. *Go to sleep,* he must be saying. *Go to sleep.*

Or, maybe, *Let it be.*

Bee picks up Attie's car seat, walks into her bedroom, and closes the door. Tomorrow, she will call the police and tell them everything she knows. She will not sleep, not tonight. She will stare at the ceiling, close her eyes, and try to disappear.

Diana

Diana sits on her patio and sips a glass of wine from a chipped coffee cup. The wine is pale orange, like a jewel, and it comes from behind the counter of Yannis's small restaurant at the pier, where she eats a plate of stuffed grape leaves and charred octopus almost every night. She drinks one glass there, then brings the rest home so that she can sit and watch the sunset turn the ocean into brushstrokes of slate and olive and amber. The beach is always empty, except for parallel lines of small shells and shreds of driftwood, left behind by the waves.

She pulls a thin blue-and-white poncho around her shoulders. The night air is warm and thick, but there is a cooling breeze from the ocean. Even after all these years in Greece, she has not gotten used to the vastness of the water spreading out in front of her. It dislodges something inside her, some invisible but important piece of her internal architecture, and makes her shiver.

Two hundred miles from her spot on the patio in Sigri, over

the clusters of white houses with orange roofs, across the water, is the sanctuary she spent all those years studying. When she left the university, she had the idea that she would come to Brauron, walk among the cypress hills the arktoi haunted in their crocus-yellow robes, and they would return to her, as if they were waiting for her arrival. She would know their secrets at last, and they would keep hers. But she was young then, and she didn't know that a secret will lodge inside you always, no matter how much time passes.

After the summer of the fire, the summer the girl disappeared, Diana tried for three years to finish her project on the arktoi before she gave up her job at the university. Or, more accurately, before her funding ran out. No one begged her to stay, not even Mark, and Leo didn't seem to notice, since by then he was living with Derek in his new apartment by the river, with no garden, no fountain. He was supposed to come to her house every Sunday for dinner, but most of the time he made excuses. Diana tried to tell herself that she understood. He didn't know what she had done for him, and she could never tell him, so the silence between them grew and festered. On the rare Sundays he did decide to come, it was almost impossible not to follow him around the house or pull her chair next to his as they ate their takeout.

When she finally decided to sell the house on Stillwood Lane and move to Greece, Leo didn't protest, as if he already understood that the distance between them was insurmountable. He was eighteen, about to start college, and it was her chance to get away from Texas, that street, staring every day at Mary Rowan's garage. She gave Leo all of her savings to pay for college, plus whatever was left after she bought the ticket, and mailed the rent to the man in Athens who turned out to be nonexistent, leaving her with nothing except a bag full of scholarly journals and an absurdly outdated, forty-pound typewriter that she ended up leaving at the bus depot. "I don't want your money," Leo told her. But she mailed it to him anyway.

He was angry. He must have thought that she was abandoning him. He is a grown man now, with no trace of the small boy he once was, and he will never understand the way she has kept his secret about that girl, all these years, the way it eats her away from the inside, like rust corroding iron. She is only doing what he asked, when he left her those flip-flops, one in the fountain pipes, one in the closet. She is saving him. She didn't need to, as it turned out, because even though Mary Rowan never went to the police the way Diana told her to, they stopped asking about the girl. Leo would have been safe without Diana after all. But she keeps his secret.

Here, in this tiny village at the edge of the Aegean, she can look across the ocean at her old idea, which is easier than looking at her old life.

Diana works most days at the natural history museum in Sigri, where she gives tours to groups of Americans and Europeans. The work is familiar, except that there are no amphorae, and almost never any children. There are maps, and slabs of wood, twenty million years old. Nearby, there is a petrified forest, with white, salty-looking stumps scattered across the landscape, like the unfinished columns of a temple. Diana finds them soothing. Her life, the secret she keeps, will be small, infinitesimal, compared to theirs.

Yannis always sends her home from the restaurant with a white cloth napkin that he wraps around the bottle like a baby's swaddle. "To keep her warm," he says, his eyes alight with the joke, and Diana washes the napkin and brings it back to him, dried to crepe in the sun. It is one of the ways that she gives the days their shape: dinner, a bottle of wine, this small and single human connection, wash, repeat.

She moves her cup and spreads the wrinkled napkin on the table like a newspaper. It is a map, with folds that she can follow with her finger. Here is the house where she used to live, on Stillwood Lane, in Austin. Here is the road that curved its way through the neighborhood and ended on Burnet Road. Here is the university, its quad enclosed with pale stone buildings that look, she knows now, like the stone the ancient Greeks used for their temples.

It is a map, or a newspaper. Diana tips her cup and lets the last few drops of wine wet the napkin. She rolls it into a tight scroll and unrolls it again. When she found the newspaper in her old fountain, wrapped around that girl's shoe, she thought her heart would clog, too, all the blood and lymph and love that should course through her stopped in its tracks. But the fountain worked fine, once she finally finished it. The water trickled through the pipes and bubbled over the stones, as it was supposed to. The realtor called it a "little oasis of your own" in the listing. And once she burned the field with Mary Rowan, the clog inside her shifted just enough that she could breathe.

It is like Sappho said. She has hauled a bucket of spring water from a sewer.

She has also had too much wine. Her head is pounding, and her eyelids feel weighted. The ocean is smooth tonight, an unbroken blanket of blue. She tips her head back, letting its weight sink into the woven rope of her chair. She is there, almost asleep, gazing absently, when she sees it.

In the water, there is a dark shape, like a seal, moving closer to the shore as she watches. It breaks apart—there is one head, then another—and she can see that it is not a seal at all, but a small boat that is bobbing unhappily in the waves. It is almost completely dark, and Diana's entire body is tuned to the movement on the water. She hears, in the distance, the cry of a small child.

They are stumbling on the shore now, refugees, their skirts like shrouds woven around their legs. There are three of them, a woman and two small girls. They are pulling the boat onto the shore, and one of the girls keeps losing her footing in the surf.

Inside Diana's cottage, there are blankets. There is a pantry full of food. It isn't much, but it will be enough to help this small trio through the night. She is just about to stand up from the table when she sees another dark shape in the water behind them. And another. And another.

There is a line of small ships, heading for her beach. Where do they come from? She reads the news, so she knows the answer: Syria, Turkey, Iraq. They land here, on this tiny island in the Aegean, because they believe that whatever greets them here will be better than whatever they left behind. They are women, children, pushed away from the shore by young men who whisper promises and press envelopes of money into their shaking hands. They wrap their children inside their skirts to keep them warm.

They are filled with the courage of bears.

Diana has not been a good mother, a good wife, a good scholar. Her project on the arktoi was a failure, too abstract, too massive. She has not been as brave as she should have been. She has lied to save her son, and she has lost him. She tried to turn poor Mary Rowan into a liar too. She has been a fool.

But she can do this one thing. She can bring water and

blankets to these women and their children, shivering in the water. She can invite them to her home. She can ask them their names.

Diana stands. She will go down to the beach. She will do what she can.

Bee

Austin, Texas
2011

Bee is walking to the Vaquero to buy milk. It is early, not even six, and the neighborhood lawns are draped in garlands of fog. Trickles of sweat hurry down the small of her back and halt at her waistband, where they pool and spread. Attie is strapped to Bee's chest, that soft cheek smooshed against her sternum. Attie isn't sweating, exactly. She is just getting stickier.

There are no cars on Stillwood Lane. In the middle of the road, a black plastic bag is teasing its way up the street. It catches a gust of wind, then stills, a nervous animal caught in the open. Or a shredded kite, bumping along behind a child who is running too slowly to get it aloft.

When Bee and Gus and Leo were small, there was a kite festival in Zilker Park every spring, and always someone would try to make the world's largest kite out of stapled trash bags, or the world's smallest one of toothpicks. Only the regular ones flew, their tails trailing as high as jet wash in the sky. Otherwise it was all wishful thinking, bad design, as if people forgot that the thing they were building wasn't just an idea or a piece of whimsy but something meant to exist in the real world, something meant to work. To fly.

Bee has to do better at existing in the real world. Charlie has a point; she sees this now. For the past two months, having Attie allowed her to convince herself that the disconnect she has felt for years was only exhaustion, or the result of the radical transformation from self to mother, but the truth is that Gus's story means something more. She has spent most of her life not listening, not paying attention.

Now she sees the truth. Deecie Jeffries is still missing, and Bee's father might have had something to do with it. She is on the side of some barren highway, in the trunk of an abandoned car in a junkyard. In the frame on a website, or in someone's memory. But still missing.

She is somewhere, nowhere, like Bee has been, all these years.

Bee is coming out of the Vaquero with the milk when she hears her name. When she turns, Gus is walking quickly on the road behind her. Sweat stains his T-shirt in a dark triangle. Disturbed at the interruption, Attie begins a loud snuffle against Bee's chest.

"Wait," Gus says, even though Bee has already stopped. Air brakes hiss as trucks ease their way into the turn. The air here is thick with diesel. "Are you leaving already?" His voice is strained, and he is winded, as if he has been running for miles instead of a few blocks down a flat street.

"I wasn't planning to walk to the airport. I'm just getting milk." As she says it, she realizes that this is what she does to Charlie, all the time: he asks for some piece of her heart, and she gives him something hard and recalcitrant instead, a scorched spot where softness should be. She tries again, grabbing Attie's hand to make her wave a pretend goodbye. "Our flight is this afternoon. Charlie probably misses us by now."

"Oh. Okay." A single car pulls into the parking lot, its headlights cutting the early-morning light and washing over Gus's frame. "Hey, I wanted to ask you about something." He is watching a giant Target truck wedge itself between two smaller ones. It pulls up and then back again, then settles with a wheezing sigh.

He knows what Mary wrote on the website. Bee has to explain. She says, "Gus, I'm so sorry. I shouldn't have deleted what she wrote. I know I need to tell the police about Dad. I'll call them this morning. All of this—it's such a mess. I should never have made you talk about something you never wanted to say. I made everything worse."

Gus is looking at her strangely. "What are you talking about?" he asks.

Bee's heart sinks. "The message. On Drawthemback.com. I know it was Mom. She said that they never interviewed all the truckers. I have to tell the police that Dad must have had something to do with Deecie Jeffries. If it wasn't Leo, then it has to be him. It makes sense, doesn't it? Her family should know."

Gus's eyes are wide. He shakes his head. "But you deleted it, right?"

"Gus, I still have to tell them. To help them." She has made so many mistakes. She could have given the Jeffries family the note. She could have called the police days ago.

Gus looks down the street, toward the spot where the field used to be. The neon cowboy on the Vaquero sign flashes orange and red on his cheekbones. When Gus speaks again, his voice is echoey and small. "Do you really think . . ." he begins.

She nods. There is nothing to say that will make this better. She wishes she were back in her bedroom in Maine, her quilt over her head, the sound of Charlie's shower drowning out her thoughts. She wishes she had never come.

Before she can think of something to say, Gus takes a deep breath. "You're right," he says. "If it helps."

They walk back toward the house in silence. Gus carries the milk, and Bee hooks her thumbs into a loop on Attie's carrier so that she will not be tempted to try to hold Gus's hand. They move slowly, gingerly, as if the sound of their footsteps will shatter something fragile between them.

They are almost at Stillwood Lane when Gus says, "That's not what I wanted to ask, though. I wanted to talk to you about the whole Mom thing. She asked me to stay here, right, to help her with the house and everything. She needs . . . I was going to ask you if you thought it was a good idea. Just to—I don't know. Watch her. Maybe find her somewhere else to live, eventually. Somewhere she can be taken care of. Last night was . . ." He stops. "I know I'm not exactly the right person to take care of anyone. But I thought I could try."

He is scuffing the rubber toe of one of his sneakers on a crack in the sidewalk, like a shy child. Bee recognizes the look on his face. It is the same one she makes, when she is excited about something but afraid to show it, a smile with a shrug built in. One hand stretched out to another.

"You'll be great with her," she says, and she means it. "Thank you." Gus isn't the same person he was when they were children, or when she and Leo sent him away from the farm, or when he appeared on Google pages, formless and possibly criminal. He is entirely new, every cell replaced.

"You think?"

She nods. "Maybe you could come see us sometime. I could get you a ticket, for Christmas or something, if you want."

Gus looks down at Attie, whose hair is dark and slick, plastered to her scalp in thin curls. Above him, a row of sparrows perches on a gently bouncing wire. It is so early still. Bee feels creaky and unfamiliar to herself, like she put on someone else's body when she got dressed this morning.

"Yeah," he says quietly. "I'd love that." He gives Attie a pinky and smiles as she wraps a fist around it. They stand together silently for a moment. Then he asks, "Do you remember that old fence? The one that used to run along the side of the field?"

"Yeah, of course. Where you and Leo hung out. You always said it wasn't for girls." Bee tries to sound like she is joking, like she is not wounded by this ancient exclusion, but her chest tightens when she says it out loud.

"I know. We should have invited you." He pauses. "But that fence—it felt like the only place I could talk about it. There was this tunnel that ran alongside it, under the bushes, and Leo and I would go there and talk. Or I would go alone, just to be out of the house. It felt safe. You know? Bee, we needed help. But we didn't know how to get it. Telling anyone felt like . . . hurting them."

Bee's mouth opens once, twice, but nothing comes out. She thinks of the plastic bag, skipping out of reach, then waiting for her, like the scrap of an idea. She imagines herself running after it, catching up to it, trapping it with her foot.

She doesn't know all the details of what happened to her brother, or the terrible damage her father inflicted on others during his life. Maybe she never will. Now at least she is with them, with Gus and Leo, on the same side of the story. It changes everything. All those nights of searching for something that she couldn't name have finally brought her here.

Attie sneezes, the spray hitting Bee's clavicle. She pulls out a ripped paper towel from her pocket to wipe her chest and remembers her flight. She should text Charlie. Relief, or maybe joy, tightens the space behind Bee's heart, her eyes.

"Let's go home," Bee says to Gus, to Attie. They turn down Stillwood Lane. Attie is bouncing gently in front of Bee's chest, her arms waving like a metronome as they walk.

Bee

Leo's farm is less than an hour from Portland, past the warehouses that edge the bay, past Kittery and the naval shipyard and down a dirt road that crosses a marsh and ends in front of a leaning red barn. There is mud everywhere, splattered on the sides of the barn and reaching all the way to the bottom edge of the sign that hangs there. *Lionheart Farms*, it reads in swirling orange script. *Flowers for All Occasions.* Below it is a hand-painted flower that might be a lupine, might be a bluebonnet. Above the *i* in Lionheart, there is a tiny, almost invisible bumblebee.

Bee has not seen Leo since they kissed. Months ago now, in another world. In all these days, though, she has wondered. It is the note that is bothering her. The shoes that Leo found in the field.

The farm is quiet. There is a truck parked next to the barn, but there is no movement except for a faint, sticky breeze coming from the ocean. The sky is bright blue and cloudless. Bee takes her time getting Attie out of the car because she is sweating a little in the unexpected spring heat, and because her heart is sputtering. Attie fell asleep the moment Bee started to drive, and now she is placid. Every day she becomes more herself, with skin that is dry and warm, not damp with the sheen of their shared fluids. Bee is amazed to see that there is an essence in her that remains steady and unchanged even as her body shifts and stretches, a wise and inquisitive nature that is entirely her own. It makes Bee sad to think that it might disappear someday, or be lost.

When Charlie picked her up at the airport, he hugged her gingerly, like he was afraid she might break. She told him everything: about Gus, and the call she made to the Travis County police from the airport. About her mother, and the way the house on Stillwood Lane was crumbling around her, like a metaphor come to life.

She knows that if she looked at his web history, she would still find searches for remedies for exhaustion and vitamins and postpartum depression and restorative vacations. Bee wants to tell him not to worry. She can feel herself return to him, crawling back to him through a long, narrow tunnel.

Today, she will say goodbye to Leo, and then all the mistakes she has made will be righted. Almost all: she will not tell Charlie about the kiss. Some truths are only cruelties, in the end.

Bee pulls Attie to her chest and slams the car door. There is a small white house just beyond the barn, almost hidden behind a flapping wall of white bedsheets. He must be in there. Maybe he is eating lunch. Or maybe he isn't here at all, and the silence is not the sound of rest but of absence.

Bee holds Attie and pats her back so she will stay quiet. She wants to frame this scene: the barn, the sheets flapping like white sails, the road rutted with mud, the small, curtainless house. The ocean, a brushstroke in the background. This farm is a Wyeth painting, remote and windy and full of feeling. It is the painting she would make of her own interior life, if she had the skill. It is a painting about being lonely.

"Hey." Bee starts at the sound, and Attie lets out a tiny noise. Leo is standing next to the cottage, his hand raised. He appears and disappears behind the line of white sheets when the breeze gusts. Bee takes a step toward him, but he is already beside her, bending awkwardly over Attie to give Bee a hug. "How did you find me?" he asks, and Bee almost answers before she realizes he is joking. She will not joke. She will ask Leo exactly what happened on the night Deecie disappeared, and then she will say goodbye to him and go back to Charlie.

"Looks like Attie survived her fall from the bed. She's beautiful, Bee." Leo rubs his neck and smiles, the one she loves, with just part of his mouth, the other part resisting.

Go. "Leo, I came here to ask you something. When I was in Texas, I found a note from Deecie under the rug in my bedroom on Stillwood Lane. A note to you. Do you know how it got there?"

He does not move, but his smile dims. The wind is gone. Behind him, the sheets droop on the lines.

Leo kneels and picks up Attie's sock, which has fallen from her foot. It is small, edged with lace, a gift from Bee's mother that at first seemed absurd and now seems unbearably dear. He holds it out to her, an offering in his scarred, dirt-covered hand.

"Sorry, my hands are dirty," he says. "Here."

She takes the sock and wrestles it onto Attie's squirming foot. She wants to ask Leo about the scar on his hand, and the one twining down his chest, but she is here to say goodbye. She will have to accept not knowing. There is a whole span of his life that she knows nothing about, and there will be another. It is not a tragedy, even if it feels like one.

He lets her finish with the sock, and then he begins to talk. He does not hesitate. It is as if he knew she was coming, as if he has practiced for this very moment, the way she used to practice the apology she now realizes she never gave. "I didn't know her," he says. "Not really, I mean. She went to our school, you know? And sometimes she used to do these routines, on the metal railing, and I would clap for her, if I was there in the field to see it. But we never talked, or anything." There is a smudge of grease on his shirt, and he scrapes at it absentmindedly. "I guess Gus told you. We were running away from . . . from your dad. We stopped at the fence for a minute, to smoke a cigarette and figure out how to get Mr. Moynihan's keys out of his pocket so we could take his car. We thought your dad was asleep. But he must have figured it out because he came outside, around the corner of your house, from the backyard. Looking for us. I saw him first, right when he got to the edge, so I told Gus to run. We split up and looped all the way around the field so he wouldn't see us, and by the time your dad got to the fence and realized that we weren't in the field anymore, we were back in our rooms. Safe, kind of." Leo pauses and bites his bottom lip until it turns white. "But I ran right past her. Deecie. She was standing in the middle of the field, just staring. And I thought—the next day, when they said she was missing, I thought someone would think we had done it. Because we were there."

"But that doesn't make sense. Why would anyone think you were guilty?"

Leo pauses. Beneath his tan, his skin is pale, so the scars stand out more vividly, like someone has drawn pale purple branches on his skin. "I don't know. I was always in trouble, back then. I think I felt guilty," he says. "I'm the one who saw her. And I'm the one who found that note. Right before your dad came. It was stuck in the fence, wedged there between two flip-flops, like a little present for me. And then the next day, she was gone."

"But you could have told the police. You could have told anyone. Someone would have helped you."

Leo lets out a breath. "We wanted to help. We went back to see if there was anything the police missed. But there was nothing there."

He crosses his arms, hugging himself. Bee wonders if there is someone in the farmhouse, someone who can comfort him when she is gone. Then he says, "I know that what I did doesn't make sense. But it did at the time, you know? I didn't know what happened to Deecie. Your dad told us that if we said anything he would—Bee, he had a gun. We were scared. And all I could think about was Gus. He told me that I wasn't allowed to tell anyone about what your dad was doing to him. We promised each other. But I knew that someone needed to know. I used to try, so hard, to tell my mom. I would do stupid stuff, like write it out for her on the back fence with the watering hose when I knew she was watching. I think I even got in trouble at school so she would ask me what was wrong. But she never asked me anything. It's like she didn't notice, or she didn't care. So I took the shoes, and then I put them—where I knew my mom would find them. We were working on this fountain together, fixing it. I put one of them in there, in a pipe that was clogged with leaves, so I knew she would have to go back to it. I put the other one in the closet with the towels. I thought that when she found them, she would ask me about them, where they came from, maybe she would even get mad, and then I would have to tell her, about being there, and about Gus, and your dad. I wouldn't be breaking my promise to Gus if she figured it out herself. And if I told her, then she would have to do something. She would have to help him. She wouldn't just—she couldn't just ignore it. Not if she knew something like that."

"So what happened?"

Leo lowers his head. "She found them," he says. "But she didn't do anything. She never even asked me about it. It was like she couldn't be bothered."

What kind of woman would ignore something like that? What kind of mother? Bee looks down at the top of Attie's head, at the crown, where the hair swirls into a hint of a curl, a little wave kissing her forehead. Is there anything Bee wouldn't do to protect her? She thinks of her own mother, hidden behind the living room curtain, her voice wavery and uncertain.

Maybe Diana Nastasi wasn't ruthless, but practical. Protective.

And then it hits her. Diana Nastasi must have come to the same conclusion Bee did. She must have thought that Leo had something to do with Deecie's disappearance. She was trying to save him, the way Bee was when she flushed the note down the library toilet. But they didn't ask the right questions.

This is her chance to untangle everything, once and for all. She will ask the right question, finally.

"Leo, why was that note in my room?"

"Oh." Leo shrugs and looks out over the fields, in the direction of the ocean. "That was stupid, Bee. I thought . . . I was just a kid when I left that there."

"Leo. Wait. You left it there for me?" Her breath is shallow. "I was supposed to find it?"

"Like I said, Bee. It was stupid. You had no clue it was there. And you were a kid." He looks down. "I couldn't make sense of anything. I was afraid of your dad, of hurting anyone. I didn't know how to ask for help." He shoves his hands into his pockets. "To be honest, I'm not even sure I do now."

Bee looks behind him, to the line of sheets, the thin line of ocean beyond. She knows what it's like to feel like you don't make sense, not even to yourself. She pictures Leo, fifteen years old, his heart pounding as he climbs into Bee's bedroom window. Lifting up the flap in the corner of her room, finding the sheet of paper that Gus told him was there. Sliding a new one in its place. Hoping that Bee would find it there. That she would put it together, somehow, and they would finally get the help they needed.

But she never saw it. And Gus and Leo were alone, for all these years, while Bee pretended to make a real life without them. She thought that if she could just keep moving forward, she could eventually get far enough away from her childhood that it wouldn't matter anymore. She didn't understand that this secret, the one she could always sense but never see, made it impossible to go anywhere at all.

Her life isn't real without Gus and Leo. Her brother, her old friend.

She twirls one of Attie's curls on her finger. Leo is staring, hungrily almost, at both of them. Bee takes a deep breath. "Do you want to hold her?" she asks.

He nods, and takes Attie in his arms, where she settles. One hand reaches up to pat his chin, and—oh, this world and its small miracles—he smiles.

By the time Bee gets home, it is dark. The house is lit from top to bottom. Bee can see through the first-floor windows to the kitchen, where there is a pot steaming on the stove. Upstairs, Charlie is moving around behind the curtains in the bedroom. He is folding laundry. She can see him move from the bed to the dresser and back again. A minute later, he appears in the kitchen window, then vanishes again when he opens the refrigerator's tall chrome door.

She should go inside. But out here, in the dark, she can see her life for what it is: warm, with the possibility of happiness right there in front of her, lit up and glowing. Maybe she could set up an easel out here in the driveway, try to paint it, the way the darkness makes the light almost holy. Or she could put one next to her bedroom mirror, try a self-portrait. She wouldn't be expecting anything.

Behold, she thinks, watching Charlie move behind the windows, and it is only the steering wheel that stops her from lifting into the night sky. *Behold.* Attie will grow up in this house, and she will become a girl, and then a woman, right in front of Bee's eyes, so quickly that it will seem like witchcraft, and she will forget her old self, like you might forget a line in a play but be left with a sense of how it felt to say it, or what it meant. Or how it felt to be young, sitting in the dark, while the world around you glowed.

Attie will forget her old self, but Bee will remember everything.

Attie is asleep in the car seat behind her, her lips glossy with drool and her cheeks warm and pink. Bee can see the girl she will become, the image as clear as if she were with Charlie inside the house. Attie is eight, or maybe nine, or maybe thirteen. She lifts a finger to her lips. She holds a towel in her arms, folded and round, and Bee notices that she is cradling it, like a baby, or a pet rabbit. Her lips are moving, but Bee can't hear what she is saying.

It doesn't matter. When Attie is ready to tell her, she will listen.

Austin, Texas
1987

The flicker of light is gone now. Maybe it was her imagination. *"Go,"* she thought she heard him say, before he turned and ran, right past her, his body brushing hers like wind. But maybe she never saw him, maybe he never saw her. Maybe he never thinks of her at all.

Deecie feels foolish, like she has waved to the wrong person in a crowd. She draws a circle in the mud with her big toe, trying to halt the tears that are coming now, for no reason. She has nothing to cry about. She does not even know this boy. Feeling like you know someone is not the same as knowing them. It's not even close.

The field around her is made of a thousand shadows. There are deep purple ones where the bushes are, and there is a strip of brownish black on the other side, where the street that mirrors hers must be. Someday, she will walk up and down that street, to see if the boy lives there. To see if she is a different person there, better at gymnastics, or better at math. Someone her mother would have stayed for. Someone her father would trust.

If she had the night vision of the animals that rustle in the bushes around her, she would be able to see if the boys were still there, standing by the gray fence and watching her. She would at least be able to see a glistening set of eyes. But there is nothing, just the sound of mice and tiny insects crawling and calling to each other in their own world, an inch from the dirt. Behind her, the streetlights are buzzing like cicadas, and her house is glowing with lamplight. After she came inside, her father told her to brush her teeth, go to sleep. He was watching the Sunday-night movie when she slid open her window, slowly, so he would not hear her. Soon he will turn out the kitchen lights, and the house will go dark, and then the whole street. She has an hour, at least. Maybe all the way until morning.

But she doesn't want to go home. If the boys are gone, she will at least get to be here, in the field, for the last time, before it turns to pavement. She lies down. Her T-shirt sticks to the warm, wet dirt, and the whole sky is a dark blanket someone is spreading out above her, tinted rose and orange from the lights of the city. Beneath her, somewhere, is the backpack she buried once, when she was little. She can't quite remember where she put it, so it's not a time capsule anymore, just a piece of trash, or maybe it's a home for an armadillo who is using her old baton as a tiny balance beam.

She smiles, picturing it. There is something crawling toward her left ear, but she does not swat it away.

If her father wakes up and finds her bed empty, he will look out into the field first, but he won't see anything. He will ask the neighbors down the street, who have a girl her age. He will call her mother, who lives in Georgia now with her new family and does not know where Deecie is, not tonight, not on any other night. He will get in his car and circle the neighborhood, looking for her in the shine of his headlights. He will think that he can find her himself.

The skin of her arms is beginning to itch. The ground feels like it is made of ants and the hairy legs of centipedes. Deecie makes herself lie still. The itches pass through her and reappear somewhere else on her skin, and she lets them. This is how animals must feel. They are a part of the earth, able to live outside all the time without being bothered by itches and feelings and rules.

Her knees are covered in tiny cuts that feel cold when the night breeze blows over them, and she is starting to shiver, so she crawls down into the concrete bowl of the drain. She is lying there, breathing and looking at the sky, feeling the edges of her body dissolve, when she feels a low rumble beneath her.

"*Go,*" he said, or maybe it was *no.* The word comes to her again, and she tries to decide.

It does not matter what he said. He was not talking to her. He does not even know she is alive. He barely even glanced at her when he ran past. She does not need to run: where would she go? She will spend the night in this field, and then she will go home, and in the morning the field will shimmer with light, and she will come outside and practice her routine again, again, and if she never stops, the bulldozers will never start to dig, and one day he will look across the field and she will be a blur, a perfect cartwheel turning endlessly across a shining metal rail.

The ground is not just rumbling now. It is speaking, in a low growl, and it exhales a cold breath down the dark opening of the drain. When the water comes, at first Deecie thinks she can scramble to the side. It is just the way they told her it would be, in school, in the diagrams that hang on the bulletin board outside the principal's office. *A Storm Drain Is Not a Playground*, the signs say. *Beware of Flash Flooding, Even on a Sunny Day!*

It is not water at first, just sticks and mud, but it comes so fast, widening out of the drain like paint from an overturned bucket and then turning to a sickening gush of brown foam. Deecie's first thought is that it is not a sunny day, but the middle of the night, so of course it can't be a flash flood. But then a branch hits her, so hard that she is stunned for a moment, and when her body returns to her, she is underwater, inside the second drain at the other end of the channel, so much closer to the fence, where the boy would be if he were still here, waiting for her, which he isn't. There is no one here to grab her hands, which are torn now from her attempts to clutch the ground, a passing branch, anything at all.

She is a giant black bird, flushed from the field by a volley of arrows, but she has no wings. The water will take her from Shoal Creek to the mighty Colorado. To the Gulf. With the floodwater filling her ears, her mouth, Deecie pulls her hands close to her body and shuts her eyes. She imagines that the darkness inside her lids is the dark blue blanket of the night sky, unfolding forever above the field she loves.

She will miss it. But she is not afraid, not really.

She is just a girl, disappearing.

ACKNOWLEDGMENTS

For my entire life, I have loved books, but until I wrote this one, I had no idea how many people were involved in shepherding each one in its winding journey from mind to shelf. It makes me love my bookshelves even more. I have had the very good fortune of being led on this path by loving, kind, intelligent guides: first, my agent, Kerry Sparks, who has been my unflagging, ferocious advocate from day one and who always believed that this was possible, even when I was not so sure myself. My editor, Bridie Loverro, read this manuscript many, many times with her exacting and creative eye, and I am so grateful for her precision, her patience with my stubbornness, and her generosity. Jeffrey Henderson generously allowed me to use his translation of *Lysistrata* on page 49 and William Logan provided the beautiful translation of Sappho on page 144. The remarkable people at Zibby Books, Zibby Owens and Kathleen Harris in particular, have created extraordinary energy for all things literary, and I am proud beyond measure to receive their creativity and support.

Now I think I understand what a "labor of love" really is.

I want to thank the Williston Northampton School for its enthusiastic backing of my creative work, both in the classroom and on the page. The school's generosity has allowed me to attend the Tin House Workshop, the Writers' Colony at Dairy Hollow, the Juniper Institute, the Bard College Institute for Writing and Thinking, and the Iceland Writers Retreat, where I had the chance to learn from workshop leaders and fellow writers alike. My colleagues and my students inspire me and make me laugh every day; it is a blessing to do a job that doesn't feel like work.

I also owe a huge debt of gratitude to my teachers. At Amherst College, the Middlebury Bread Loaf School of English, and the Episcopal Academy, I was fortunate to learn from people who gave the classroom the full force of their creative energy. I hope to be half the educator that John Powell and Phil Spear were to me. And to my first and best teachers: my mother, who taught me that it is a sin to watch television during the day when you could be reading instead, and my father, who taught me the Greek alphabet when I was seven and the Roman poets when I was seventeen. Thank you both for putting intellectual joy at the top of the household to-do list.

To the Sawyers of all stripes, the Raines family, the Fords, and the Darling-Pearcys: thank you for your enthusiastic support and your love. My brother, Ben, inspires me every day with his selflessness and intelligence. My husband, Matt, has been my most trusted (and most patient!) reader, wine pourer, plot fixer, and cheerleader. He is funny, authentic, and honorable; marrying him is by far the best decision I ever made.

Last and most important, I want to thank Will and Anna. You tease me, but it's true: I really am that delighted every time I see you. I have no idea how I got so lucky. I hope you read this book (please?) and remember to be like a summer field: keep changing. Never forget yourself.

SARAH SAWYER is an English teacher at a boarding school in western Massachusetts, where she finds endless humor and inspiration in her colleagues and students. She has held both the Joseph C. Mesics Instructorship and the Henry and Judith Zachs Faculty Chair. Sawyer is a graduate of Amherst College and the Middlebury Bread Loaf School of English, and she lives in Easthampton, Massachusetts, with her family. *The Undercurrent* is her first novel.

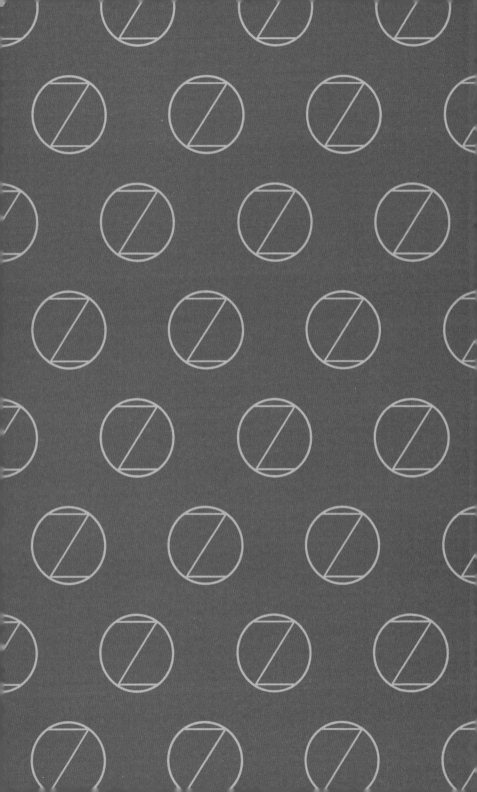